Enchanted IVY

Also by Sarah Beth Durst

ICE

IVY

SARAH BETH DURST

MARGARET K. MCELDERRY BOOKS
NEW YORK LONDON TORONTO SYDNEY

MARGARET K. McELDERRY BOOKS

An imprint of Simon & Schuster Children's Publishing Division

1230 Avenue of the Americas, New York, New York 10020

MARGARET K. McELDERRY BOOKS is a trademark of
Simon & Schuster, Inc.

For information about special discounts for bulk purchases, please
contact Simon & Schuster Special Sales at 1-866-506-1949 or
business@simonandschuster.com.

The Simon & Schuster Speakers Bureau can bring authors to your
live event. For more information or to book an event, contact the
Simon & Schuster Speakers Bureau at 1-866-248-3049 or visit
our website at www.simonspeakers.com.

Book design by Debra Sfetsios-Conover

The text for this book is set in Brioso Pro.

Manufactured in the United States of America

10 9 8 7 6 5 4 3 2 1

Library of Congress Cataloging-in-Publication Data

Durst, Sarah Beth.

Enchanted ivy / Sarah Beth Durst.—1st ed.

p. cm.

Summary: To achieve her dream of attending Princeton
University, sixteen-year-old Lily Carter accepts the challenge of
seeking the Ivy Key to a magical realm, where she finds herself
caught in a power struggle between two worlds, with her family
at its center.

ISBN 978-1-4169-8645-4 (hardcover)

ISBN 978-1-4424-0961-3 (eBook)

[1. Adventure and adventurers—Fiction. 2. Magic—Fiction.
3. Princeton University—Fiction. 4. Locks and keys—Fiction.
5. Princeton (N.J.)—Fiction.] I. Title.

PZ7.D93436Enc 2010

[Fic]—dc22

2010009340

Yes, I went to Princeton. I went because of the trees. Junior year of high school, I walked onto campus, saw the arch of elm trees, saw the massive oaks, and I was sold. Perhaps not the best way to choose a college, but that's the way it happened. Anyway, that moment changed my life and inspired this book. So thank you to the Princeton trees, the dorms, the classes, the professors, and the tulips in Prospect Gardens. Thank you to my roommates and my friends at Forbes, Quad, Triangle, and Theatre Intime. And thank you to the Housing Department, who assigned me to a room next door to my future husband. (We meant to send you flowers on our wedding day—sorry we forgot!)

Special thanks to my amazing agent and fellow Princetonian, Andrea Somberg, and my incredible editor, Karen Wojtyla, as well as Emily Fabre, Paul Crichton, Justin Chanda, Anne Zafian, Elke Villa, Lucille Rettino, Catharine Sotzing, and all the other wonderful people at Simon & Schuster who made this book a reality. You guys are all dream makers.

Many thanks and much love to my family, who inspire me on a daily basis, to my husband, who is the heart of everything I am and do, and to my children, whom I love unconditionally and always will, no matter where they go to college—unless, of course, it's Yale.

Although Yale has always favored
The violet's dark blue,
And the many sons of Harvard
To the crimson rose are true,
We will own the lilies slender,
Nor honor shall they lack,
While the Tiger stands defender
Of the Orange and the Black.

—From "The Orange and the Black," Princeton University fight song;
lyrics by Clarence Mitchell, 1889

CHAPTER One

"Almost there," Grandpa said.

Pressing her nose against the car window, Lily frowned at the strip malls, gas stations, and industrial parks as they rolled by. "Really?" she said. She'd expected to see something a bit more picturesque than Wal-Marts and Home Depots en route to her dream school—at least a stately forest or a field with a few photogenic cows. And she should hear trumpets playing, plus a massive choir announcing in verse the approach of her destiny.

Maybe she'd built up this moment a bit too much.

"Just a few more miles and then I will don my illustrious blazer," Grandpa said.

Grandpa's orange and black striped Princeton University Reunions jacket hung from the back of the driver's seat. Wondering why he'd mentioned it, she met Grandpa's eyes in the rearview mirror. He shifted his eyes toward Lily's mother, who sat slumped in the passenger seat in front of Lily. *Oh, of course,* she thought. If they were almost there, then it was time to cheer up Mom. "You know it looks like a psychedelic zebra's pelt, right?" Lily said.

"You'll see worse," Grandpa promised.

"I doubt the skinless zebra would agree with that," Lily said.

Grandpa nodded solemnly. "The Class of 1969 wears a vest and headband covered in orange and black yin-yang polka dots."

Lily faked a shudder. "Oh, the horror!"

In front of her, Mom laughed. Her wild, tangled hair (today, dyed a beautiful soft green) shook like willow leaves in the wind. It was the first time since leaving Philadelphia that Mom quit looking half-wilted and smiled. Mom hated car rides. She felt caged, she said, inside all the steel and plastic and glass. If it wasn't for worries about how it would react with her usual medication, Mom would have taken a Valium for the drive.

Normally, Mom avoided car rides altogether, but this wasn't a normal weekend. It was Princeton Reunions weekend. Reunions weekend! Lily couldn't believe Grandpa had offered to take them. He always attended, even in off years like his forty-ninth reunion. It was his "thing," his once-a-year break from mothering both Lily and Mom. But this year, he'd said that Lily should see her future alma mater.

Not that she'd even applied yet. She was a junior, three

weeks away from final exams, but Grandpa claimed this place was her destiny. No pressure, though. Yeah, right.

Grandpa pointed to an intersection. "Next left," he said.

Lily's heart thumped faster. She shouldn't be this excited, she knew. It wasn't as if she even had an application interview. At best, she'd take a campus tour and then spend the weekend with a bunch of seventy-year-olds who were pretending to be fifty years younger. But she found herself craning her neck for her first glimpse.

As they turned onto Washington Road, the industrial parks, motels, and malls of central New Jersey fell behind them, and all Lily saw was green, green, and more green. Her breath caught in her throat. Now this was more like it! Elm trees lined the road to Princeton University. Their branches arched over the car in a grand canopy of translucent green that stretched for half a mile. Leaves swayed lightly in the wind, and Lily wanted to reach her arms up and catch the wind in her hands. Her fingers bumped the roof of the car. Self-consciously lowering her hands, she contented herself with staring out the window. Ahead, she saw a stone bridge over a lake and, beyond it, a sprawling boathouse. Crew boats lay crisscrossed on an asphalt shore. It looked like a photograph from a college brochure, and Lily felt light-headed as she drank in the view. It was perfect!

Across the bridge, Grandpa stopped at a traffic light. "We're here," he announced.

"Home," Mom said happily.

Lily closed her eyes as her perfect moment shattered.

"No, Rose," Grandpa said in a calm and patient voice. "This is Princeton University, not our home. We're here for my Fiftieth Reunion. Do you remember?" Opening her eyes, Lily studied Mom and wondered if she'd remember or fake it.

Mom frowned for an instant and then said, "Of course. Yes, yes. I'm sorry." Her chiffon sleeve fluttered as she waved her hand at the window and said, "It's very pretty here."

"I have always thought so," Grandpa replied gravely. "Did you take your medicine today?"

Lily answered for her: "She did. But I have another here. . . ." Unzipping Mom's purse, she drew out a single-dose medicine vial.

"I'm fine. Fine," Mom said, false cheer in her voice. "Just a little hiccup." Mom had nicknamed them that: brain hiccups. A harmless name, as if that would make everything okay. "You can put that away."

Lily's fingers curled around the medicine vial. Mom had been happy for . . . what? Five minutes? Three? Lily slid the vial into her pocket, easily accessible if Mom needed it, and then she forced herself to look out the window again.

Grandpa turned right at a library with a roof like metal wings and drove past an observatory and a concrete stadium flanked by metal tigers, Princeton's mascot. At a PRIVATE PARKING sign, he turned left into a gravel lot and parked.

"Vineyard Club," Grandpa said. He pointed at a tree-choked hill.

Leaning forward, Lily saw hints of brick gables and peaked windows through the screen of trees, and her breath caught in her throat. Vineyard Club was the most exclusive and prestigious of all Princeton eating clubs. Grandpa had been a member.

Following her grandfather's lead, Lily stepped out of the car. She inhaled the smell of Princeton: the earthy scent of pine and the sweet perfume of tulip trees, undercut with the sour stench of stale beer. It smelled exactly like it should. She smiled.

"Oh, freedom!" Mom cried as she jumped out of the car. She spun in a circle with her arms stretched in a V over her head. Her sleeves flapped around her. "I hear the world singing!"

Grandpa chuckled. "No more cars until Sunday," he promised, coming around to the trunk. He lifted out their suitcase. Lily claimed the duffel bag. Without prompting, Mom fetched Grandpa's hideous jacket and her purse from the backseat. Lily and Grandpa both watched her.

Mom's smile slipped. "I'm fine. I won't ruin your weekend."

"This way," Grandpa said, pointing toward a path through the trees. "We're expected."

Grandpa hadn't said they were meeting anyone. Swinging the duffel bag over her shoulder, Lily hurried to follow Grandpa across the parking lot. "Expected by who?" Lily asked.

"By whom," Grandpa corrected. He flashed her an enormous grin. "I have a surprise for you."

The last surprise from Grandpa had involved escargot for dinner. (Lily had tried one; Mom had flat-out refused.) Surprise before last was a six-foot saguaro cactus that Grandpa had ordered for the shop. (Mom had loved it; Lily had found a desiccated scorpion impaled on a thorn.) For all his aura of being a respectable business owner, Grandpa tended to plan bizarre surprises. Now he had a twinkle in his eye as though he thought he was Santa Claus. "No snails this time," Lily said.

"No snails," Grandpa said. "Just a few people I'd like you to meet."

"Really?" She'd never met any of Grandpa's college friends.

The path through the trees opened onto a slope of perfectly manicured lawn, complete with a volleyball net and Adirondack lawn chairs. As Grandpa strode up the hill, Lily tried to picture him as a college student—subtract the salt-and-pepper beard, darken the white hair to black, erase the tanned wrinkles . . . She wondered if he'd learned his I-own-the-world-not-just-a-flower-shop walk here. She imagined herself striding across the lawns as if she belonged.

Coming up behind her, Mom hooked her arm through Lily's. "I wonder what secret life your grandfather has been hiding from us. I'm thinking a dozen girlfriends."

Lily grinned. "At least a dozen." Her grandpa was a handsome man, after all. "First, we'll meet Buffy, Muffy, and Fluffy, triplet bottle-blonde octogenarians who live on a yacht.

And then will come Margaret, the divorcée with the hard shell hiding a soft, vulnerable heart. And of course Penny, the rich widow who loves sequins and feather boas . . ." As they climbed the stone steps to Vineyard Club, Lily trailed off. Here was her first close-up look at Grandpa's infamous club.

Mom didn't notice that Lily's attention had shifted. "Don't forget Clarisse," she said, "the brainy brunette. And Martha, ex–third wife of his third-best friend . . ."

Gazing up at the ivy-covered brick, Lily breathed, "I think I'm in love."

It was a mansion. No other word for it. Vineyard Club was a Victorian-style mansion with peaks and gables of aged brick, all trimmed with ivy. All the windows had wrought-iron frames, and most were stained glass. She craned her neck to try to see the pictures in the stained glass, but all she could see from this angle were colors. Sapphire- and ruby- and emerald-colored bits of glass flashed like jewels in the sunlight. "Can I move here now?" Lily asked. "Seriously, I want to live here."

Like a formal butler, Grandpa swung the door open and gestured inside. Lily peeked in and saw mahogany: walls, floor, tables, chairs, bar and bar stools, all beautiful dark wood. It was . . . ugh! She recoiled as the stench of stale beer rolled out and over her like a tsunami wave. "Before I move," she said, "we fumigate it."

Grandpa inhaled deeply. "Smells like senior year."

Was that the year his scent glands died? Retreating to gulp in fresh air, Lily turned back toward the brilliant green lawn sloping down behind them . . .

. . . and saw the boy.

He stood underneath a pine tree by the parking lot. He wore jeans and a black T-shirt, and he had orange and black tiger-striped hair. Clearly, judging by his school-spirit hair, he was a Princeton boy—the first one she'd ever seen. She felt like a bird-watcher who had glimpsed an elusive and rare specimen.

Oddly, he seemed to be staring back at her.

She was sure it was her imagination. He had to be admiring the architecture. Or waiting for a girlfriend. Guys like that had girlfriends. They didn't notice rumpled-from-a-long-drive high school juniors who were hanging out with their relatives. Lily opened her mouth to ask Mom if she thought the boy was looking at her, but then she stopped. Mom might like the hair. Lily didn't want to waste Reunions weekend on a search for orange and black hair dye.

Lily followed Mom and Grandpa inside and instantly forgot about the tiger-haired boy. She was inside Vineyard Club! She stared around her, feeling as if she needed to memorize every detail.

The taproom of Vineyard Club felt old but more in a finely-aged-wine sort of way than in a plumbing-never-works-right kind of way. Black-and-white photos of men in suits and ties (and women in the newer photos) adorned the wood-paneled walls. She studied the nearest photo, imagining herself in the group of students.

Don't get carried away, she told herself. She had no idea if she'd be accepted to Princeton, much less the über-exclusive Vineyard Club. What if they saw that B from ninth-grade history? What if she hadn't done enough extracurriculars? She'd thought she had an okay list: student council secretary (but never president), twice chorus for the school play (never the lead), part-time employee at Grandpa's flower shop (not optional), one year of tap dance (big mistake), yellow belt in tae kwon do (Grandpa's idea after the tap-dance fiasco), catcher for junior varsity softball. . . . Maybe she should have done more. She should have pushed to fit in one more AP class this year. Or joined the debate team. Or discovered the cure for cancer.

Grandpa led them across the sticky floor to the stairs. "We're on a hill, so the taproom is essentially the basement," he explained. "The rest of the club is upstairs."

The wooden steps were worn from hundreds of feet over a hundred years. More photos lined the staircase. Mom lingered on the fourth step. "It's you but it isn't," she said cryptically.

Lily froze. *Please, not another brain hiccup.* She was having them more and more often these days. "Are you okay, Mom?"

Grandpa doubled back. "Come on, Rose," he said gently. He lifted her fingers away from a photograph and then guided her upstairs. He didn't look at Lily.

Maybe it hadn't been a hiccup. Sometimes it was hard to tell when Mom was being artistically enigmatic or actually crazy. *Please hold it together,* Lily prayed silently at Mom, *at least while we're in the club!* She followed Mom and Grandpa upstairs.

Stained-glass windows cast red, green, and gold shadows across leather couches and high-back chairs. An Oriental rug covered the floor. Sections of the rug were worn to threads that looked like tan scars against the faded scarlet swirls. One end of the room was dominated by a stone fireplace with a massive marble mantel. It was flanked by an oil painting and a cream-white door. The other end of the room held a shiny black piano, as well as a doorway to a billiard room. It was all very grand and all very—

"Dead," Mom said, as if completing Lily's thought. "It needs sunlight. Fresh air!" She waved her hands at the stained-glass windows.

A new voice spoke. "But then we'd lose our carefully cultivated aura of stuffiness." All three of them pivoted to see an elderly gentleman enter through the cream-white door. "Gentleman" was the absolute right word for him. Dressed in a starched Brooks Brothers shirt and sporting a meticulously trimmed beard, he looked like someone who would know which fork was the salad fork while blindfolded with his hands tied behind his back.

Grandpa dropped their suitcase with a thump. "Joseph!" He strode across the room with a wide smile on his face.

"Richard, we're glad you made it." The two men clasped hands and then patted each other on the back in a stereotypical grown-man hug. Clearly, this was one of Grandpa's college friends. Lily tried to picture the two of them as boys here in this club, and she failed. This man had never been young. He looked past Grandpa to Lily. "And you've brought your precocious granddaughter?"

Lily nearly glanced behind her to see whom he was talking about. Yes, she took care of Mom a lot, and she managed the flower shop under Grandpa's supervision, but that was due to necessity, not precociousness. Precocious kids had dimples. And wore pigtails and sailor suits and recited Shakespeare in twelve languages by age two . . . Oh, God, what if that was her competition for Princeton admission?

Grandpa beckoned her over. "Lily, I'd like to introduce you to my oldest friend, Joseph Mayfair." Lily deposited the duffel bag next to the suitcase and joined Grandpa.

"Did you have to say 'oldest'?" Mr. Mayfair said with an affected wince. He extended his hand to Lily. She shook it, and he closed both hands around hers, effectively trapping her hand. "Pleasure to finally meet you."

She shot Grandpa a look. He knew she didn't like to be talked about behind her back. She got enough of that at school. Grandpa looked unrepentant.

Mr. Mayfair continued to clasp her hand. "Are you ready?" he asked.

He sounded so intense that she felt a butterflies-in-the-stomach flutter. "Ready for what?" She considered how to squirm her hand away without being rude to this stately gentleman.

Grandpa scowled at his friend. "I know the rules," he said. "I haven't told her anything."

Nodding approval, Mr. Mayfair released Lily's hand. She flexed her fingers as she looked back and forth between Grandpa and Mr. Mayfair. Grandpa had never involved a stranger in his surprises before; they were a family-only tradition. Of course, this man wasn't a stranger to Grandpa. Lily might not have heard of him, but Grandpa had claimed him as his oldest friend. For the first time, it bothered Lily that Grandpa never talked about his college friends. She didn't like the thought of her beloved grandfather having any secrets from her, especially since he seemed to have told this man about her.

Joining them, Mom held out her hand. "I'm Rose Carter, Richard's daughter."

He clasped her hand. "My dear, we are acquainted," he said. His voice was soft and gentle. "Do you not remember?"

Uh-oh, Lily thought.

Mom's lips pinched into an O. Silently, she shook her head.

As soon as Mr. Mayfair let go of Mom's hand, Lily took it. She spread her fingers over Mom's whitening knuckles.

"You have known me for many years," he said. "I even officiated at your wedding. . . ." He looked as if he wanted to say more, but he halted. "I'm sorry. I'm distressing you."

"Not at all," Mom said, all politeness and cheerfulness.

"Richard, she shouldn't be here," Mr. Mayfair said. "She should be home."

Grandpa shook his head. "She chose this, and I promised to see it through. I'm not going back on my word now."

Lily thought that was a rather melodramatic way to put it. She squeezed Mom's hand. A smile was still plastered on Mom's face, as if she didn't mind that people were talking about her.

Grandpa turned to Mom and asked, "Will you stay right here in this room until we return?" He spoke carefully, making sure the words sank in. Everyone had to be extra clear with Mom. Mom could forget where she was and wander off. Two summers ago at the beach on the Jersey Shore, Mom had insisted on fetching ice cream by herself. They found her an hour later, watching the carousel a mile down the beach. She said she was waiting for the horses to fly. After that, Lily didn't like leaving her alone anywhere.

"Mom . . . ," Lily began.

Mom squeezed Lily's hand and then let go. "I'll be right here when you return," she promised. "I'll practice my piano!" She pointed at the grand piano.

"You know you don't play piano, right?" Lily said.

"Hence the need for practice, practice, practice!" She wiggled her fingers in the air. Lily grinned and then kissed her mother's cheek. Mom was such an amazing person. Her own mind betrayed her on a near-daily basis, and she still found the strength to be gracious and funny. "I shall be a virtuoso by the time you return," Mom said.

Grandpa escorted Lily to the cream-white door by the fireplace. Mr. Mayfair preceded them and then halted before the door. In a low voice, he said to Grandpa, "She didn't even recognize me."

In an equally low voice, Grandpa said, "Her rate of decline is worse than we expected."

"Perhaps we should—"

Grandpa interrupted. "My family, my decision. We must act now."

Mr. Mayfair regarded him for a moment, then nodded and opened the door. Before Lily could ask Grandpa any questions about this odd exchange, she heard Mr. Mayfair announce, "It's time."

A knot formed in the base of Lily's stomach. "You know I hate surprises," she said under her breath.

"No, you don't," Grandpa said just as softly. "You love them. And I promise this will be the best surprise of all." He held the door open for her, and Lily ducked under his arm. She halted in the doorway.

A dozen men and women waited inside a private library. Each was positioned as if for a painting ("Old Boys at Princeton," Lily instantly dubbed it—if there was such a thing as an Old Boys' Network, this was it). A man in a black suit posed before a marble fireplace. Hands clasped behind his back, he regarded the cold ashes in the hearth with the solemnity reserved for a funeral. Another man leaned pseudocasually against the frame of a stained-glass window. He held an open book loosely in his hands. Lily noticed he was holding it upside down. A third man, portly and elderly, filled a thronelike chair that had armrests shaped like tiger heads. He puffed on a pipe, and smoke drifted in lazy curls over his head. Two women with impeccable posture perched on a red leather settee, and another woman with an ivory-tipped cane occupied a wingback chair. Others were perched on chairs and sofas or standing beside bookshelves.

The room itself overflowed with leather-bound books and Tiffany lamps. Above the marble fireplace was an oil painting of St. George and the Dragon. The stained-glass window depicted a tableau of knights and scholars around an emerald-green dragon with ruby talons. The green glass dragon wore a silver chain around its neck.

Lily heard awkward piano notes drift in from the main room. One of the younger men winced at a particularly inventive chord, and Mr. Mayfair shut the door.

Silence fell over the room.

Lily strained to hear the plunk of piano keys, but no sound penetrated the door. Her own breathing echoed unnaturally loudly in her ears. She wondered why a random room was so well soundproofed. She glanced at Grandpa. He was beaming, his smile as broad as the Cheshire Cat's. It wasn't reassuring.

As if he were introducing her to a concert audience, Grandpa said, "This is my granddaughter, Lily!" Pride swelled his voice until he nearly crowed. "She is ready for the test!"

Test?

What test?

No one had mentioned a test. She hadn't agreed to a test.

Snap! Lily jumped. The man at the window had shut his book. Now he straightened and smiled at her, not unkindly. "Splendid. Welcome, Lily. Are you ready to claim your destiny?"

"Presumptuous," the heavyset woman in the wingback chair said. She thumped her ivory-tipped cane on the floor for emphasis, but the ruby-red Oriental rug muffled the sound.

Lily opened her mouth to defend herself—she couldn't be presumptuous when she didn't even presume to have the least idea of what they were talking about. Before she could speak, Grandpa squeezed her shoulder. "She was born for this," he said.

The woman sniffed. "We shall soon see."

This could be some sort of admissions interview, she thought. Lily's heart hammered faster. If Grandpa had arranged an alumni interview, he should have warned her. He knew how important Princeton was to her! If this had anything to do with admissions—

"Oh, for pity's sake, Joseph," the man with the book said. "Put the child out of suspense before she pees on the floor from nerves."

Lily felt her face redden. She wasn't *that* nervous.

Should she be?

Honestly, these people could make a rock nervous. All of them were staring at her as if they were a pride of lions and she was a plump gazelle. She wanted to shout, *Stop looking at me!* But thankfully, before she blurted out anything she'd regret, all eyes shifted to Mr. Mayfair.

He drew himself straighter, and Lily suddenly understood what the term "presence" meant. This man had presence. You couldn't not look at him. It felt as if all the oxygen in the room had been pulled toward him. "Lily Carter, you are here because your grandfather, Richard Carter, has recommended you for the Legacy Test."

She dragged her eyes away from Mr. Mayfair to look at Grandpa. He was still smiling in that rather alarming way.

"First, we must ask you not to speak of this test to anyone beyond this room," Mr. Mayfair said. She thought of Mom and wished she could still hear the piano notes.

The man with the book chimed in. "It isn't a pain-of-death sort of command. We'd simply prefer that the media not catch wind of our little tradition. They would misunderstand. *Willfully* misunderstand, I might add."

Everyone nodded so solemnly that Lily thought maybe she'd misheard and he'd said it *was* a pain-of-death command. Standing here in this room, she could believe it. She felt as if she were surrounded by royalty. These people radiated self-confidence. She had the sense that each of them could fill a room with his or her presence if he or she so chose. Together, they made the air feel thick.

"Can we have your word that you will keep the contents of this conversation private?" Mr. Mayfair asked. In the same kind voice he'd used with Mom earlier, he added, "Of course with the exception of your family."

She didn't dare do anything but nod.

He smiled approvingly, and Lily's knees shook. She didn't know why it mattered to her that he approved, but she felt a flood of relief when he smiled. "The Legacy Test is offered only to the very select few," Mr. Mayfair said. "Passing means automatic acceptance to Princeton University."

She stared. Obviously, she must have misheard. Automatic acceptance? As in no grades, no SATs, no essays? Just "yes, you're in"? She looked from face to face, ending on Grandpa's. He looked as if he were about to burst into a song and dance routine, which was wholly uncharacteristic of him. "Grandpa? Is this a joke?" She'd heard rumors that legacies were sometimes favored, but she'd never imagined a formal process.

"Surprise!" Grandpa said.

Surprise? Surprise?! That was all he had to say? "Why didn't you tell me?" She could have prepared! She could have studied! She could have at least worked herself up into a fine state of nervous nausea!

"He was not permitted," Mr. Mayfair said.

Yeah, right. Since when did Grandpa need permission from anyone for anything? He ran his own business. He ran their family. *If he tried,* Lily thought, *he could run the world.* He was the strongest, smartest man that Lily had ever met . . . but maybe she'd only seen Grandpa next to ordinary people. Maybe next to giants, he wasn't so tall. That was a disturbing thought. She felt as if she were betraying Grandpa to even think it.

Lily realized that everyone was staring at her again as if waiting for her to say something, but she had no idea what she was supposed to say. "What's the test?" she asked at last.

She heard a whoosh as the Old Boys exhaled en masse. Several smiled, and a few even chuckled. Mr. Mayfair graced her with an avuncular smile, and she basked in his approval. "The test varies from candidate to candidate," Mr. Mayfair said. "For you, Lily . . . you must find the Ivy Key."

She flashed back to a treasure hunt at a classmate's fifth-grade birthday party. Back then, the prize had been gummy bears and a yo-yo.

The woman with the ivory-tipped cane said, "Find the Key, and your future will be assured. Your destiny, secure."

"You will still need to complete an application form, of course," the man with the book said. "Appearances, my dear. Must keep up appearances. But you will be guaranteed a yes response."

Her head spun. She wished she were sitting down.

The man with the book laughed at her expression. "All you have to do is pass."

"And if I don't pass?" Lily asked.

One of the perfect-posture women said, "If you fail, you are free to apply with the rest of the applicants. This test is outside the purview of the admissions committee. But if you fail here, you should not expect an invitation to join Vineyard Club. Indeed, you would not be welcome."

Success meant her dream come true; failure meant exclusion from this (admittedly nice) clubhouse but still a shot at her dream come true. Yeah, she could totally live with that. No wonder Grandpa was smiling so widely he looked like he might burst. She felt the same expression spreading across her face. She was smiling so hard that her cheeks ached. She felt as if a hundred birthday presents, including the pony she'd wanted in third grade and the lime green Volkswagen she wanted now, had landed right in front of her. "What's the Ivy Key?" she asked. "What does it look like? What does it open? What do I do to find it? How do I start?"

At her flood of questions, Mr. Mayfair and several others smiled indulgently.

"That's the test, my dear," the man with the book said.

But . . . it could be anything! A locker room key, a dorm room key, a key to a top-secret safe in the university president's office where he kept world-domination plans . . . How would she even know if she'd found the right key?

"Do you accept our challenge?" Mr. Mayfair said. His eyes bored into hers. His expression was so intense that there was only one possible answer.

"Yes, of course, I accept!" she said.

All the Old Boys applauded.

$\mathcal{M}$r. Mayfair opened the library door, and music—or sort of music—poured in. Piano notes fell over one another like a rushing waterfall. The cascade of chords exactly matched how Lily was feeling. She pictured herself years later with gray streaks in her hair and an alum's black and orange jacket, remembering this day and saying, *Here, right here, this moment—this is when my life changed.*

Better not screw up.

As Mom hit another discordant jumble of notes, Mr. Mayfair's smile slipped. He leveled a look at Grandpa that Lily would have labeled "meaningful" if she could have identified what it meant. "Are you certain?" he asked Grandpa again. "Once she knows—"

"I am," Grandpa said firmly.

"Very well then. It begins now," Mr. Mayfair said. "Good

luck, Lily Carter." He shut the door, leaving Lily, Grandpa, and Mom alone.

As soon as the door closed, Mom sprang off the piano bench. "She's starting?"

Grandpa beamed. "She accepted the test!"

"Oh, sweetie, yay!" Mom skipped across the room and enveloped Lily in a hug.

Lily felt her jaw drop. "You knew about this?" *Mom* had kept a secret? Lily was torn between being annoyed and impressed. How long had Mom known about the Legacy Test? Days? Weeks? Years? "When did Grandpa tell you?"

As soon as the question was out of her mouth, Lily wished she could suck it back in. She knew better than to ask Mom to remember anything.

Mom's shoulders slumped, and her face collapsed. "I . . . I don't know."

"Never mind," Lily said quickly. But the damage was already done.

Shooting Lily a look that made her feel as if she'd poisoned a baby, Grandpa patted Mom's hand as he guided her toward the door. "We'll be checked in at the Fiftieth Reunion tent," he said to Lily. "Ask for our room number at the registration desk when you need to sleep."

She trailed after them. "Wait, can't I come with you? I don't know where to start!" Stepping out the front door of Vineyard Club, she blinked into the midday sun. As her eyes adjusted, she noticed that the tiger-haired college boy was leaning against the brick wall in front of the club. His hands were shoved deep in his jeans pockets, and he stared up at the cloudless blue sky.

Grandpa shook his head. "You're going to pass with flying colors, and I don't want anyone to doubt that you did it on your own." He sounded fierce.

Lily wondered how many favors Grandpa had had to call in to arrange this. Mr. Mayfair had said only a select few were chosen, and she knew she wasn't anything special. "I won't let you down, Grandpa."

He softened. "That's my tigerlily. Remember that I believe in you, however the test ends and whatever mysteries you unlock along the way."

The striped-haired boy was regarding them with mild interest, but Lily told herself to ignore him. This was more important than any college boy. "Can you at least tell me what the rules are?" she asked. "Is there a time limit?"

"You have until the end of Reunions," he said. "Sunday, we go home."

Before she could ask any more questions, he turned and strode down the walk. Mom blew her a kiss and scurried after him. Feeling like a toddler left at preschool for the first time, Lily watched them head out the gate and onto the sidewalk.

The tiger-haired boy watched them too.

The street that Mom and Grandpa were walking down (Prospect Avenue, according to the street signs) was lined with other mansions in both directions—more eating clubs, she guessed. She saw an oversize cottage, a *Gone with the Wind*–like house with white pillars and a broad porch, and a squat brick monstrosity with an orange and black cannon on its front lawn. All were past their peak glory. Paint chipped off the grand entrances, and plywood covered several windows. One had a couch on its roof. She couldn't imagine how or why anyone would put a couch on a roof.

I'm so not ready for this, she thought.

As she watched Mom and Grandpa pass the club with the cannon on the lawn, Lily wanted to chase after them. But Grandpa's words rooted her where she stood. She couldn't let him down, and if she ran after him in full view of Vineyard Club . . . She pictured the Old Boys peering out the windows, clucking their tongues in disapproval. The heavyset woman with the ivory-tipped cane most likely already had a notebook full of Lily's inadequacies: drops her *r*'s at the end of words, wears uneven socks, doesn't curtsy at greetings, isn't clever enough or pretty enough or perky enough . . . *Stop it,* she ordered herself. She could do this. Grandpa believed in her. She was just freaked out because she hadn't pictured herself alone on a college campus so soon.

But she wasn't alone. There was the tiger-haired boy.

She grinned at herself. Yeah, right, as if she could walk up to a real-life college boy and ask him about the Ivy Key. He still leaned against the brick wall, as coolly casual as a modern James Dean. She couldn't talk to him. She wasn't in the same league as guys like that. She was barely from the same universe. It was enough that she'd have to walk past him.

And she *would* have to walk past him. Soon. If she kept dithering here on the steps of the club, the Old Boys would pronounce her the worst candidate they'd ever seen and blackball her admissions application to every college except those online schools that advertised in movie theaters. Lily ordered her feet to walk. She was hyperaware when she passed the college boy, but she willed herself not to look at him. If she looked, she'd stare.

On the sidewalk, she halted. *Right or left?* she wondered. She selected right. She didn't want Grandpa to think she was following them.

"Other way," Tiger Boy said behind her. His voice was soft, sort of velvety.

"Me?" she asked, pivoting to face him. Up close, his hair looked amazingly natural. It was soft orange and black, muted like the fur of a tiger-striped cat. Stray bits fell over his eyes. She imagined brushing them away from his face. She looked down and studied her sneakers instead.

"Main campus is left," he said. "Just ordinary houses to the right. Very boring. Unless you're invited to a barbecue."

"Barbecues are good," she said. Oh, God, what was she saying? Why was she talking about barbecues? "Unless you're a vegetarian, of course."

"Of course," he agreed amiably.

She felt herself blushing. The first college boy who'd ever talked to her must think she was an idiot. She told herself it didn't matter what he thought of her, even if he was extremely cool-looking and had a dreamy voice and was a student at her dream school. . . . "I'll go left," she said.

"Good choice," he said. A small smile played on his lips. "You should take a tour."

Her blush spread down her neck. She felt as if the words "high school student" were stamped on her forehead. "I'll be fine," she said. "Uh, thanks."

"Look for someone walking backward, and that will be the Orange Key Tour."

She opened her mouth to say no, thanks, she didn't have time for a tour right now, but then the name of the tour sank in: Orange *Key* Tour.

He winked at her and then ambled off across the street.

She stared after him for a moment and then shook herself. Clearly, he—whoever he was—had given her a clue.

Filled with purpose, Lily headed left, down the street toward campus. She was swept up in a steady stream of alumni that flowed into and out of the clubs. As Grandpa had promised, she saw worse outfits than his blazer: orange jean jackets, black and orange trench coats, orange satin smoking jackets. She crossed the street within a flock of alums dressed in crossing-guard orange Hawaiian shirts.

Slowing with the crowd, she began to wonder if she was wrong. The tour name could have been a coincidence, not a clue. She could end up wandering around all weekend until her nerves snapped and she resorted to stealing car keys from drunken alums and toting them in a Santa Claus sack to Vineyard on Sunday. . . . She climbed a set of steps that led to a brick archway. Above her, the arch was decorated with stone gargoyles. Little carvings of monkeys curled into rosettes. One side of the arch had a frieze carved into the shape of a tiger's head. Four stone monkeys crawled over the tiger's face.

One of the monkeys turned its stone head and looked at her.

Lily lost her footing on the steps. She caught herself on the railing, and an alum steadied her elbow. "Are you all right?" he asked.

"Fine, thanks," she said automatically.

The alum continued on.

She was most definitely *not* fine. Clutching the railing, Lily stared at the monkey gargoyle. It didn't move.

Of course it didn't move, she told herself. *It's stone.* She must have imagined it.

Lily climbed the remaining steps and leaned against a wall inside the archway, out of sight of the gargoyles. A plaque on the wall labeled the building as 1879 Hall.

Please, don't let me have a brain hiccup.

She was genetically predisposed to them. She took a half dose of the same medication as Mom to prevent their onset. Until now, it had worked. But until now, she'd never had such an important weekend. Her raised stress levels . . . *No*, she thought. She wasn't going to let Mom's illness beat her. Not here and not now. Lily reached into her pocket and pulled out Mom's medicine vial. She uncorked it and chugged the syrupy silver liquid. It tickled her throat as she swallowed.

Now she was safe from hallucinations and memory lapses and any behavior that would make a college admissions officer look at her as if she were less welcome than dog poo on an Oriental rug. She had double her usual dose in her. Or was it triple? Grandpa was always so careful with the dosage, and Mom's doses were twice the strength of hers. . . .

Oh, crap, she thought.

Lily flipped open her cell phone and then stopped. Grandpa would not be happy if he found out she'd panicked five minutes into her test. She should wait to see if any abnormal symptoms developed before she called him.

Pacing back and forth, she waited for signs of a seizure, heart attack, or frothing at the mouth. But aside from a ringing in her ears (which she decided was a distant radio), she felt fine.

She needed to calm down. Yes, this was an incredible, once-in-a-lifetime, unexpected opportunity—and calling it that was *not* helping. Lily took a deep breath. She needed to treat this as if it were an outing with Mom. She had to remain calm, stay in control, and try not to do anything stupid.

Like overdose on antipsychosis medication.

Stop it, she told herself. Done was done, and now she had to continue on. Her best bet for where to find an Orange Key Tour was the center of campus. Tucking both the empty medicine vial and her cell phone back into her pocket, she strode out of the arch without looking at the gargoyles.

Almost immediately, the ringing in her ears worsened. It sounded like dissonant notes, blurring into a steady hum. It peaked as she reached a campus road hedged with rhododendron bushes and evergreens. She guessed she was hearing overlapping music from the various Reunion tents beyond the shrubbery. Grandpa had said that each Reunions class had a fenced-off area with its own swing band, country band, disco band, or DJ. That was a much more likely explanation than that the hum was a side effect of too much medication. She pushed aside worries about overdoses and brain hiccups and instead focused on her first view of the heart of campus.

Ahead was a plaza with a soaring cathedral. To her right were Gothic classrooms draped in wisteria. To her left was an ivy-edged walk lined with lampposts. Following a campus road, she passed the cathedral plaza and headed for a wide green lawn flanked by twin, white marble, templelike buildings. This was the Princeton University that she'd been dying to see. Gothic turrets. Gleaming marble buildings. Massive oak and elm and sycamore trees. Lawns so green that the grass looked as if it had been combed and cut by a master barber rather than a lawn mower. And a flock of tourists trailing like ducklings after a woman who was walking backward.

Take that, Old Boys! she thought.

Picking up her pace, Lily trotted across the green lawn toward the Orange Key Tour. She attached herself to the rear of the tour as prospective students, their families, and tourists circled an ivy-clad building. She heard the tour guide call it Nassau Hall, the oldest building at Princeton. Looking up at the yellow stone building with the white bell tower, Lily missed her grandfather. She was supposed to see the campus with him. She'd missed out on that moment.

But if she found the Key before Saturday afternoon, she could still march with Grandpa in P-rade, the annual alumni parade through campus that Grandpa always talked about. She shouldn't feel bad; she hadn't missed all the warm, fuzzy bonding moments. And if she won acceptance to Princeton, that would, of course, be the ultimate moment.

The tourists clustered in front of Nassau Hall. Green copper tigers flanked steps that led to tall blue doors. Lily inched closer to hear the guide, a ponytail-wearing student in a Princeton field hockey shirt, say, "After commencement, all the new graduates walk out FitzRandolph Gate."

As the guide pointed behind them, the tour (Lily included) rotated en masse to gawk across the oak-speckled yard at the formal entrance to Princeton. Permanently open, the wrought-iron gate marked the line between campus and the banks, coffee shops, and Rolex stores of the town of Princeton. It was crowned with the Princeton seal and framed by stone pillars, each with a stone eagle on top.

Leaning against one of the pillars was the tiger-haired boy.

Eyes widening, Lily stared at him. Maybe it wasn't the same boy. Maybe orange and black hair was a popular fashion statement on Reunions weekend.

The tour guide continued to talk, "Legend has it that if you walk out that gate before graduation day, you won't graduate. Ask any student, and he'll say that's just a myth. But ask that same student to walk out that gate, and he'll say no way. We all walk out the side gates." She pointed to twin gates that flanked the main gate. Made of the same spirals of black iron, they were crowned with lamppost-style lights instead of the Princeton seal. Lily barely glanced at them. Instead she watched the tiger-haired boy walk toward her between the oaks.

He was definitely the same boy. Had he followed her? Why on earth would he?

"I don't even like to come *in* the FitzRandolph Gate," the tour guide said. "What if I tripped and fell backward? So not worth the risk." Several tourists chuckled.

As he came closer, Lily could see his eyes. She hadn't looked at his eyes before. She'd been too busy looking at his hair, her feet, and the sidewalk in the vain hope that he wouldn't notice how fiercely she'd been blushing. He had beautiful eyes. They were tawny, a brown so light that they were nearly golden. All Lily could do was stare at them.

"You found the tour," he said in his soft voice.

"Yes," she said, still staring. His eyes were the same color as a lion's eyes. She'd never seen eyes like his. They were flecked with gold and bronze specks.

"I'm Tye," he said.

"Lily," she said.

"Nice to meet you, Lily." He sounded as if he meant it. She liked the way he said her name, all drawn out. His voice was as warm and smooth as hot chocolate.

In as sunny a voice as she could manage, she asked, "So . . . are you stalking me?"

"Pretty much," Tye said cheerfully. He flashed her a quintessential bad-boy smile. It made his eyes look like warm honey. She felt herself blushing for the second time. "I'm here to be your guard," he said. Before she could process that rather stunning statement, he added, "Tour's on the move."

"Oh!" she said. She turned to see the flock of tourists disappear through a brownstone arch. She hesitated. If she chased after the tour, would he leave? "I should . . . You're my *guard?*"

"You're taking the test, right?" he asked. For the first time, he looked unsure of himself. He looked even cuter when he was confused than when he smiled, if that was possible.

"You mean the Old—" She stopped herself before she said "Old Boys." They might be the Old Boys' Network, but she bet they wouldn't appreciate being called that. "Yes, that's me.

I mean, I'm taking it." God, could she sound any more like an idiot? Just because he had nice eyes didn't mean she had to lose all grip on the English language. "I should catch that tour."

"Good idea," he said, and he walked with her to the arch, through an ivy-choked courtyard, and out under a second arch. Distracted by the fact that he was accompanying her, she nearly plowed into the back of a middle-aged woman who was pointing a camera at an array of Gothic buildings across the plaza. Lily skidded to a stop mere inches away.

"Ahead and to your left is Firestone Library," the tour guide was saying to the flock, "and ahead and to your right is the University Chapel. We just passed through the courtyard of East Pyne, the Foreign Language Department. If I could draw your attention to the top of the East Pyne arch . . ." She pointed, and everyone rotated to view the arch.

At the top of the brownstone archway was a gargoyle shaped like the face of a blindfolded woman. Stunted arms jutted out under her chin to hold open a stone book. Every tourist aimed a camera up at the gargoyle.

"So . . . I'm on the right track to find the Key?" Lily asked Tye. She leaned closer to him so that the tourists wouldn't overhear. This close, she breathed in his scent. He smelled like a rain forest, or like the flower shop after Mom had misted all the plants. In his jeans and black T-shirt, he hadn't seemed like the scented-aftershave type of guy.

He flashed his lopsided smile. "Depends on what you want to open."

Enigmatic much? "Thank you, Cheshire Cat." Maybe he didn't understand that her whole future rested on this.

His smile vanished, and he self-consciously ran his hand through his tiger-striped hair. "What do you mean by that?"

Who dyed their hair crazy colors and then acted shy about it? Mom never flinched at the odd looks she got. Of course, that was Mom, queen of getting odd looks. "That wasn't a hair comment," Lily said. "I like your hair."

His grin returned. "Thanks."

She wondered if he thought she was flirting.

The tour guide continued. "Some of the campus gargoyles, like the Literate Ape on Dillon Gym, are humorous. Some are more classically inspired, like the Chained Dragon, which we'll see in just a moment on the University Chapel. Others represent the university experience, like this perennial favorite here, the Unseeing Reader, who symbolizes opening the eyes of students."

Keeping her voice low, Lily asked Tye, "Why do I need a guard?" She was on a campus tour at a suburban school, not wandering alone in the inner city. "Are you supposed to protect me against vicious squirrels and roving gangs of prefrosh?"

"Something like that," he said.

The tour guide was talking about a bulldog (Yale's mascot) carved into a drainpipe on the chapel, supposedly a joke from the architect, a Yale graduate. "Everywhere you look on the Princeton campus, you'll find treasures like these," the guide said. "Some call our gargoyles the 'true professors of Princeton.'"

Lily winced. Okay, that was cheesy. She hung back as the tour proceeded on to the chapel. "Am I really supposed to be on this tour?" she whispered to Tye. "She seems as likely to say something useful as a gargoyle." Lily nodded up at the Unseeing Reader.

"I wouldn't be so sure of that." His golden eyes twinkled at her. "You never know what a gargoyle might say." He waved up at the gargoyle as if the Unseeing Reader were an old friend that he always greeted.

High up on the arch, the Unseeing Reader's stone fingers twitched.

Lily felt blood drain from her face. It had to have been a flicker of light, a cloud crossing the sun, even though the sky was blemish-free blue. "Did you see—" She stopped. She didn't want him to think she was a lunatic or, worse, to report back to the Old Boys that she had her mother's problems.

Tye was watching her with an unreadable expression.

"Never mind," she said. Clasping her shaking hands together behind her back, Lily willed herself to stay calm. She'd taken a triple dosage. She might have a seizure or a heart attack, but she could *not* have a brain hiccup.

The fingers twitched again.

"Oh, crap," she said.

She couldn't pretend she hadn't seen that. Out of the

corner of her eye, she glanced at Tye. He was still watching her, his tawny eyes intense.

Above, the gargoyle spread her fingers. A shard of stone slipped between them and plummeted toward the plaza. Without thinking, Lily stretched out her hands. The stone landed neatly on her palms. She stared at it. It didn't feel like a hallucination.

"What does it say?" Tye asked.

Her head shot up. "How do you know it says anything?" She didn't wait for him to answer. "The Old Boys . . . Vineyard Club . . . they rigged the gargoyle," she said flatly. She waved the stone shard in the air. "This is a clue. And you knew it was and let me think I was . . ." Instead of finishing the sentence, she swatted his arm. Her fingers brushed against his bare skin. She felt tiny static shocks dance on her fingertips.

His eyes widened, and he reached out as quick as a cat and caught her hand. He held it for a second, and she felt prickles run up and down her arm. "Who are you?" he demanded.

"Nobody," she said. "I'm Lily. Lily Carter."

He was staring at her with a gaze so piercing that she felt yet another blush rise up over her neck and face. A second later, he dropped her hand and blushed too. "Sorry," he said. He seemed at a loss for words. She flexed her fingers. *Strange,* she thought. Her hand felt tingly. "You, uh, you think the 'Old Boys' are controlling the gargoyle?" he asked.

"Puppet or robot." She didn't care which, so long as it wasn't a hallucination. Lily studied the shard, a flat rectangle.

Carved on one side were numbers and letters: *921.45 Wil.* She showed it to Tye.

"Cryptic," he commented.

"It could be a date, except the punctuation isn't quite right," she said. "And what about 'Wil'? What does that mean?"

"Abbreviation?" he suggested. "Acronym?"

"Research time," she said. She was a stone's throw from the university library. The prospect of winnowing through that much information was daunting, but the answer had to be in there somewhere. It couldn't be a coincidence that she'd received this clue so close to—

Oh.

Of course.

"It's a book catalog number," Lily said. Looking up at the Unseeing Reader, she asked, "I'm right, aren't I?"

The gargoyle didn't answer.

Love at first sight, Lily thought as she and Tye approached Firestone Library. First, it was beautiful, all gray stone and turrets. But second and even better, it was lopsided. It had a single off-center tower that looked as if someone had stolen half of Notre Dame Cathedral and then stuck it on top of the library without measuring first. She loved it. It was grand and quirky at the same time, and it was utterly different from her home library. Not that she didn't love that library too. Her home library was a drab hunk of concrete from the seventies, but it was also her first-choice refuge whenever Mom was acting too "artistic" to handle. Lily typically holed up in the nonfiction section. She liked to thumb through the books and imagine what she would do once her life was her own . . . *if* it was ever her own.

If Princeton said yes, she would have her own life. Since this was Grandpa's alma mater, she was allowed to apply here, even though coming here would mean leaving home. (Princeton was too far from Philly for an easy commute.) All of the other colleges on the Grandpa-approved list were in or just outside Philadelphia. If she went to one of them, she'd live at home and commute to class. Mom and the flower shop would continue to dominate her world, and nothing would change. Passing this test was the key to her future.

"So is the Key in there, or just a clue to the next clue?" Lily asked Tye.

"They really have *you* looking for the Key?" he asked.

She bristled. "You don't think I can find it?"

"It's not that," he said quickly. "It's . . . you're a surprise, you know. Going to be fun to figure you out."

For about the five millionth time since she'd met Tye, she felt herself blush. "Not much to figure out," she said. "There's nothing mysterious about me." Mom was the one who was full of riddles. Lily was as ordinary as peanut butter and jelly. Possibly peanut butter and bananas.

"Yeah, right." He cupped his hand around her cheek, and she felt her skin tingle again with that fuzzy electricity. She froze, scarcely breathing. She'd never had a boy cradle her face in his palm, even if he was regarding her more like an interesting scientific specimen than an object of adoration. He released her. "I'll be back before you've found your next clue."

"You aren't coming with me?" she asked. Inwardly, she winced. She shouldn't beg him to stay with her. Just because he was the cutest guy who had ever talked to her . . . On the other hand, shouldn't he come with her? He *had* said he was her guard. "Don't you need to protect me from extra-fussy librarians or dangerously dust-ridden books?"

He flashed his lopsided smile. "Just watch out for rogue book carts."

She opened the library door. When she glanced back over her shoulder, he'd already walked away and was looking up at a gargoyle of a cloaked man with a flute. She had only a second to wonder what he was doing before a family of four approached. Rather than continue to block the door, she scooted inside.

The library foyer was a warm honey-colored wood, the same color as Tye's eyes. *Quit thinking about him,* she told herself. If she passed the test, she'd have plenty of time to moon about college boys with nice eyes. Right now she had a book to find.

Lily marched across the lobby only to stop at a set of turnstiles. Security guards were checking student ID cards. She considered her options: One, she could claim she was a student and try to bluff her way through (not a good idea—she was a lousy actress); or . . . She couldn't tell the truth. The Legacy Test was supposed to be a secret.

As she tried to think of a plan, she half listened to the family of four touring the library lobby. The woman was reminiscing about hours spent here on her senior thesis. The father bounced a toddler in a tiger-cub outfit on his hip while the girl gazed up at her mom with wide brown eyes. They looked like a poster for the Perfect Family. Lily knew a few families like that at home. The mothers always chatted politely with Lily's mom, but they'd look at Lily with pity when they thought she wouldn't notice.

The looks had only gotten worse in recent years, as Mom forgot more and more. Lily watched the alum gesturing as she described the carrel where she'd written her thesis. Lily bet that no one had ever looked at that woman with pity. She wondered if Tye would look at her with pity once he knew about her mom.

Focus, Lily, she told herself.

She spotted a sign that said VISITORS. One short conversation later (including liberal use of the words "prospective student"), and she was in possession of a temporary visitor's pass. She sailed by the guards, bypassed the reference room with its vaulted ceiling and Gothic windows, and headed to the elevators that bore the label, STACKS. There was a handy-dandy guide beside the elevator door identifying which floor had which set of books. The

900s were on C-level, it said, three floors below ground level. *Piece of cake,* she thought.

As she rode the elevator down, she wondered how large this library was to have three levels under ground. She pictured secret catacombs deep below the earth.

The doors slid open on C-level, and she saw her imagination wasn't far off. She stepped off the elevator to face darkened rows of bookshelves. Catacombs indeed.

Behind her, the elevator whirred as it rose, and then there was silence. No voices. No footsteps. No scratch of pencils, no click of laptop keys, no rustle of pages. *Kind of creepy,* she thought. She walked forward, and her shoes slapped loudly on the floor. It was so phenomenally quiet that she felt as if she should tiptoe. She wished Tye had come with her. She didn't like the feeling that she was the only person on the entire floor.

Only the center aisle was lit. Each aisle had its own light switch (either to conserve energy or to increase creepiness). Shadows shrouded the books. Lily hurried down the center aisle, reading the call numbers on the labels: 870s, 880s, 890s, 900s, 910s, 930s. She halted and backtracked. The labels jumped from 919.98 Zoo to 930.0 Abr. Worse, the 915 shelf and the 930 shelf were flush against each other so that you couldn't walk down the aisle to check for the 920s. How did anyone . . . She spotted a crank on the endcap of the row.

Oh. Right.

Stepping back, she noticed that every other bookshelf was

42

flush against its neighbor and each had a crank to separate the shelves. It doubled the number of bookshelves that could fit on the floor. "Clever, Lily," she muttered to herself. "Way to impress the Old Boys." At least Tye wasn't here to see her flummoxed by sliding shelves.

As she turned the crank, the shelves groaned and lurched sideways. She imagined a horror movie where the villain squeezed his victims between movable bookshelves. *Attack of the Killer Librarian.* Definitely a low-budget movie.

The bookshelves creaked and then settled in their final positions. Silence wrapped around her again. Lily shivered. She never thought she'd be freaked out by a library. On the other hand, she'd never been in a dimly lit, preternaturally silent library buried three floors below sunlight and fresh air. Walking quickly down the row, she scanned the shelves for the call numbers. Like the label had said, the books jumped from 919 to 930. "Where—?" she began to ask out loud.

Screech! The bookshelf shifted toward her.

"Hello? I'm in here!" she called. "Please stop turning the crank!" The shelf rattled closer. She darted down the row and burst into the center aisle. "Hey, I said—"

No one was there.

The crank continued to turn unaided until the bookshelves slammed together. She leaned forward to examine the crank. She didn't see a motor. So how—

Clang, screech!

Across the aisle, a second bookshelf shuddered, then

shifted. Lily backed away as the crank whirred faster. Jolting sideways, the bookshelf slammed against the next shelf. Books rocked, and then the library fell silent again.

Okay, she thought, *this is seriously creepy.* Maybe she should return to the nice, sunny lobby and ask the librarians at the information desk where to find the 920s. She liked that idea. Lily headed for the elevator.

Metal shrieked, and a bookshelf shot across the center aisle to block her path. Several books tumbled off the shelf and landed at her feet. Her heart hammered in her rib cage. "This isn't funny," she called. "You can stop now!"

She didn't hear anyone. Maybe it was a malfunction. Or it could be part of some automatic air-out-the-books maintenance routine, the library's version of an automatic sprinkler system. Not that she'd ever heard of such a thing, but there had to be a nice, logical explanation for why the shelves were suddenly acting possessed.

Lily speed-walked down a row. As she reached the end, the bookshelf sprang back and slammed against the brick wall. She ran back to the center aisle. All around her, dozens of bookshelves lurched forward and sideways. Metal crashed and shrieked. Books tumbled to the floor. She screamed as a set of shelves crashed together in front of her.

"Help!" she yelled. "Someone, anyone, help!"

She zigzagged through a moving maze. As shelves slid, she plunged through gaps. Aisles and rows slammed shut behind her.

Up ahead, Lily saw an old card-catalog cabinet. Hip height, it was an island in a storm. Lily raced toward it, ducking her head as books sailed off the flying shelves. The bookshelves zoomed around her faster and faster. Reaching the cabinet, she scrambled on top. A shelf smashed into the brick wall on one side of her, and then a second shelf crashed into the wall on the opposite side. A third shelf sailed directly toward her. Lily screamed and threw her hands in front of her face—

The shelf halted inches from her fingertips.

Everything fell silent again. All the bookshelves were still. Crouched on top of the cabinet, Lily listened, but all she heard was her own breathing, fast and loud.

She had to get out of here. Now. Before it started again.

Sliding off her perch into the narrow space between the cabinet and a bookshelf, Lily yanked books off the lowest shelf. She could clear a shelf, crawl through, and then run for the elevators. She'd emptied half the bottom shelf before she noticed the call numbers on the spines of the books: 921.

"Bastards," she said out loud.

Lily clapped her lips shut before she said anything worse. The Old Boys could be listening. She bet they were watching her right now through video cameras, chortling to one another as they sipped port in their leather chairs. They'd succeeded in scaring their newest candidate with mere bookshelves.

What sort of college admissions test involved terrifying

the applicant half to death? Lily took a deep breath and told herself to focus. She could tell them what she thought of their practical joke *after* she had her automatic-acceptance guarantee. For now, she had to find that book.

Lily ran her fingers over the book spines. 921.45 Bre, 921.45 Div, 921.45 Lin, 921.45 Zar . . . She didn't see a 921.45 Wil. She stood up and checked the other shelves.

A few book titles caught her eye: *Rituals and Music of the Northern Ogre Clan, On the Behavior of Brownies, Goblin Genealogy.* She plucked a book at random off the shelf and flipped through it. *Mermaids, a Life Cycle of.* It mimicked a research book, complete with charts and graphs and footnotes. It even had drawings of mermaid skeletons and diagrams of mermaid respiratory systems. Someone had put a lot of work into this parody. Replacing it, she selected another book. This one, *Chimeras of Today,* was the same: hundreds of pages of detailed "research." She returned it to the shelf and noticed that none of the books in this section had a publisher's logo on the spine. Maybe this was some sort of odd, self-published fan fiction stash? Or, ooh, maybe these were instruction manuals for some kind of elaborate homegrown Dungeons & Dragons game. Or fake dissertations. She bet the authors were the Old Boys themselves. If her grandfather (who read only literary fiction by either semidepressed writers or authors who eschewed all adverbs) had written one of these, she was going to tease him mercilessly.

Lily scanned the section. Cane . . . Card . . . Carr . . . aha!

She pulled a book off the shelf and read the title: *Dryads, a History* by William Carter.

She felt as if the world froze as she stared at the author's name. Grandpa's name was Richard. This book was written by a William Carter.

It was written by her father.

For an instant, she thought she must be hallucinating. But that was impossible. She'd taken the medicine. It was only that the book had surprised her, that was all. She hadn't expected to encounter anything that her father had done or touched. Her fingers traced lightly over his name, embossed in gold print on the soft black leather. Her hands trembled.

She shouldn't be so surprised. She knew that her father had been a student here. That was one of the few facts she did know about him. She didn't know what he'd looked like. (Mom had destroyed the photos years ago, though she had no memory of doing it or why.) Lily didn't even know his real name. (He'd changed his last name to Mom's when they married. Grandpa said her father had had "issues" with his own family.) He'd died in a car accident a few months after Lily was born.

Hands still shaking, Lily opened the book. She flipped through sketches of trees—everything from bonsai to evergreens, each with a figure beside it. The figures were clearly fantastical. Some had leaves for hair. Others had twigs for arms. She skimmed a chapter entitled "Powers of a Tree

Spirit, Mastery of Plants" and decided her father had been a creative man. Also, kind of a dork.

She didn't see what any of this had to do with a key. Setting her father's book down on the card catalog, she pulled out the *W* drawer. She rifled through the cards, looking for an author whose last name began with "Wil" and call numbers that matched the ones on the Unseeing Reader's clue. One minute later, she had it:

Author: *Wilson, Woodrow.*

Title: *The Gargoyles of Princeton: Lessons from the Literate Ape.*

"You guys think you're hilarious, don't you?" she muttered. There was no way that Woodrow Wilson, former president of the United States, had written an entire dissertation-length book on gargoyles . . . unless he'd been a member of Vineyard Club? Could these books be part of a hundred-plus-year-old in-joke?

She studied the subtitle: *Lessons from the Literate Ape.* She chewed on her lower lip, thinking. She'd heard that name before. Hadn't the tour guide mentioned a gargoyle called the Literate Ape?

This had to be her next clue.

She couldn't wait to tell Tye.

CHAPTER Three

Lily fled Firestone Library into bright, beautiful, and not-at-all-creepy sunlight. As she emerged, she heard ringing in her ears again—she hadn't realized that it had stopped inside the library. She shook her head as if she could shake out the sound and scanned the plaza for Tye.

She scolded herself for being so eager to find him. He'd joked about rogue book carts, but he hadn't warned her about the bookshelves. She had to remember that, as cute as he might be, he wasn't necessarily on her side.

She spotted him across the plaza. One foot on the chapel steps, he was looking up, talking to someone she couldn't see. He was probably talking about the pathetic high school girl who'd had to be practically hit over the head with the Orange Key Tour clue and who'd nearly had heart failure over a few remote-controlled bookshelves.

Approaching him, she caught a few words: "... old worm ...

I don't know why I even try . . . certainly not to *you* . . . even they aren't that stupid . . ." Oddly, he didn't seem to be talking to anyone. He was focused on the gargoyles above the arch, a ribbon of stone leaves and grapes interspersed with foxes and birds and lizards. She didn't see what was so fascinating about them. The only gargoyle that caught her eye was an S-shaped dragon, curled between the grape leaves and vines. Its curved neck was caught in a stone chain, and it looked out over the plaza with sad puppy-dog eyes.

Coming up behind Tye, she asked, "What's up with the obsession with the gargoyles here? The tour guide, the Old Boys, you . . ."

He spun around so fast that it was nearly a leap. "Hey! You're back. Great!" He flashed his patented lopsided grin and then quickly guided her by the elbow away from the chapel, as if he were steering her away from a patch of poison ivy. She felt a tingle on her elbow like static electricity.

"Any luck in the library?" Tye asked.

Lily nodded. "I'm supposed to go to the Literate Ape."

"Huh," he said.

She was surprised that the Old Boys hadn't briefed him already. "That was the clue from the special catalog that the possessed bookshelves guided me to."

His eyebrows shot up.

"It was very *Scooby-Doo*."

He looked blank.

"You know, Scooby, Shaggy, Mystery Machine. 'If it

weren't for you meddling kids . . .'" She trailed off. Okay, she'd made herself look like enough of a tool. "Never mind. I, um, have to go find a rock now."

"He's on Dillon Gym," Tye said. "You don't know about the Princeton gargoyles?"

"The true professors of Princeton?" Lily mocked the tour guide. She shook her head. "What do they have to do with the Key and the Legacy Test?" *Come on,* she thought, *give me a hint!* The Old Boys seemed to have a theme here with all the gargoyles, but she didn't see the connection to a key.

"You really don't know," he said, more to himself than to her. He grinned at her as if she'd done something marvelous. "And here I thought today was going to be boring." He clapped a hand on her shoulder, sending tiny tingles down her arm. "Let's go find some answers."

He headed for the East Pyne arch and waved again at the Unseeing Reader. Lily glanced up at the gargoyle and wondered if the Old Boys who'd supplied the clue knew about her father's book. She wondered if Tye knew about it. Gathering up her nerve to ask, she followed him through the archway into the ivy-choked courtyard. "Can I ask you something?"

"Yes, this is my natural hair color."

She grinned. "I'm serious."

"Okay, shoot," he said, stopping.

Shadowed and cool, the courtyard felt like a secret alcove. She was hyperaware that she was alone with this intense, cool, and intriguing boy and that she had his full attention. The humming-ringing-singing in her ears sounded extra loud. "Um . . . ," she said. "There were these books in the library. . . ."

"I'm told libraries have such things," he said solemnly.

She ignored that. "Different books. Strange books. One of them was by—"

A weight smashed hard into the center of her back. Lily lurched forward and slammed down knees first on the slate flagstones. Pain shot through her knees and up her thighs. All the air whooshed out of her lungs.

"Lily!" Tye yelled as he dove toward her.

She screamed as tiny pricks stabbed into her shoulder. "Ow, ow, ow—get it off!" Lily swatted at her back, and her hand smacked into leathery skin.

Tye yanked the animal off her back and flung it across the courtyard into the ivy. She heard a smack as it crashed to the ground several yards away. Tye knelt beside her and started swearing. "Look at me, Lily. Can you focus? It bit you. Oh, shit." He pressed his fingers to her neck, feeling for her pulse.

Over Tye's shoulder, she saw a . . . what the hell was that? Monkeylike, the animal was hairless and green. It wore half-shredded children's clothes draped over its leather body.

"You have bite marks," Tye said. "It must have started—"

The creature snarled, exposing sharklike pointed teeth, and then it lurched toward them. "Behind you!" Lily cried. Clawed paws scraped over flagstones.

Smooth as a cat, Tye spun and launched himself forward to intercept. Lily scrambled to her feet as Tye wrestled the monkey-thing to the ground. The creature slashed at Tye. He yelled as its claws scraped his arm.

Squirming out of Tye's grasp, the creature ran on all four paws toward Lily. She backed off the path into the ivy. Vines snagged her ankles, and she kicked them free.

Tye scrambled after the monkey-thing and wrapped his arms around its hind legs. It kicked, claws raking Tye's shoulder. "No!" Lily screamed. Reaching for a rock or a stick, she plunged her hand down into the ivy.

The vines slithered around her fingers as if they were snakes. She glanced down and screamed—the vines writhed like tentacles all around her.

The creature kicked hard, broke out of Tye's grip, and charged again at Lily.

"Stop!" she yelled.

Ivy vines uncoiled from Lily's ankles and shot out in front of her like striking cobras. They wrapped around the monkey-thing's torso and yanked the creature flat onto the ground. Tye pinned it down as the ivy encircled the thrashing creature, until the vines wrapped it so tightly that it lay cocooned.

Lily stumbled backward as black spots danced through her vision. Leaning over, she put her hands on her knees and squeezed her eyes shut. *Don't faint*, she ordered herself. Her leg muscles trembled and spasmed. She sucked in air.

Panting, Tye said, "Knew there was something about you."

She raised her head. He was kneeling on the monkey-thing's back. Blood dotted his arm. His sleeve had been shredded. The vines lay still now, wrapped tightly around the . . . whatever it was. "What the hell is that?" she asked. "And what do you mean, 'something about' me?"

"It went for you, not me," Tye said.

The creature fixed its hungry yellow eyes on Lily. Its face was disconcertingly human, except that its skin was as leathery and green as a reptile's. It licked its teeth, flecked red with her blood. She shuddered. If Tye hadn't been here . . . She pulled out her cell phone. "I'll call . . ." Police? Animal control? What was it, a mutant monkey? She guessed she should call 911.

"No!" he barked.

She jumped and nearly dropped the phone, catching it before it plunged into the greenery. At the same moment, she realized that she was still standing on the vines that had been writhing like snakes a minute ago. She scurried to the center of the flagstones, a safe distance from the ivy. Absently, she noticed that the ringing in her ears was gone.

"You have no idea what this is, do you?" he said. He didn't wait for her to answer. "No police. This . . . creature . . . it has to stay secret. Understand? The safety of a lot of people depends on it." His golden eyes pleaded.

"But why? What is it?" Lily walked toward him to get a closer look.

"Keep back," Tye said. "You can't let it bite you again."

"Is it rabid?" She twisted her neck, trying to see the bite marks on her shoulder. She touched them and winced as they stung. *Don't panic,* she told herself. She never panicked with Mom; she wouldn't panic here. "You can't hold it there forever. We need help." She flipped open her phone and dialed.

"Dammit, Lily," he said. "Who are you calling?"

"My grandfather," she said. The phone rang. "Pick up, pick up, pick up . . . ," she murmured. Voice mail answered. "Grandpa, I need you," she said. "Call me back ASAP."

"Richard Carter, right?" Tye asked.

"He's supposed to be at the Fiftieth Reunion tent," she said. "Where can I find it?" She wondered how he knew her grandfather's name.

Tye considered it for a moment, then nodded. "All right, he could help. Fiftieth tent is on the other side of Nassau Hall and Alexander Hall, next to Blair Arch." She blinked at him, and he pointed. "Straight that way."

"I'll be right back," Lily promised. She turned and took off at a run.

He called after her, "If you feel faint or weak or anything, go through the gate!" Or at least that was what she thought he said. She didn't stop to ask what he meant.

Lily ran across a campus road and in front of a building that looked like a half-shrunken cathedral. Straight ahead of her she saw a semicircle of Gothic dorms cordoned off by a newly erected wood fence. As Tye had said, there was an arch next to the fence, but the tip-off was the enormous sign that said CLASS OF 1960 in fat orange letters.

She stopped just inside the fence to catch her breath. She made a mental note to take up cross-country. Any one of the tanned long-legged runners from her high school could have sprinted that distance without panting like an overheated puppy. She hoped she'd been fast enough.

A man and a woman, both decked out in psychedelic zebra coats, sat at a registration desk. The woman flashed her teeth, white and perfect against her tanned and wrinkled skin, and said, "May I help you?"

"Looking for my grandfather," Lily said, panting. "Richard Carter. Is he here?"

The woman consulted a list. Lily felt the seconds tick by as the woman squinted at the list, forming names on her lips as she read. Finally, she looked up. "Carter with a *C?*"

"Yes," Lily said. *How else would it be spelled?* she wanted to shout. Her fingers itched to take the list. Tye was waiting for her.

The woman elbowed the man next to her. "Do you have A through *E?*"

"Richard Carter," Lily said. "He checked in with my mother. You'd remember her. She has green hair."

"Heavens!" the woman said. "On purpose?"

The man smiled warmly. "Oh, yes, Richard! Good man.

Splendid to see him. We were in Greek Myths 101 together. Top of the class, he was."

Yes, very nice, but . . .

"Carter," the woman repeated, and then recognition dawned on her face. "Oh! The FitzRandolph Gate Tragedy."

"The what?" Lily asked, and then she heard a familiar laugh boom across the tent. He was here! "Never mind," she said. She scanned the tent. Alumni milled around the lawn and under the tent. Kids played tag between the tent posts and around tables with folding chairs. Across a dance floor laid over the grass, she saw her grandfather. He was talking with someone she couldn't see.

"Grandpa!" she called.

At least twenty grandfathers in zebra-pelt jackets glanced over at Lily. She jogged across the tent, weaving between wheelchairs and partyers, toddlers and teenagers. Closer, she called again, "Grandpa!"

Her grandfather turned. So did the man he was talking to—Mr. Mayfair. Lily faltered as Mr. Mayfair frowned at her. His forehead was creased into deep craters, and his lips were tightly pursed—disapproval was etched onto every feature. *He has nothing to disapprove of*, she told herself. She wasn't here because of the Legacy Test. She was here to help Tye. He couldn't hold that creature forever. She forced her feet to walk across the rest of the tented area.

Grandpa frowned at her. "Lily, I told you—"

She showed him the bites on her shoulder. As she'd

discovered in third grade when she'd broken one of Grandpa's antiques, blood made an excellent conversation stopper.

Gripping her arms, Grandpa spun her around and examined her shoulder. "What happened?" he demanded. "Are you all right?"

"Those look like bites," Mr. Mayfair said with a note of concern.

"Lily, what bit you?" Grandpa sounded frantic. She frowned at him. Grandpa *never* sounded frantic. He hadn't even been fazed that time that Mom had insisted a pixie had infested their shop's roses. That had been one of Lily's worst moments—Mom had refused to admit it had been a hallucination—but Grandpa had stayed calm.

Lily half wished that monkey-creature had been a hallucination. "Well, it kind of looked like a wrinkled monkey, but it was green and hairless. . . ."

Grandpa checked her pulse and peered into her eyes. "Your breathing is fast, and your heart rate is up," he said. "Do you feel dizzy? Faint?"

Lily shook her head. "I ran here. Just catching my breath." She wondered why he didn't ask more about the creature. He understood that it was green, right?

Grandpa continued to prod her shoulder. "Did you take any extra medication today?"

Lily's eyes widened. How could he tell? "Are there side effects? Did I overdose? I know I shouldn't have. I was afraid of a brain hiccup. I took one of Mom's doses."

"It saved your life," Mr. Mayfair said. Lily gawked at him, but Grandpa didn't wait for her to digest that extraordinary statement.

He scowled at his oldest friend. "How could this happen? Your security—"

Mr. Mayfair spread his hands. "Perhaps you should take her home—"

"Or perhaps you should assign a guard," Grandpa interrupted.

Lily spoke up. "My guard has the creature pinned down in the East Pyne courtyard. But I don't know how long he can hold it. He needs help. He didn't want me to call 911...." Both men were staring at her. She trailed off. "What?"

Mr. Mayfair and Grandpa exchanged looks, and Mr. Mayfair said, "We didn't assign a guard."

"He said—," Lily began.

"Did he tell you his name?" Mr. Mayfair asked.

"His name's Tye," Lily said. "He has orange and black hair. Light-colored eyes. He said he was my guard. He knew Grandpa's name."

"Of course he did," Mr. Mayfair said, half to himself. To Lily, he said, "That boy cannot be trusted."

Lily looked from Grandpa to Mr. Mayfair and back to Grandpa. "But he saved me," she said. "He pulled the creature off me. It clawed him. He's hurt and waiting for help."

"I know this is upsetting," Mr. Mayfair said kindly. "You should know that you can stop this test at any time."

Lily opened her mouth to reply, but Grandpa beat her to it. "She cannot," Grandpa said. "This is her destiny. She was born for this."

Lily shut her mouth.

Grandpa smiled at her. "I promised your mother years ago that you would have this chance." And then his smile faded. "I need to check on Rose. If Lily was targeted—"

"You left her alone?" Lily looked around. She'd expected Mom to be nearby.

Grandpa nodded wearily. "She's in the room. She claimed she'd stay." For an instant, Lily thought, *He's old.* She had never seen him before as old, but now she noticed that the wrinkles on his cheeks were as deep as creases in a walnut shell. To Mr. Mayfair, he said, "Lily needs a guard. Could you—"

Mr. Mayfair squeezed Grandpa's shoulder. "You don't even have to ask. I'll see that she's taken care of."

"Thank you," Grandpa said gravely. He kissed Lily on the top of her head and then strode toward one of the gothic dorms.

Lily started after him. "Wait!" She should help him with Mom. But Tye also needed her. . . . "Tye's expecting me," she said to Mr. Mayfair. "I'd planned to bring Grandpa."

Mr. Mayfair beckoned to a clump of college boys. One, a blond, broke away from the pack and walked across the tent. Under any other circumstances, Lily would have been content to stare and stare. He was angelically beautiful: perfect blond hair, piercing blue eyes, and a Superman cleft chin. She half expected sunlight to burst through the tent in a halo around him and a heavenly chorus to swell in song. He was that perfect. Introducing him, Mr. Mayfair said, "My grandson, Jake. Jake, this is Lily Carter."

Jake smiled at her, the kind of smile that could make daffodils burst into full bloom. "Nice to meet you," he said. His voice was as warm as summer sun.

"Hi," she squeaked. *Snap out of it,* she told herself. He was just a cute boy. Okay, a godlike boy. She couldn't let that distract her from the fact that she'd been attacked by a monkey-thing and that Tye was waiting for her to return with the cavalry.

"Jake, Miss Carter encountered a Feeder," Mr. Mayfair said. "She'll lead you to the attack site in East Pyne."

Feeder. That thing had a name.

"Dispose of the Feeder and stay by Miss Carter for the remainder of her test. Don't interfere or aid her with her test, but do see to it that she remains safe from bodily harm. Understood?"

"Yes, sir," Jake said. The "sir" was not the least bit ironic. Lily had the sense that if they weren't in public, he would have clicked his heels and saluted.

"The tiger boy will be there," Mr. Mayfair continued. "I'd like to ask him a few questions."

Jake nodded. "He'll be taken in."

The way Jake said it sounded almost ominous, as if Tye would be in an interrogation room with a single bare lightbulb. Lily frowned and opened her mouth to object.

"Respectfully," Mr. Mayfair said. "He saved our candidate here. We owe him a debt." He favored Lily with a warm and reassuring smile. Lily smiled back, very glad that he'd been here with Grandpa.

"Consider it done," Jake said. To Lily, he asked, "Ready?"

She still had about three billion unanswered questions, but she nodded anyway. Liar or not, Tye needed help as soon as possible. Her questions could wait. "Thank you," she said to Mr. Mayfair.

"You're most welcome, my dear," he said.

"Tell Grandpa to call me if he needs help with Mom," she said.

Leading the way, Jake wove through the crowded tent. Lily followed behind. Once they exited the fenced-in area, Jake broke into a jog. She hurried to catch up. Her side cramped almost instantly.

In a perfectly conversational tone, as if they weren't running, Jake asked, "How are you enjoying your visit to Princeton?"

He had to be joking. "What's a Feeder?" she asked.

"I'm not at liberty to discuss that," he said. He smiled at her as if to say it was nothing personal. The smile made her heart do a little flip inside her rib cage. "I'm not supposed to aid or interfere."

"It *attacked* me," she said. Her calf muscles burned as they trotted across the campus road and headed toward Nassau

Hall. "I think I have a right to know what it is." She pointed at East Pyne. "They're in the courtyard."

"Stay behind me," Jake said, picking up speed. "You're not trained."

"Trained for what?" Lily asked.

He ran through the arch first. She raced after him and then bumped into his back as he abruptly stopped. "Sorry!" she said. She peeked around him. The courtyard was silent and peaceful . . . and empty.

The Feeder was gone.

So was Tye.

CHAPTER *Four*

Jake knelt next to the torn and mangled leaves. He fingered a battered vine.

"Careful," Lily warned. "The vines . . . well, they moved. Like snakes." She winced as she said it. It sounded so ridiculous. But she'd seen them writhe and watched them cocoon that Feeder thing.

He frowned at the ivy. "Dryad? What did the Feeder look like?"

"Green hairless monkey," she said. "Did you say 'dryad'? As in Greek myths?" She thought of the library book by her father.

"Can't be," he said. "Not with that description. Are you certain the vines moved?"

A knot of shredded ivy lay beside an indent in the soil. The vines looked like a cocoon ripped open. Ragged greenery was strewn about. "I didn't imagine it!" she said.

And she certainly hadn't imagined a dryad.

He held up his hands, palms out. "I believe you."

"Sorry," she said. She hadn't meant to yell. But the creature had been real. She hadn't had a brain hiccup. Lily touched the bite marks on her shoulder to reassure herself and winced again as they stung. The creature must have escaped, and Tye must have chased after it. She pictured it barging through a Reunions tent filled with toddlers and grandfathers. "We have to find them." She spun in a circle, as if she'd see a clue as to which direction they'd run.

Jake smiled.

"It's not funny," she said. "Tye could be hurt. An innocent bystander could be hurt."

"I'm sorry," he said, smile disappearing. The tips of his ears turned pink. She stared, awed that she had made this golden boy blush. "It's only . . . I like your attitude. That's all."

She continued to stare. She was more used to people telling her she needed an attitude adjustment.

"You don't have to worry about the Feeder, though," Jake said. "We have teams to chase it." He pulled out a phone and flipped it open.

"You have teams?" Lily asked. This happened often enough to need *teams*? Like intramural sports? Varsity creature-chasing?

"Got a code thirteen, last seen in East Pyne courtyard." He closed the phone, flashed her his megawatt smile, and said, "See? All set. You can continue your test."

She couldn't just resume her test as though nothing was wrong. Tye was missing, and that thing was still out there! She didn't know these "teams." How did she know they'd take this seriously? "It's not like I encountered some overly aggressive squirrel. It wore clothes."

"It will be taken care of," he said. "Trust me."

He had the most trustworthy face she'd ever seen. It was like being told "you're safe" by a superhero. He must have inherited that aura of competence from his grandfather. Still . . . "You sound like this happens all the time," she said.

He hesitated, and his forehead crinkled as if he were thinking very, very hard about how to answer. "Not all the time," he said at last. "Everyone's test is different. I've never heard of a Feeder attack as part of the test, but it would be too much of a coincidence otherwise."

Lily gaped at him as she tried to wrap her mind around what he'd just said and everything that it implied. "This was *intentional*?" she said. She thought of Mr. Mayfair's and Grandpa's reactions, more concerned about her guard than the creature that attacked her. She thought of how Tye had said that the Feeder had wanted Lily, not him. What the hell kind of test was this? Ordinary admissions tests didn't include mutant monkeys. The SATs didn't bite. "I could have been seriously hurt," she said. If Tye hadn't been there . . .

"I'll make sure no other Feeder bothers you," Jake promised.

"There are *more* of those things out there?" She thought

of how Grandpa had left to check on Mom. Maybe he hadn't been worried about Mom's usual flightiness. Maybe he'd been worried about Mom's encountering a Feeder. Lily pulled out her cell phone and dialed Mom's number. No answer. She tried Grandpa's. No answer either. "I have to check on my mother," she said.

"Hey," Jake said as she hurried out of the courtyard. She heard him jogging to catch up to her. "What about your test?"

Screw the test, she thought. If Mom was in any danger because of Lily's test . . . If creatures like that were loose on the campus because of her test . . . If Vineyard Club was responsible for allowing vicious, unnatural creatures to roam around in highly populated areas because of her test . . . She hadn't agreed to that. "Admissions tests shouldn't involve blood," she said. She'd fill out an application form and submit her essays just like everyone else. She had a decent shot at getting in on her own merit, right?

"You're safe now," he said, "and so's your mom. Your grandfather is with her—he was heading for the dorm, wasn't he? You don't have to worry."

Lily snorted. That was like saying, *Hey, you don't have to breathe today.* "She doesn't travel much," she said, a massive understatement. They should never have brought Mom here. "She's used to her and me being together." Mom rarely left the triple-decker that was their home. She worked on the first floor in the flower shop, Grandpa lived on the second floor in his antique-laden apartment, and Mom and Lily lived on the third floor (the attic, really). They'd made it into their sanctuary and filled it with items that made Mom feel safe. The apartment was littered with art: leftovers from Mom's pottery phase (they had a shelf full of lopsided vases), her mosaic phase (she'd retiled the bathroom to resemble a Turkish bath), and her mobile phase (they'd hung a dozen spiraling mobiles of birds and sailboats and kites). Skylights flooded the apartment with sunlight, and every shelf, table, and windowsill held plants. Morning glories crawled over their kitchen window, and a miniature rose garden covered the entire dining room table. Without all of that, Lily knew that Mom wouldn't feel safe here, but she'd never thought that Mom actually wouldn't *be* safe here. Lily walked faster. "My mom takes care of me. Like any other mom. But I also take care of her. That's how it works. I have to check on her." And if her Legacy Test had endangered Mom, then she'd quit.

Maybe she should quit anyway. The Old Boys were clearly deranged, and Lily hadn't signed up to play head games. She wondered if they'd planted Dad's book to mess with her, too. Maybe he hadn't written it. She wondered if Mom would know.

"No one can fault you for caring about your mother," Jake said. "I'm sure the officers won't penalize you for deviating from the test." He didn't sound confident, and for an instant, Lily wondered if she was being overly anxious. Mom was most likely fine. Grandpa was with her, as Jake had pointed out. Lily tried to imagine how she'd explain to Grandpa that she wanted to quit. It would kill her to disappoint him.

Entering the 50th Reunion tent again, Lily slowed at the registration desk, but Jake flashed the couple a brilliant smile and ushered Lily past. "You know which room?" she asked him as they crossed the tent.

"Everyone was briefed on where you'd be," Jake said.

"Oh," she said. She bet "everyone" would be briefed again if she quit the test, mortifying Grandpa.

As she followed Jake into a dorm and up a cement stairwell, she heard a familiar voice belting out show tunes. *Mom*, she thought. *She's okay. Off-pitch, but okay.* Grandpa must have already come and gone; Mom wouldn't be singing like that if Grandpa was there. Lily felt the muscles in her back slowly unclench. She hadn't realized how worried she'd been.

"You don't have to come with me," Lily said to Jake. Introducing Mr. Mayfair's gloriously gorgeous grandson to Mom was not high on her list of things to do.

"I can't guard you if I'm not with you," Jake objected.

"Can't you—I don't know—scan the hall for green monkeys and then wait?" she asked. "Mom won't tell me how she's really doing if you're there." With other people, Mom was all sunshine and cream. If Mom had seen a Feeder, she wouldn't admit it in front of Jake. And she'd never agree to talk about Dad. "Please," Lily said. "I'll be fine. Does that sound dangerous?" She pointed toward the room where the singing was the loudest. "I mean, other than to one's eardrums?"

Jake laughed. "Yell if you need me," he said. "I'll be right here." He leaned against the wall and crossed his arms so that his muscles bulged. Oddly, the obvious I-am-buff move *did* make her feel safer.

"Thanks," she said, and meant it.

Lily knocked on the dorm room door, but the singing didn't falter. She tried the knob, and it turned easily. She sighed as she opened the door. Honestly, couldn't Mom at least remember to lock the door? "Mom . . . ," she began. She stopped and stared.

Oh, this was not good.

Mom had dragged one of the spartan metal dorm beds to the center of the room and was standing on the mattress. She had markers and pens and pencils strewn all around her bare feet, and she was drawing on the ceiling as she sang "Everything's Coming Up Roses."

Lily shot a look back at Jake. She didn't think he could see into the room from where he stood. She smiled brightly at him. "Everything's normal," she said to him. "Just a sec!" She scooted inside and shut the door quickly behind her. "Mom!" Mom held a Sharpie. Permanent marker. "We don't live here! What are you doing?"

Holding up one blue-stained finger for silence, Mom added another leaf and then smiled up at her handiwork.

Mom had drawn an intricate mural of intertwining black leaves on the ceiling. Flecks of blue danced between the leaves like glimpses of sky.

"Come down from there." Lily pointed to the floor for emphasis. "Where's Grandpa? Did he see this?"

Mom frowned down at her. "Lily! Is that blood on your shirt?" She climbed off the bed and cooed at Lily's shoulder. "Sweetie, are you okay? What happened?"

Lily plucked a fresh shirt out of their suitcase. "I'm fine," she said automatically. She changed shirts and then waved at the ceiling. "What are you doing?"

"Since we're here for a few days, I thought I'd make it feel more . . ." Mom trailed off, finally noticing the expression on Lily's face. "Oh. I didn't think." Mom looked down at the Sharpie in her hand. Blue and black ink covered her fingers. "I'm so sorry, Lily. I know how important this weekend is to you. I didn't mean to add to your stress."

Of course she didn't. She never meant to. Sighing, Lily looked up at the ceiling with its thousands of tiny leaves. Buds poked between the branches. She thought she saw creatures, too: squirrels and birds, tiny winged men and wide-eyed elf girls. "It's beautiful," she said.

Mom sank down on the mattress and stared up at her leaf mural. "I just had to . . . you know. It wasn't . . . quite . . . home."

Sitting down next to her, Lily rubbed her neck, feeling at least seventy years old. "We'll buy some white paint before

71

we leave. It's fine. Really, it could be worse." At least Mom hadn't gotten herself mauled by a monkey-thing and herded by unruly bookcases. Lily was in no position to judge. "We shouldn't have left you alone here until you settled in."

Mom patted her knee. "Don't be silly. You have your test."

Lily hesitated, unsure how to tell Mom that the test was insane. She was so used to shielding Mom from bad news. Lily flopped back onto the mattress. Springs poked into her back. "Ow."

"Seriously ow," Mom said, poking at the bed. "When you come here, you can bring your futon and a lot of pillows. We can make it look more like home, once it's your own room." She waved her hand at the ceiling.

"I still don't think they let you draw on the walls."

Mom winced. "I let you down."

"It's okay. Really." Funny thing was, staring up at the ceiling of swirling leaves *did* make Lily feel better. She felt calmer. "It's been a strange day. After you left Vineyard Club, I met this boy with orange and black tiger-striped hair. . . ."

"Hmm."

"Not as nice as green hair," Lily said quickly. "Don't get any ideas."

"Nothing is as nice as green hair," Mom said solemnly. She leaned back on the mattress beside Lily. Their hair overlapped. "Is he cute?"

Lily sat up. "Mom!"

Mom laughed. "You're such an easy target. How can I resist?"

"Ha. Very funny." Lily lay back down slowly this time so that the springs didn't stab her spine again. "Yes, actually, he's very cute. He's also a liar."

"I'm intrigued. Tell me more."

Lily launched into a description of the day, but she stopped when she reached the part about finding her father's book. She rarely mentioned Dad to Mom. There was usually no need—he wasn't part of their lives, and with Mom's memory . . . it was best not to mention him.

Mom touched her shoulder, near the bite marks. "Did someone hurt you in the library?" she asked gently. "You can tell me, Lily. I'm your mother. You don't need to protect me."

Yes, I do, she thought, but she didn't say it out loud. She never said anything like that out loud. "I saw a book . . . ," Lily began.

Mom patted her reassuringly. "And it had no pictures?" Her voice dripped with false sympathy.

Lily laughed. Mom would get along well with Tye, she thought. Sobering, she said, "It *did* have pictures, as a matter of fact. Of trees. And kind of magicky tree spirits."

"And puppies and rainbows?" Mom asked. "Are you certain you were in a *college* library?"

"Dad wrote it," Lily said quietly.

Mom fell silent.

Lily told her about all the fake dissertations. "Dad's wasn't the only one. There were dozens, maybe even hundreds. Why would anyone take the time to write a several-hundred-page joke? It doesn't make any sense." She propped herself up on one elbow so she could see Mom's face. Expressionless, her mom stared at the ceiling. "Mom? What is it?"

Mom picked up a marker, crossed the room, and began to draw vines on the white plaster around the window. *Uh-oh,* Lily thought. Clusters of grapes and leaves blossomed over the vines. The marker tip bent as she bore down on the wall.

Lily jumped off the bed. "It's okay, Mom. You don't need to remember. I didn't expect you to. Please, stop." *Dammit,* she thought. She shouldn't have said anything.

A doglike face emerged between the vines and grapes. "You should know more about your father," Mom said. She drew faster. "I should be able to tell you what his smile looked like, what his voice sounded like, what he liked for breakfast, what made him laugh. . . ." In slashing strokes, she drew a curved, snakelike neck. "But. I. Don't. Remember."

Lily wrapped her arm around Mom's shoulder. "It's all right. Really, it doesn't matter. Forget I said anything. Let me tell you about some of the Reunions jackets I saw. Much worse than psychedelic zebra."

Shrugging her off, Mom continued to draw. She added bat wings to the snakelike body. "All I remember from the day he died is the ambulance. I don't remember our car or the accident. I don't even remember where we were." She added clawed talons. "I don't remember the day we met. I don't remember the day he proposed. I don't remember the day we married." She drew scales shaped like tears. "I know we once walked through a garden of red and yellow tulips with a fountain in the center." She switched pens and sketched linked ovals around the animal's neck—a chain that was held in one talon. "And I remember how he made me feel. Safe. Like he'd be my knight in shining armor. Like he'd fight dragons for me."

Mom finished the final link of the chain, and then she sank down on the floor and hugged her knees. Lily dropped down beside her, wrapped her arms around her mother, and stared at the drawing of the Chained Dragon gargoyle that she'd seen on the arch of the University Chapel.

"Wow," Lily breathed, and then fell silent.

For a long while, they simply sat like that, without looking at each other, eyes fixed on the dragon. Questions swirled in Lily's head, but she didn't dare ask a single one.

A half laugh, half chirp burst out of Mom's lips. "It's very . . ." She waved her hand as if the gesture would finish the sentence. Lily watched Mom attempt to dredge up a smile, but the fake smile faded after only a few seconds. "Oh, Lily, sometimes I think the only reason I hold on at all is you and your future. You're going to pass this test. I know it. And then you'll have everything I can't give you." Turning to her, Mom gripped Lily's wrists. "You can't know how much that means to me. I *need* to look forward. I can't look back." Mom was crying now. Silent tears. "I'm getting worse, Lily. I can feel it. Every day, I slip further away. But when I think about you . . . your future . . ."

"I'll pass! I promise!" Lily hugged her. "I have the next clue already: the Literate Ape. I can win this. It's only a weird treasure hunt. Piece of cake." The Feeder hadn't really hurt her much, and the bookshelves had only scared her. She could do this. "Please, don't cry!"

Mom turned her head aside, as if she thought that if Lily couldn't see her cry, then it didn't count as crying. Stroking Mom's leaf green hair, Lily looked up at the drawing of the Chained Dragon and wondered what the Old Boys had in store for her next.

Shutting the door, Lily leaned against it. She wanted to bang her head repeatedly, but she bet that would alarm Jake. She smiled wanly at him. "She'll be fine," Lily said. Mom had sworn up and down that Grandpa would be checking on her soon.

"Of course," Jake said. As Mom began to sing again, Lily saw pity in his very blue eyes and felt as if he'd seen her underwear drawer, complete with the pairs reserved only for laundry emergencies. She guessed he must come from one of those oh-so-perfect families without any hint of . . . without anyone like Mom.

"I need to find the Literate Ape," she said. *And the shreds of my dignity and self-respect,* she added silently. At least she hadn't told him that she'd considered quitting. She ducked her head, unable to meet his eyes anymore. Her face felt hot. Passing him, she headed downstairs. He fell into step behind her. She felt his sympathy-filled eyes soaking into her back, labeling her pitiable. She didn't look back at him as she pushed open the door to the dorm and walked into the sunlight.

Outside again, she lifted her chin up to feel the warmth on her face. As always, the touch of the sun soothed her. She braved a look back at Jake. "Which way to Dillon Gym?" she asked.

Jake hesitated. "Grandfather instructed me not to aid you. Campus directions aren't classified, but I don't think I'm supposed to give you any information. . . ." He dithered adorably for a moment longer until she let him off the hook by tapping the shoulder of a nearby alum.

"Excuse me, could you please tell me where I can find Dillon Gym?" Lily asked the alum.

The orange-clad grandfatherly man pointed at the Reunions gate. "Straight out to the campus road and then downhill." His hat, she noticed, had beer cans strapped to either side and a straw that bent down to his mouth.

She thanked him and turned back to Jake. His ears were pink as he blushed. "Guess I could have told you that," Jake said. "It's my first guard assignment. I don't want to make a mistake."

Lily couldn't blame him. She felt the same way about nearly everything she did. Jake trotted alongside her as they left the dorms area. "Are you in Vineyard Club?" she asked. She quickly added, "You don't have to answer if you don't want to."

"I'm more . . . in training to be a member," he said. "You join eating clubs at the end of sophomore year. I just finished my freshman year." He puffed out his chest like a rooster, proud of his member-in-training status. She stifled a smile.

"Is Tye in Vineyard Club?" she asked. She skirted around patches of ivy, keeping to the far side of the sidewalk. The ivy vines lay still and quiet.

Jake snorted. "Absolutely not."

"You *do* know him."

"I know *of* him," Jake said. "Never met."

"Who is he?" Lily asked. "Why did he say he was my guard? What did he want?"

"I . . . um . . . ah . . ." His face reddened. Lily remembered he wasn't supposed to give her any information. She opened her mouth to apologize, but before she could, he pointed straight ahead. "That's Dillon Gym," he said.

Following his finger, she saw a building that looked like a medieval fort. If it wasn't for the DILLON GYMNASIUM sign by the road (which, admittedly, was a big tip-off), she never would have guessed it was a gym. "Don't worry," she said. "I won't tell anyone you told me."

"I think it's all right, but thank you," he said gravely.

"You really care about this, don't you?" she said.

"As much as you do," he said.

She didn't have a reply to that. She wondered what he'd say if he knew that her mom's sanity was tied to Lily's admission into Princeton.

Lily faced Dillon Gym. Four gargoyles jutted out over the entry arches: a football player, a dour-faced man in medieval garb, a tiger with a shield, and an ape in graduation robes and spectacles. Like the Unseeing Reader, the ape held an open book.

She halted underneath the ape gargoyle. Looking up at his stone chin, she waited for him to produce a clue like the Unseeing Reader had.

He was as motionless as . . . well, as stone.

Lily squinted up at the gargoyle. Sun wreathed his stone head like a halo. She wondered if the clue was in the book that he held. After all, she'd been sent to the library to find a book—maybe this was the book she was supposed to find. If so, she'd have to climb up there to be able to see it. She nearly laughed out loud at that thought. There was zero chance she was coordinated enough to scurry up the stone. She wasn't a rock climber. Or a squirrel. She'd end up clawing uselessly at the walls while Jake laughed until he collapsed on the sidewalk.

This is ridiculous, she thought. The ability to impersonate Spider-Man had nothing to do with college aptitude. "Can you lift me up?" she asked Jake.

"I can't—"

"—aid me," she finished. "Sorry. I promise I won't get you in trouble." Craning her neck, she looked up at the windows above the arches. She might not be able to climb up to the Literate Ape, but maybe she could climb *down*.

With Jake behind her, Lily walked into the gym. She mentioned the words "prospective student" to the guard and was waved through. Inside, Dillon Gym looked and sounded like every other gym in the world. College guys and girls ran back and forth over basketball courts. Sneakers squeaked, and players grunted and panted. Lily spotted stairs and went up to the second floor with Jake trotting behind her. She noticed several of the female basketball players eyeing him as they passed. Jake didn't appear to notice, which Lily liked.

Upstairs was a gymnastics room. She poked her head in. It was empty. She crossed over mats and shimmied around a balance beam to get to the windows. In the mirror that covered one wall, she watched Jake follow her. He looked rather confused.

"What are you doing?" Jake asked as she opened a window.

"Going to check out that ape," she said.

"People will see you," he said, "and you could fall." He sounded genuinely concerned, and Lily wanted to pat his hand to reassure him.

"It's one story up," she said. "I'll be okay. But thanks." She'd climbed out onto the roof many times at home, and that was the third story. Her mother even climbed out with her. They liked to lie on the roof side by side under the stars and invent their own constellations.

Jake continued to look worried.

"You could wait below and catch me if I look like I'm going to splat," she suggested. "It would be a very guardlike thing to do, preventing splattage."

He smiled, and his face lit in a warm, melt-polar-ice-caps kind of way. "I haven't had any training courses on preventing splattage. You'd be putting your life in my hands."

She noticed he had really nice hands. Imagining him catching her, she failed to think of a witty response. "Okay," she said.

"Okay," he said. And then he blushed.

"Do you have a camera?" she asked.

Still blushing, he asked, "What?"

"If anyone looks curious, you can pretend I'm posing for a photo."

"Got one in my cell phone."

"Great," she said.

For a long moment, they stared at each other. Jake cleared his throat. "I'll just . . . go down now," he said.

Lily watched him exit the room. She couldn't believe this Greek god of a boy was talking to her, much less blushing when he talked to her. *Don't read anything into it,* she told herself. *He's just a naturally sweet guy.* Below, she saw him emerge under the arches. He waved up at her. Smiling, she waved back.

She climbed out the window above the ape gargoyle. Dangling her legs down, she stretched her feet until she felt stone with her toes. She lowered her weight down onto it and then knelt on the back of the gargoyle. Once she was lying belly down on the statue's back, she peered over the ape's shoulder at the book.

The stone pages were blank.

Her heart sank. She'd been sure that was the answer!

Below, Jake had his cell phone out and was snapping pictures. She wondered if he thought she was crazy for climbing up here, especially since the book was blank. She usually tried so hard to appear not crazy. None of Mom's hippie clothes. Just jeans, ordinary T-shirts, tiny earrings, and lip gloss. None of Mom's offbeat habits. No knocking on wood or climbing trees at the park with the six-year-olds. No flowers in her hair. No singing off-pitch at high volume in the veggie aisle of the supermarket. No weird aversion to cars or movie theaters or basements. But if Lily's looking crazy at her dream school would keep Mom sane (or at least close to it), then Lily had no choice but to dance naked in the full moonlight, so to speak. "Now what?" she asked herself. "What's my next clue?"

Underneath her, the stone shuddered. A soft voice said, "I am."

It wasn't Jake. She looked behind her at the window. No one was there. "Who said that?" she asked. She had the sinking feeling that she wasn't going to like the answer.

The stone vibrated again, and the voice said, "I am your clue."

She bent sideways to look underneath the gargoyle for a

microphone and speaker. She didn't see anything. "Mr. Ape," Lily said in an even voice, "are you talking?" She wasn't going to let the Old Boys rattle her this time. They'd rigged another gargoyle somehow.

"Professor Ape, if you please," the gargoyle said in the same soft-as-sand voice. "I have tenure." He chuckled as if he'd made a joke.

"Nice to meet you, Professor Ape," she said. "So am I talking through a microphone to someone in Vineyard Club, or is this a recording? Are you interactive?"

The gargoyle sighed. "I would appreciate it if we could dispense with all the 'you're joking' and 'this can't be true' and 'I must be dreaming' nonsense. Can we simply agree that I'm a magical being from a parallel world and pronounce this lesson done?"

She laughed. At least the voice's owner had a sense of humor.

He sighed again, and the stone beneath her shifted. She wondered how they achieved that effect. "One of *those*. Very well. Please proceed with your speech about how I can't be real and how I must be an elaborate ruse involving puppetry and/or robotics. I'll hibernate until you're finished. I must conserve my magic."

Someone in Vineyard Club liked fantasy novels a little too much. But she could play along. "What do you mean, 'conserve your magic'?"

His voice brightened. "Ah, you've decided to be sensible!

Marvelous! Let's begin then." He adopted a professorial voice as he began to lecture, "First, you must understand that there are two worlds. Parallel worlds, if you will. In many ways, they are nearly identical, but the one primary difference is that your world is inhabited by humans and other related creatures, while my world is inhabited by, for lack of a more precise term, what you would call 'magic creatures.' Are you with me so far?"

"Parallel worlds," she repeated. "Magic creatures." She tried to sound serious and failed. She wished she'd read more fantasy. Mom had stacks of Tolkien rip-offs tucked into every corner of the apartment, but Lily hadn't read a book like that since *The Lion, the Witch and the Wardrobe* in fourth grade. She'd lost her taste for it the first time Mom's hallucinations involved an elf. Now she felt as if she were bluffing her way through a test she hadn't studied for. *Oh, wait,* she thought, *I am bluffing my way through a test I haven't studied for.*

"No need to sound so skeptical," he said. "You're talking to a gargoyle."

Or, more accurately, she was talking to some guy in the basement of Vineyard Club. How gullible did they think she was? Lily glanced down at the sidewalk and wondered if Jake was in on the joke. He was too far away to hear the gargoyle's soft voice. She wondered if he knew about this whole parallel-world story.

"For the record, we academics do not approve of terms

such as 'magic creatures.' It smacks of Tolkien and literary invention."

"Gargoyles read Tolkien?"

"I am a literate ape," he said modestly.

She laughed.

"Despite many similarities," the gargoyle continued, "the worlds are not compatible. There's a particular airborne element that exists only in the nonhuman world. Denizens of that world—my home world—have evolved to be dependent on that element, which we call 'magic' for the sake of convenience. We need a certain amount of magic in our bloodstream to survive, and we need a higher concentration of it in order to fuel our magical abilities."

"Very interesting," Lily said, trying her best to sound polite. Someone had clearly spent a lot of time crafting this whole scenario.

"Do you have any questions so far?" he asked.

Yes, she had a million: What did all of this have to do with college admission? Why had the Old Boys invested so much time in this role-playing game? How had her father been involved? Why had Mom drawn the Chained Dragon gargoyle? Where were Tye and the Feeder? And what breed of idiot thought that releasing an uncontrollable mutant monkey with claws, teeth, and a taste for blood on a crowded campus was a good idea? But she didn't dare ask any of those questions. She had to humor these people until her admission was secured. Lily stuck instead to a relevant question: "If you're from the magic world and need magic to survive, how are you here talking with me right now?"

"Ah, an excellent question!" He sounded pleased. "There are two ways for my kind to survive in your world. One: With significant training and the correct preparation of rituals, we can transform ourselves into stone. Essentially, we hibernate, slowing our breathing, our heart rate, and the decay of magic in our system. Many of the gargoyles on this campus, such as myself, are magic creatures who have chosen to undergo the elaborate rituals and physical inconveniences in order to remain in this world as ambassadors and teachers to those humans designated to interact with our world." He paused as if waiting for her to say something.

"That's, uh, very nice of you," she said.

"How kind of you to notice!" Again, he sounded very pleased. "I think I like you."

She hoped Grandpa was listening to this. In effect, this was her admissions interview. So far, she seemed to be acing it. She shot a look down at Jake. He was shooing away a curious tourist.

"The second way for a magic creature to survive in this world is to become a Feeder," the gargoyle said. "Feeders drain magic out of others in order to survive. Commonly, this is done via a bite since the magic inhabits the bloodstream."

So the attack *did* tie into this whole fantasy game. She touched the puncture marks on her shoulder and winced as they stung. The fact that the Feeder had drawn blood highlighted how serious the Old Boys were about their fake scenario. She wondered how far they were willing to take it. She pictured Tye holding down the vine-wrapped creature. They'd already taken it far enough.

"Their prey is humans," Professor Ape said. "All humans have a trace of magic in them, but only a trace. Once it's gone . . . the human does not survive. A single bite will kill a human."

She'd been bitten and survived, so the Old Boys had already slipped up in their story. She guessed that the voice behind the Ape didn't know that. She wasn't going to point it out.

"Unfortunately, draining humans is addictive," Professor Ape said. "Once a Feeder has experienced it . . ." He sighed, his stone body rippling.

"What does all this have to do with the Ivy Key?" she asked.

"I *knew* I liked you! No dithering about impossible versus possible. So refreshing! The knights did well to allow your candidacy," he said. "If you'll pardon the pun, you've 'keyed' into the correct question: What does a key have to do with parallel worlds?" He sounded exactly like her AP Chem teacher, waiting for an answer.

She considered it. If she were to invent parallel worlds, how would she involve a key? Keys opened doors. "It's the key to a doorway between worlds," she said.

"Right you are!" he exalted. "In this case, substitute 'gate' for 'door,' and you have it!"

She wanted to cheer. She felt as if she'd nailed a pop quiz

for a class she hadn't even been taking. She glanced down again at Jake, wondering if he could tell how well she was doing. He snapped a photo with his camera phone and then gave her a thumbs-up sign.

The ape continued. "Once, our two worlds were separate, but three hundred years ago, a gate was opened between our worlds. A golden era began that lasted nearly a century. Hundreds traveled freely between the two worlds, exchanging knowledge and culture. Princeton University was founded to facilitate this exchange." He paused as if picturing the shiny goldenness of this "golden era," and then he heaved a sigh that shuddered through his stone body. "But then, due to fear and ignorance on both sides, the gate was suddenly and irrevocably closed with disastrous consequences. Humans, trapped in the magic world, weakened and died. Magic creatures trapped here either died, became gargoyles, or became Feeders. And so it was . . . until the first Key was discovered."

Beneath her, the stone stilled.

"So, where can I find this key?" Lily asked.

No answer.

"Professor Ape?"

Silence.

She knocked on the back of the gargoyle. "Excuse me? Hello? Where do I go next?"

Below her, Jake called up, "Incoming—twelve o'clock!"

Lily looked up and saw a security guard jogging toward the gym. She bet he wasn't going to like the explanation that she was up here to talk with a gargoyle. "Jake? Remember how you're going to keep me from splatting on the pavement?"

He positioned himself beneath the Literate Ape. Lily swung her legs off the gargoyle. She tried not to think about the cement sidewalk below. She wrapped her arms around the ape's neck and lowered herself down. Her toes touched Jake's shoulders, and he gripped her calves.

"Got me?" she asked.

He grunted in response.

She released the gargoyle. For an instant, she dropped. But then Jake's arms tightened around her legs, and she slid straight down into the circle of his arms. Her feet touched the sidewalk, and she looked into the very blue eyes of the very gorgeous boy who was now holding her tightly against his chest. "Knight in shining armor," she said.

He widened his eyes.

She heard the security guard shout, "You! Stop!"

"You promised you weren't going to get me into trouble," he said, his arms still around her.

"Technically, you're only in trouble if you're caught," she said as the security guard neared. "How about we run?"

"Good idea," he said.

Together, they ran.

CHAPTER *Five*

"*He's* not following," Jake reported.

Under the shade of a fir tree, Lily stopped. She bent over, hands on her knees, and caught her breath. They'd sprinted up a hill and past another Reunions tent to a path surrounded by fake wilderness. The trees, shrubs, and vines were staggered to resemble a bit of forest, but unlike a real forest, they'd been carefully trimmed and circled with mulch.

"You were amazing!" Jake said. "Most people panic the first time they talk with the Literate Ape. But you . . . you took it in stride! He even seemed to like you." He was regarding her as if she'd flown solo across the Atlantic without an airplane.

Lily felt her cheeks heat up. "Uh, thanks," she said. She hadn't done anything so special. Certainly nothing to warrant that expression on his face. "I just . . . want to pass." Closest she'd ever gotten to seeing that expression on a guy's face was when she'd dumped a container of chocolate milk directly on

Melissa Grayson's head after Melissa had called Lily's mom a loony. She'd gotten applause and then a chat with the school psychologist. But that had been second grade. If it happened now, most of her high school class would agree with Melissa, and no amount of chocolate milk would change that. At least Lily's mom didn't vacation in Hawaii without her or fail to show up to parent-teacher conferences due to a manicure appointment like Melissa's oh-so-perfect mother.

"You really might pass!" Jake said.

"Your confidence in me is overwhelming," she said drily.

"I'm sorry," he said. "But most don't. Most can't handle it."

"You did, right?" she asked.

"Of course," he said.

He didn't elaborate, so she walked forward down the winding path. It opened onto a manicured garden of red and yellow tulips. Strips of flower beds curved into a shieldlike shape. Green blanketed the space between the tulips, and in the center was a fountain with candy blue water and a sculpture of a half horse, half man. Sunlight bathed the tulips so the petals glowed. *Mom would love this,* Lily thought. She should bring her here.

Or maybe Mom had already been here. She'd mentioned a tulip garden with a fountain. This place, like the Chained Dragon on the chapel, could be somehow lodged in Mom's memory. "Where are we?" Lily asked.

"Prospect Gardens," Jake said. "Straight ahead is the student union, and beyond that are the eating clubs. To our right are dorms. To our left, Firestone Library, the chapel, East Pyne, Nassau Hall. You have your next clue?"

Unfortunately, she didn't. She knew that Feeders were bad and that the Old Boys liked Dungeons & Dragons a bit too much, but she didn't know what she was supposed to do next. She couldn't admit that with Jake still beaming at her, though, so she dodged the question instead. "Did you talk to gargoyles in your test?"

"Oh, yes, but I spent the entire conversation with Professor Ape searching for a speaker and microphone," Jake said. "I even pried up a flagstone in the walk below. Grandpa subtracted the repair cost from my trust fund."

"Oh." She tried to imagine cavalierly tossing around words like "trust fund" and couldn't. "Your grandfather didn't help you?"

"It wouldn't have been ethical," he said.

"Right. Sorry."

Side by side, they circled through the garden. Ringed with evergreens, the flower beds were half in the shadows. Tulips swayed in a breathlike breeze.

"Grandpa did train me," Jake said. "Pop quizzes over breakfast on the prior night's homework, martial arts classes since age four, summer trips to Europe with enough museums to put an artist to sleep. He wanted to ensure that I had a chance at a future here. Failure wasn't an option for him or for me."

She thought of Mom. If passing this test would keep

Mom from slipping away—if walking through fire would keep Mom from slipping away—Lily would do it. "Not so much an option for me, either."

"Yeah, I get that."

Their eyes met, and Jake smiled. She smiled back.

Voices carried across the garden as a string of chattering and laughing students passed by and then exited. A couple holding hands strolled after them, pausing for a photo in front of the yellow and red tulips.

"So, where to?" Jake asked.

She thought for a moment. She didn't know where to find the Key, but she *did* know what the Key (supposedly) opened. The Literate Ape had talked about a gate, and there was only one famous gate here: the entrance to Princeton, the gate that no student ever walked out through. It would be just like the Old Boys to pick the most ornate, most famous gate on campus as their special gate. "This way," she said.

Lily headed up a set of stone steps. Jake followed her behind a row of manicured bushes to a rose garden. She saw red and yellow and soft pink buds. Only one or two had begun to open their petals. At home, Mom had coaxed all their roses into bloom already. She claimed her success was due to the fact that she sang to them. Lily credited the skylights that turned their apartment into a greenhouse. As soon as her test was over, she'd bring Mom to this garden. Maybe it would stir up memories of Dad. The memories couldn't be gone forever, could they? There had to be some way to bring them back.

"Do you like it here?" Lily asked. "At Princeton, I mean."

"Love it," he said. "I can't picture myself anywhere else. I think I was a prefrosh from birth. My grandfather used to sing me Princeton songs instead of lullabies. I have these clear memories of him tucking me in while belting out a fight song. . . . I know it sounds corny, but I always felt this was, like, my destiny."

"Not corny at all," she murmured. She thought of her grandpa singing Princeton songs in the flower shop on slow days.

Up ahead, she saw a familiar road. She'd walked this way before—the campus road led to the chapel and library plaza. She picked up her pace, weaving among members of a marching band dressed in orange and black plaid and wearing straw hats. As she crossed the plaza in front of the chapel, she imagined returning to Grandpa and Mom with the news that she'd passed. She'd be able to make Mom happy, a semimiraculous feat.

Up on the arch over the chapel door, she spotted the Chained Dragon. Nestled in the stone greenery, he was the size of a terrier, curved into a backward S with bat wings splayed flat against his back. A thick stone chain was carved around his neck. One of his talons clutched the chain.

Scale for scale, Mom had drawn him exactly. She'd even captured the sad, lonely look in the dragon's puppy-dog eyes. How had Mom remembered this carving so precisely when she couldn't even remember Lily's father's face? Of all the things to remember, why this?

Lily didn't realize she'd stopped walking until Jake burst out, "You can't be ready to talk to him!"

Both of her eyebrows shot up. So . . . the Chained Dragon was another rigged gargoyle, like the Literate Ape. Perhaps Mom's subconscious had given her a clue. "Why not?" she asked.

"Did Professor Ape tell you about the dragon?" Jake asked. He seemed agitated. "Anything about his history? You can't talk to him yet!"

She guessed she was meant to approach the dragon much later in the test. Skipping ahead sounded good to her, though. She could finish the test early and then join Grandpa and Mom for P-rade on Saturday as planned. "What about his history?" she asked.

"I . . . I can't tell you." He clearly wanted to talk. His thoughts played across his face. She watched his forehead crinkle and uncrinkle. His lips started to form words and then pressed together as if he were physically holding back the words as they tried to escape his mouth.

"It's okay," Lily said. "You don't have to tell me anything. I'll figure it out." If she wasn't supposed to talk to the dragon yet, then all the Old Boys had to do was tell the guy running the audio setup not to respond. But maybe, just maybe, they'd slip up and she'd have a shortcut to the end of this ridiculous test.

Lily marched toward the steps of the chapel. The second her foot touched the first step, she saw a stone tongue flick out of the dragon's mouth.

She halted. That had looked very realistic.

Jake caught her arm. "You don't have to do this," he said. "We can return to Professor Ape. Ask him about your next clue. It can't be the dragon. He can't be part of your test." If she didn't know better, she'd say he was genuinely freaked out by this sculpture. "He's saved for late in the training. Seniors face him. Not candidates. *I* haven't spoken to him yet."

Jake really seemed to believe what he was saying. She hadn't expected him to be such a good actor. The Old Boys must have prepped him well. She was positive now that she was on to something. "I need to get close," she said. Like with the Literate Ape, she bet the gargoyle would talk once she was close enough that no one could overhear.

Unlike with the Literate Ape, she didn't see a convenient window above the gargoyle. The ribbon of carvings that included the dragon was recessed within the arch. She'd need to reach it from below, ideally with a ladder.

Climbing the stone steps, she entered the chapel antechamber. She glimpsed the chapel's nave through the inner doors. Rows of wood pews stretched to the distant altar. Stone pillars soared to the vaulted ceiling. Everything was bathed in a soft blue light from hundreds of stained-glass windows. She wondered if Mom would remember this if she saw it. She promised herself to bring Mom here too, after the test was over.

Lily scanned the antechamber for anything resembling a ladder. Beside the open doors to the chapel was a marble staircase with a red velvet rope stretched across it and a sign that read BALCONY CLOSED. Leaning beside it was a black metal folding chair. *Good enough,* she thought. She fetched the chair and brought it back outside.

"Can you watch for security?" she asked Jake. "Ward off any paparazzi or whatever?"

"Only if you promise me you won't get too close," Jake said as she set up the chair underneath the arch. "You have to be careful."

"It's stone," she said. "I won't hurt it."

"If you look in danger, I'll knock you off the chair."

Lily blinked at him. He seemed 100 percent sincere. "You should win an Oscar," she told him. He was fully immersed in this role-playing game, treating the gargoyles as if they weren't robots or puppets . . . except he had gotten the story mixed up. The Literate Ape had said the gargoyles were the good guys. "I'll be fine." She stepped onto the chair.

A foot down from the gargoyle's tail, she looked up into the dragon's mournful eyes. *"Free me,"* a voice whispered. His voice was so faint that she rose onto her tiptoes to hear. The stone tongue darted in and out again. *"Free me,"* the dragon repeated.

His voice was snakelike. Shivers walked over Lily's skin.

The audio guy had succeeded in making stone sound truly creepy. Kudos to him. She wanted to climb off the chair and put as much distance between her and that voice as possible.

Jake hovered on the steps below her. "What's he saying? You shouldn't listen to him."

"I hurt. Oh, I hurt." The stone chain, she noticed, had been carved to look as if it were biting into the folds of the dragon's neck. It was clever of the Old Boys to use that detail. It made the dragon seem more real. *"Please, I beg of you. Save me."*

"It's stone," Lily said. "You're stone."

"Come closer," the dragon whispered, *"and I will show you how to free me."*

The Old Boys were testing her. But were they testing her compassion or her resistance to peer pressure? "I don't know if I'm supposed to do that," Lily said.

The dragon hissed. *"Free me!"*

Just a game, she reminded herself. Just a role-playing fantasy game that some bored privileged kids had cooked up over beer pong. But it was hard to remember that while the dragon's harsh, sad, awful voice shuddered through her. She felt it echo in her bones. Such a sweet little carving shouldn't sound so painful. "Why are you chained?" she asked.

A harsh, sibilant laugh erupted from the stone sculpture. The sound made her feel as if her guts were churning. *"You came on your own, young one, didn't you? The knights didn't send you to me. How delightful."*

The Literate Ape had mentioned knights too. She

wondered who they were. "The Literate Ape said—"

"*He is still here? Fool. He could be free! He has not been shrunk to this unnatural size and bound against his will.*" His tongue flicked again, gray as stone but fast as flesh.

"Who did this to you?" she asked.

"*That is not the question you came to ask,*" he said. He sounded oddly amused.

"I want to know where to find the Ivy Key."

His stone features slid as smoothly as skin as his expression changed from sad to eager. She shivered and told herself that the Old Boys were wealth personified—they could afford special effects like talking stone and sliding bookshelves. "*And you come to me? How deliciously fascinating.*" His voice changed to a command. "*Your name, little one.*"

"Lily," she said. "Lily Carter."

"*Ahh!*" His tail lashed. "*You come to me for answers because the humans lie, lie, and lie. Come closer, Lily Carter, and I will tell you all.*"

Hesitating, she glanced down at Jake.

"Lily, what is he saying?" Jake asked. "You can't trust him."

"*You of all people cannot trust humans,*" the dragon said. She realized that Jake hadn't heard anything the dragon had said. His voice was pitched only loud enough for her to hear. "*To you, their truths are only half truths. Their answers, half answers.*"

"And you'll give me whole truths?" she asked.

"*I can tell you who you are.*"

"I know who I am," she said.

His tongue flicked in and out. *"I can tell you how your father died."*

What the hell did he mean by that? She knew how her father had died: a car accident. "All I need to know is where to find the Key." And then she'd finish this test, secure her admission, and tell the Old Boys exactly what she thought of their mind games. First the book and now with the dragon . . . why so many reminders of her father? What did he have to do with this crazy game?

"Once, there were many Keys. One by one, they were destroyed." He laughed again, and she shuddered at the sound. *"I even destroyed one myself."*

The Old Boys wouldn't send her on a hunt for something that didn't exist. Would they? "Are there any left?"

"Oh, yes."

"Tell me," she demanded.

"The Key is not an object," he said. *"The Key is a being who is half human and half magic, a parent from each world. Only such a being can pass through the gate. Only such a being can allow others through the gate."*

"Where can I find this Key person?"

"Come closer, and I will whisper to you."

Shoving her foot into one of the ornate hinges, Lily boosted herself up. She reached up and grabbed the stone vines near the dragon's tail to pull herself higher—

"Lily!" Jake cried. He grabbed the back of her jeans.

Before he could force her down, the dragon's head shot

100

toward her. His jaws clamped down hard on her hand. She screamed as stone bit into her. Below her, Jake yelled. Spots burst in front of her eyes as pain coursed up her arm like fire. Bits of red orange flame darted out of the dragon's mouth and around her fingers. She screamed again.

Jake yanked her down. Stone scraped gashes along her hand as he pulled her out of the dragon's jaws. Red splattered across the wood door and stone trim. His arm around her waist, Jake half carried, half dragged her down the steps to the plaza. Her head spun.

The dragon screeched. He pushed his talons hard against the chain, and the stone stretched and strained. Dimly, Lily heard Jake: "Oh, shit. Don't die! Oh, shit, what do I do? Dammit!" He ripped his sleeve off his shirt in one quick jerk and wrapped the cloth around her hand. More swirls and spots spun over her eyes as she stared up at Jake's face. A second later, he was shouting into his cell phone—she hadn't seen him take it out. Only a few words made sense. She blacked out.

A few seconds (or minutes or years—she couldn't tell) later, she opened her eyes to see Jake's face swimming inches from hers. She was cradled in his lap. "He could have killed you," Jake was saying. "He *should* have killed you. You shouldn't have survived that."

She focused beyond him on the chapel arch. Black dots still danced over her eyes, but she thought that the dragon had grown. He filled half the arch, and the stone chain bit deeply into his thick neck. "He grew," she whispered. Stone didn't grow. Stone didn't live. Didn't talk. Didn't bite.

"He had long enough to drain you," Jake said. "Why aren't you dead?"

"*More!*" the dragon howled. "*Need more!*" He let out a scream that shook Lily's bones and echoed across the plaza. She shuddered hard.

Jake looked up at the dragon and then down at her. "You're one of *them*," he said. He shoved her hard away from him. She rolled off his lap and onto the stone plaza. She lay there, cheek against the flagstones. Every muscle felt depleted. She couldn't process his words. "God, I helped you! I even thought you—" His voice was so full of revulsion that she flinched. "You don't belong here. Monsters belong on the other side of the gate."

Gate . . . She remembered Tye's voice: *If you feel faint or weak or anything, go through the gate!* She seized on that memory. It was the only coherent thought that penetrated the dark swirls in her brain. She felt weak; she needed the gate.

Lily lurched to her feet. The plaza tipped and spun.

"*More!*" the dragon cried.

She heard other voices shouting. All she could think was *gate*. She needed to go through the gate. Every muscle shaking, she half ran and half fell across the plaza and through the East Pyne courtyard. She stumbled past Nassau Hall, and the green lawn of the yard tilted before her. Her ears roared as her vision spun.

She caught herself against an oak tree. Her fingers curled into the bark, and she breathed in the scent of the tree. It strengthened her. She pushed away from the trunk. The few people in the yard swam in and out of her field of view. She avoided them, dimly hearing them call to her, asking if she was okay, as she wove her way toward FitzRandolph Gate.

She stopped in front of the gate and looked up at the Princeton seal. It blurred into a smudge as she gazed at it. The stone eagles multiplied as her vision swam again. Beyond the gate, she saw Nassau Street. A traffic light held cars at an intersection. *Go through the gate,* Tye's voice repeated in her memory. "Why?" she wondered. But it hurt to think through the aching haze. It was simpler to obey.

Lily plunged through the gate.

Everything flashed white.

Seconds later, Lily lay flat on her back on grass, not sidewalk. She stared up at the front of FitzRandolph Gate. She saw the Princeton seal . . . but the stone eagles were gone.

In their place were twin eagles with feathers of metallic gold. The birds screeched and then lifted skyward from the stone pillars. They circled above her, shadows against the cloudless sky. She saw another bird with firelike feathers streak between them, and she saw a shape that looked like a winged lion, silhouetted against the blue. . . . *Where am I?* she thought. *What's happening to me?* She tried to scramble to her feet and collapsed forward onto her hands and knees.

She lifted her head. A tiger paced slowly toward her. His

tail lashed from side to side. Her heart started to thud so loudly in her ears that it muffled all other sound. Gritting her teeth, Lily pushed herself to standing.

Muscles shaking, she backed away as the tiger approached. *Run,* her mind whispered. *Run!* But she couldn't. She stumbled.

The tiger shimmered as if he were drawn in smudged ink. His fur rippled, and he collapsed and then stretched upward. Legs shot down, and arms reached out. Slowly, the blur solidified into a boy with orange and black hair.

"Tye," she breathed.

He caught her as her knees buckled, and she crumpled.

$\mathcal{L}$ily heard a murmur of voices, and she tried to open her eyes. Her eyelids felt as if they were glued down. She raised her hand to touch her face, and she felt cloth. She forced her eyes open and saw a white cloth wrapped around her hand.

Bandages, she thought. *How nice.* Her vision faded.

Next time she woke, she was on her back, looking up at a ceiling of wood tiles. At first, they wavered and spun, but then they resolved themselves into a static geometric pattern. She turned her head, but the motion made her vision blur again. Figures standing near her looked like streaks of white light and shadow.

She felt panic rise up into her throat, choking her. "Tye?" she said. It came out as a croak. She tried again: "Tye?"

"The were-tiger boy isn't here," said a voice that sounded

like a waterfall. Words cascaded down. *You could drown in a voice like that,* she thought.

She squinted, but her eyes wouldn't focus right. The voice's owner was a white smudge against a brown background. She thought she saw a streak of gold. "Where is 'here'?" she asked. "Who are you?"

"If she's awake enough to ask questions, then she is alert enough to answer them," another voice said in a deeper tone, tinged with a growl.

"Patience," yet another said, an airy voice this time, almost amused. "She was drained to nearly nothing. All your fine interrogation skills are useless on the unconscious."

Drained. Jake had used that word. It matched how she felt, as if the marrow of her bones had been sucked out and she were about to collapse from the inside out. Her heart hammered loud and fast in her ears, and she wondered what the airy voice meant by "fine interrogation skills." "What do you want?" she asked.

She felt a breath on her cheek, hot and fetid. A voice rumbled, "We want to know how many humans you've killed to survive."

"What?" Her eyes teared as she strained to force the blurs and streaks into shapes. "I don't understand. I've never hurt anyone."

"Impossible," the airy voice said.

Another voice said, "Tye has vouched for her."

"Children can be deceived," the deep voice rumbled. "In

this case, he may wish to be. You'll answer us now, half breed. Are you a Feeder?"

"No!" she shouted. Lily sat up and felt as if fire shot through her head. She squeezed her forehead and felt the cloth bandages on her hand. It stung where the dragon had bit her. "I'm not a Feeder. I'm not a half breed. I'm not anybody." Until today, nothing unusual had ever happened to her. She was just ordinary Lily who worked in her grandfather's flower shop, took care of her mother, and obsessed about her grades.

"You crossed the gate on your own," the waterfall voice said. "You are a Key."

Lily's vision was clearing, though her head still throbbed. She saw a horse directly in front of her. She lifted her gaze, and the horse's torso flattened into a human stomach. She stared at the intersection of human skin and horsehair, and then she looked up into an elderly man's face.

Centaur, her brain helpfully supplied.

Behind the centaur was a man with orange and black tiger fur streaking his face. Beside him, a two-inch-tall man with orange butterfly wings perched on the shoulder of a porcelain-skinned woman with black-as-night hair and sharply pointed ears. Next to the elven woman was a stack of stones, loosely in the shape of a person, that moved and breathed as if it were alive. And lastly, there was a unicorn.

Lily stared longest at the unicorn. She felt as if she were looking at a shaft of moonlight. He was iridescent white, as smooth and flawless as a Michelangelo sculpture. His golden horn shone like an angel's halo.

"How do you feel, child?" the elven woman asked. Her tone implied that she didn't care what Lily's answer was or if she answered at all. She peered down at Lily as if she were an only mildly interesting science experiment.

Lily could be dreaming. She could be unconscious, knocked out when Jake had let her fall onto the stone plaza. Or she could have lost her mind. Given her family history, that was the most likely option. It was much more likely than the idea that Professor Ape had told the truth. "I need my medicine," Lily said, attempting to keep her voice calm. "Where's my grandfather?"

"Who is your grandfather?" the tiger-faced man rumbled.

"More importantly, who are your parents?" the elf asked. She caught Lily's chin in her hand, and Lily felt the pressure of fingernails against her cheek. Lily froze. The elf was doll-like beautiful. She shouldn't have been frightening, but there was something too perfect about her face. She looked more like a department store mannequin come to life than a real woman.

"My grandfather is Richard Carter, and my mother is Rose Carter," Lily said "My father was William Carter."

The tiger man asked, "Was?"

With his tiger face, he should have looked like a costumed performer, but he didn't. The fur was real, and there was no faking the heavy jaws or the cat-slit pupils. He looked as if he'd begun to transform into a tiger and stopped partway. Under his gaze, Lily felt as if she'd been cornered by predators. His yellow eyes bored into her. "He died in a car accident a few months after I was born," she said. "I never knew him." She'd never even seen a photo. . . . Oh, God, was this why there were no photos? Could he have been—

No, she thought. If her father had been one iota out of the ordinary, Grandpa would have ferreted it out. He was too protective of Mom not to have thoroughly screened her husband.

The rock creature shifted, and Lily heard the crackle of gravel. He spoke: "What is your purpose in coming here now?" Each word thudded.

"I just . . . wanted to get into college," Lily said miserably. It sounded ridiculous given the circumstances. "I didn't do anything wrong!"

"How old are you, child?" the elf asked.

"Sixteen," Lily said.

The tiny man whistled low. "Sixteen years without magic . . ."

"Impossible," the tiger man said. "She must be a Feeder. She must be held and reeducated. We cannot allow her to return—"

The unicorn interrupted him. "She would never survive the length of time required for reeducation. The magic would overload her body."

"I'm telling you the truth!" Lily said. "I never heard of

Feeders before today. All I did was walk through a gate!" She stood up, and the unicorn leveled his horn at her, the stone man shifted forward, and the centaur tensed. She stiffened.

"You did more than that," the centaur said grimly. "You survived for sixteen years without a single visit to our world. You're a half breed. You need both worlds to survive."

Staring at the tip of the unicorn's horn, she felt her heart pound so fast that it felt like bird wings beating inside her rib cage. "I don't understand," Lily said.

"Half breeds belong to both worlds," the tiny man said.

"Or neither," the elf said. "You should only last a month in the human world before too much magic leaches from you and you die of magic loss. And you should only last a month in our world before your body suffocates with too much magic. Yet you live. An interesting mystery."

Lily forced herself to take a deep breath. "If you let me go home, I promise I'll find an explanation. I'll figure out why I'm still alive. If I'm a mystery, then let me solve it. I deserve a chance to solve it!"

The centaur and the tiger man exchanged looks. The tiny man hovered above the elf's shoulder. His fluttering wings stirred the air, swirling the sunlit dust. The stone man shifted, and it sounded like an avalanche.

"Please!" Lily said. She'd never come here again if they'd just let her go. She looked at each of them, her eyes pleading. "I'm not a Feeder. I'll find answers."

The unicorn dipped his horn low, the equivalent of lowering his sword. "I will allow it," he said.

"As will I," the centaur said.

"Yes!" the tiny man said.

The elf sighed. "Very well."

The tiger man growled. "Only with conditions."

The others nodded. Lily didn't breathe. *Please,* she thought. *Please, let me go!*

"You may return to the human world," the centaur said. "But you must find answers to our questions before you enter our world again. Otherwise we will have no choice but to believe you are a Feeder and insist that you remain here for reeducation."

She felt her knees shake. "You'll let me go?" Her voice cracked.

Back on the elf's shoulder, the tiny man braided and unbraided the elven woman's silken hair. His tiny fingers flew over the brilliant black strands. "Do you understand? You can't survive here. You'd last longer than any of us would in your world, but eventually you'd suffocate on too much magic." ·

"Discover how it is that you are alive," the tiger man said. "Or when you next come before us, you will not leave, no matter the consequences to you."

Lily swallowed hard. "I'll find answers," she promised.

"We do not condone Feeders," the centaur said. "Remind the knights of your Princeton. We support them and their cause."

The tiger man flicked a claw at her. "My son will assist you. He awaits you outside." His son . . . Tye? Tye looked much more human than this man. She wondered what her own father had looked like. What kind of monster had he been? What was in her genes?

The stone man lumbered toward the door and opened it. Lily walked to the exit. It took every ounce of self-control not to run. Behind her, she heard the unicorn say in his waterfall voice, "If you are truly innocent, then we will welcome you. Another Key is a blessing."

Lily heard the tiger man rumble, but she couldn't tell if it was in agreement, disappointment, or hunger. She wasn't about to stay to find out.

She fled the room and didn't look back.

Outside, Lily halted and stared across a college yard, complete with oak trees, sidewalks, and the FitzRandolph Gate. On either side of her were Princeton buildings, and behind her—she turned to look—the building she had been in was Nassau Hall.

"Impossible," she said.

Leaning against one of the oak trees, Tye said, "Sorry. You're not dreaming, hallucinating, or crazy." He peeled away from the tree and crossed to her. "Are you okay?"

Lily looked back at the gate. Gold eagles perched on the stone pillars, and a thick forest lay beyond. She'd crossed the looking glass into bizarro Princeton. "Just peachy," she said. She started to shake, and Tye wrapped his arm around her shoulders. She buried her face against his chest as tears poured out of her eyes. He stroked her hair. He didn't tell her to stop crying or that there was nothing to cry about or any other platitude. He simply held her until she could breathe again without sobbing.

She pulled back. "I wet your shirt," she said, touching the tearstains that darkened his T-shirt. "I'm sorry. I don't know why I did that. I'm not a crier." She was normally a bottle-it-upper. She reserved any necessary crying sessions for late at night, locked in the bathroom, where Mom wouldn't hear her.

He shrugged. "It'll dry. Don't worry about it." Strands of hair clung to her tear-streaked cheeks. Gently, he pushed the strands off her skin. She looked into his golden eyes. His face was only a few inches from hers. For a second, they stared at each other, and Lily had the insane thought that he was going to kiss her. But then he released her and said, "You're hurt. What happened to your hand?"

"Oh, uh . . . you know the dragon on the University Chapel? It bit me."

He turned her wounded hand over and examined the bandages. His fingers were soft and gentle on her wrist. "What on earth possessed you to get so close to him?" Tye asked.

"I thought he was animatronic," Lily said.

Tye grinned. "Fair enough." He was still holding her hand.

Her skin tingled. She couldn't tell if it was from his touch or from the air here. "Last time the Chained Dragon drained a Key, the magic was enough to free him. He killed a lot of people before he was caught again. You were lucky. That Key didn't survive."

She shivered.

"If you'd been an ordinary human, you'd certainly be dead," Tye said. "Good thing you're full of surprises."

"So are you," Lily said. She pulled her hand away from his. "You lied to me. You said you were my guard."

"Yeah," he said. He didn't sound the least bit sorry. "But 'Hi, I'm Tye, I'm a were-tiger' would have been the worst pickup line ever."

Despite herself, Lily laughed.

His smile faded. "You aren't supposed to exist, you know."

"Now, *that* is the worst pickup line ever." She tried to keep her voice light. "Everyone seems very disappointed that I'm not dead."

"Believe me, I'm not," he said softly. He laid his hand on hers, over the bandages, and looked straight into her eyes. He didn't have his father's eyes, she noticed. He had human eyes, except for the golden color. "I thought I was alone," Tye said.

Lily couldn't think of anything to say. His expression was so intense that it could have thawed a glacier. She felt as if she were melting into his tawny eyes.

"So, what are you?" he asked. "You don't look like you have wings or a tail. Anything strange ever happen around you? Anyone turn to stone? Anything burst into flame?"

She shook her head.

"Hey, it's okay." He lightly touched her cheek, and she felt her skin tingle again beneath his fingertips. "We'll figure it out. I have an idea that could help. Come with me."

He propelled her across the yard and around Nassau Hall. She heard a faint whispered hum as she passed the oaks. It sounded as if a radio stuck between a station and static were lodged inside her head. Maybe it was a side effect of the blood loss. Or she could have a concussion from when she had fallen onto the plaza flagstones. "Do you hear that?" she asked.

"Hear what?" he asked.

In the distance, a trio of boys with antlers exited one of the Gothic classrooms. Lily stared, hum forgotten. "What is this place?"

"It's Princeton," Tye said. "Or at least another version of it. Both schools were built when the gate was open to everyone. The two campuses were supposed to foster understanding between the worlds. You know, so that we don't end up slaughtering each other."

"Oh," she said. "You go here?"

"Father's on the council," he said, "so I've pretty much been a student here my whole life." As they crossed the campus, he told her stories about being a student at this Princeton: classmates who could vanish or sprout wings, professors who wrote with six arms on chalkboards, courses that focused on shape-shifter physics. At last, Tye stopped in front of the concrete arches of the football stadium.

"So what do you do here?" she asked. "Quidditch?"

"Not all the students fit into the usual dorms." He led her through the arches, underneath the bleachers. Ahead, she saw a football field crisscrossed with clumps of dirt as if it had been unevenly raked. "We use this place for the dragons."

Lily halted. Clutching her bandaged hand to her chest, she said, "I think I'll skip this part of the tour."

"You need to see this." He sounded serious and intense. "You need to understand that the Chained Dragon is the exception. You need to understand that we're the good guys too."

"Why?" Lily asked. "Why do I need to understand? Why show me any of this? It's not like I'm ever going to come here again." She wouldn't come back to a place where the ultimatum of death loomed over her head. She planned to avoid FitzRandolph Gate as studiously as if she were a superstitious Princeton student. "I belong in the other Princeton, in the human world."

He looked as if she'd slapped him.

"I'm sorry," she said. She wished she'd phrased it differently. She hadn't thought he would take it personally. "It's really nice of you to show me around, but . . ."

"Fly with me," he said.

Lily gaped at him. Now, *that* was a request that didn't come along every day. "What part of 'no dragons' was unclear?" she asked. "I don't want this." She waved her hand at the dragons, at the campus, at all of it. "This is not on my life plan."

"Maybe you need to change your 'life plan,'" Tye said. "You have a new destiny now. An important and amazing one. If you let me, I'll show it to you."

Without waiting for her response, he strode out onto the field.

She hesitated for a second and then followed. Above, three dragons soared through the sky. Jewel-like scales glittered in the sunlight so brightly that it looked as if someone had tossed sapphires, emeralds, and rubies into the air.

One of the dragons broke formation and glided down to the field. He skidded along the grass, churning up long furrows of dirt. As he swung his mammoth head toward Lily and Tye, Lily froze. Steam curled out of his nostrils as he breathed. His eyes were swirls of liquid gold.

"*Greetings, Tiger Boy,*" the dragon said.

Lily shivered at the familiar snakelike sound.

"Come on—ride a dragon with me?" Tye asked Lily. He flashed his lopsided grin at her. "You can't deny it's a helluva first date."

She couldn't help smiling back at him. His tawny eyes were fixed on her as if her answer were all that mattered in the world. "Just back to the gate," she said.

Tye smiled.

"And only if you promise the dragon won't eat me."

The dragon spoke. *"I wouldn't dream of it, little Key. You are not flavored to my liking."*

"Somehow I don't feel reassured," she said.

Tye held out his hand. "Trust me."

She took his hand and let him boost her onto the dragon's back. She settled onto scales as smooth as metal. Tye climbed on behind her and wrapped his arms around her waist. Lily felt his breath on her neck. She breathed in his rain forest–like scent.

Beneath them, the dragon pumped his wings. Wind whooshed around them. With a massive push against the football field, the dragon lurched into the air. He stretched his wings out, and in seconds they were soaring in the brilliant blue sky.

She saw wisps of cloud in front of them, and then damp mist surrounded them for an instant. They burst out the other side, and then the dragon dove down. Lily clutched at the dragon's scales and screamed. Tye's arms tightened around her waist. "Look beyond Princeton!" he shouted into the wind.

She looked and saw forest for miles on end. Sprawling trees, larger than sequoias, stretched their branches in every direction. She saw streams so blue that they looked like strips of sky laid through the forest. Griffins plummeted and rose in aerial dances with fiery birds. In the distance, she saw mountains etch the horizon in white and black.

This was not New Jersey.

"Do you like it?" Tye shouted in her ear.

Below, horses with bodies of foam and spray galloped down the streams and then melted into water droplets. She saw a man with angel wings leap from a tree and glide over the forest. A lone woman jumped over a fallen trunk and changed into a wolf. A swarm of bright lights lit the shadowed trees and then disappeared.

The dragon pitched forward again. Wind battered Lily's face. The forest rushed toward them. She screamed. Tye howled as if he were on a roller coaster.

Pulling up, the dragon skimmed over the tops of the trees. She heard the sounds of the forest below—a distant whispering. The air smelled like pine and rivers and earth after rain. It smelled like Tye. She let the sun warm her face, and she leaned back against Tye.

As they flew on, she saw a tower of stone beside a tumbling waterfall. Mermaids dove through the spray. Beyond the waterfall were villages of trees whose limbs had woven into houses high above the forest floor. She watched tall, pale elves, as thin as slivers of moonlight, glide across branches, and she saw monkeylike and catlike men and women scurry among them. The dragon flew farther and circled a city. Skyscrapers of mother-of-pearl gleamed in the sunlight, more beautiful than any painting Lily had ever seen.

All too soon, the dragon flew back to campus. Gliding to a landing, he tore tracks in the green as he skidded to a halt beside the gate.

"Well?" Tye asked.

"That was . . ." She tried to think of a word to describe it. Every word felt too small to fit the feeling of soaring through the wind. Instead, she leaned toward the dragon's neck and said, "Thank you."

Rumbling beneath her, the dragon said, *"You are welcome, little Key."*

Tye slid off the dragon's back first. Lily followed and slipped down the scales. Unfortunately, she kept sliding as her knees collapsed underneath her. She landed in a heap at Tye's feet.

"Graceful," he commented.

"Shut up," she said.

"And witty," he said.

"Are you going to be a gentleman and help me up, or just stand around being amused at your own cleverness?" she asked.

"Stand around, I think," he said. But he held out his hand to her. She untangled her legs and stood. "Better?" he asked.

Lily nodded. "Got my land legs back now." Unfortunately, the whispering buzz was worse. She stuck a finger in her ear and wiggled it. It didn't help.

Behind her, the dragon launched back into the air. She turned and watched him fly away, emerald scales sparkling against the blue sky. She wished she could have kept flying with him forever. That had been . . . incredible. Beyond awesome, in every sense of the word. High above the campus, the dragon was joined by a second dragon. The two twisted and danced through the clouds, scales flashing and sparkling in the sun.

"Get any hints, any feelings, about your heritage?" Tye asked.

"You mean, did I suddenly want to sprout wings or change into a wolf?" she asked. She pretended to check herself for wings or fur. "Nope."

Tye shrugged as if it weren't a big deal. "Well, you've absorbed enough. We should know soon."

She raised her eyebrows at him. "You like cryptic comments, don't you?"

"It's the cat in me."

Lily laughed despite herself.

Unamused, the gold eagles stared down at them. One ruffled his feathers, and she heard the clink of metal. On the other side of the gate was Nassau Hall, silent and stately. Lily stared up at the Princeton medallion embedded in the iron. "So I just waltz through and *poof!* I'm back in the human world?"

"Pretty much, yeah," Tye said. "That's what makes Keys so special and awesome. For everyone else . . . ordinary gate. For Keys . . . *poof!*"

"Huh," she said. He said it so casually.

"It's because Keys belong to both worlds," he said.

"Or neither," she said.

"Or neither," he agreed. "Keys need to switch worlds at

121

least once a month to stay alive. But without Keys, *no one* would be able to switch worlds, ever. Only time a non-Key can pass through is if a Key goes with him. Again note the specialness and awesomeness."

She didn't care about that. All she cared about was the fact that she could get home. "Do I walk in or out of the gate to return to my world?"

"Either direction works," Tye said. "But it's safer to walk in."

"Safer?" Her gaze shifted to the eagles' talons.

"Last time I walked out the gate, a bike slammed into me."

She grinned. A boy who could turn into a tiger, felled by a bicycle.

"Don't overdo the sympathy," he said. "I did crack a rib."

Lily schooled her expression. "Poor kitty." A thought occurred to her. "You're one, too." She should have realized it sooner. She'd been so preoccupied with the revelation about herself. "A half breed. You're a Key, too."

"Yep," he said. He caught her hand and pressed his lips to the back of it. "That's why we're destined to be soul mates."

She felt her jaw drop open.

Lightly, he lifted her jaw back up. His fingers brushed her cheek. "Guess I should have waited a bit before springing that on you," he said. "Go ahead home. Your grandfather must be worried about you. You should tell him you're okay. And that you passed the test. You're a Princeton girl now."

She gawked at him, stunned twice in less than thirty seconds. She hadn't thought about it, but she *had* passed the Legacy Test. She'd found the Key. And she'd also found an adorable college boy with dreamy eyes and feline superpowers who had mistaken her for soul-mate material. *He must have been joking,* she thought. Yeah, that seemed a lot more likely. "Okay . . . I'll, um, see you soon?"

He flashed her his cocky lopsided smile. "You can count on it."

She stared at him for a moment longer and then she walked through FitzRandolph Gate. Everything flashed white.

CHAPTER *Eleven*

"Welcome back, little Key," one of the stone eagles said. "I have alerted Vineyard Club of your return. Remain here, please."

"Uh, thanks," Lily said. She looked up at the eagles. The sky behind them was a crisp blue, empty of clouds and dragons. The forest was gone, replaced by Nassau Street. Pedestrians walked past banks, jewelry stores, and coffee shops. She heard the whoosh of cars, in addition to the now familiar radio hum in her ears. The air tasted thinner, as if she'd suddenly switched altitudes, but her skin still buzzed with the fizzy feeling of magic.

She heard a shout. "Lily!"

Grandpa jogged across the yard toward her. A half-dozen men and women trailed behind him. "You knew!" she shouted to him. "You knew about"—she flapped her hand at the gate—"all of this!" She'd never imagined he'd keep any secret from her, much less anything so major.

Beaming with a smile so wide it should have split his face, Grandpa swept her up and swung her in a circle. "You did it!" He set her back down.

"Grandpa . . . ," she began.

"Careful what you say; we can't talk freely here." He kissed her forehead. "Oh, my tigerlily, I am so very proud of you!" Grandpa was practically singing. She'd never seen him so gleeful. It was as unexpected as talking gargoyles.

Swarming around Lily and Grandpa, the alums chattered loudly about Reunions: the new class's Reunions jackets, the number of Old Guard (70th Reunion and older) who had returned, the fireworks display that was planned for Saturday after P-rade. Inside the circle of chattering Old Boys, Lily and Grandpa were swept across campus. It felt as if they were guarding her—or hiding her—with their bodies and their voices.

Under the cover of their babble, she asked Grandpa, "Why didn't you tell me?"

His smile dimmed. "You had to discover the truth on your own. That's the point of the Legacy Test: to determine if you can handle the truth by offering you the opportunity to discover it. It's a tried-and-true method."

"It sucks," Lily said.

He clucked his tongue. "Language."

"It's cruel and manipulative, and you *lied* to me," she said. "What am I? What was Dad?"

"A loving father," Grandpa said. "That's what's important." Putting his arm around her, he squeezed her shoulders. "Lily, you have to trust me. The secrecy was necessary. All of this is larger than you or me."

"Does Mom know about 'all of this'?"

Grandpa sighed. "She used to. She's forgotten so much."

Quietly, Lily said, "She's getting worse, isn't she?"

"There's hope, Lily," Grandpa said. "Soon, I will explain to you both. But first, we need to celebrate what you've achieved! Tonight, we'll celebrate at Vineyard Club, and then tomorrow morning, I'll take you and your mother to Pj's Pancake House for a celebratory breakfast. You'll love it there. You can sign your name on the table. It's tradition there, not vandalism."

"Where is Mom? You didn't leave her alone again, did you?" Aside from the fact that the campus was infested with vampiric monsters, Mom might have one of her "ideas." She could decide to tame squirrels or climb the vines on one of the Gothic classrooms to commune with the sun from a closer angle—she'd done similar things before. "And what do you mean, 'there's hope'?"

"She's being watched," Grandpa said. "Lily, focus on yourself for once. You did it! You passed!" He beamed at her again.

As they crossed the street, she tried to push aside all the million questions and revel in that fact. She really had done it: automatic acceptance to Princeton! So what if her dream school had a few quirks she hadn't expected? She could avoid walking through the main gate (which wouldn't be hard since it was a common student superstition to circumvent that gate), avoid eye contact with gargoyles (again, not hard since most people didn't try to chat up stone sculptures), and avoid being attacked by rampaging monkey-things (always sound advice).

They turned onto Prospect Avenue, and she heard the steady static in her ears mix with a buzz. It undercut the chatter of the alums around her, but before she could pinpoint the source, she was swept down the sidewalk toward Vineyard Club.

"Lots of people are waiting to congratulate you," Grandpa said. "You are more important than you know. We haven't had reliable access to the magic world in many years." He pointed to the club. Mr. Mayfair and his grandson, Jake, flanked the front door, holding it open as if they were honor guards. Last time she'd seen Jake, he'd shoved her away while she'd bled. He'd found a new blood-free shirt since then. Softly, Grandpa added close to Lily's ear, "Go easy on Jake. His parents were killed by the Chained Dragon. Seeing you survive was a shock."

Lily halted halfway to the door. "Oh, God, how awful."

"It was years ago," Grandpa said. "But still, it was a terrible tragedy. Jake's parents . . . they'd had a messy divorce and were only beginning to find peace."

So much for her image of Jake's perfect family. She realized

Tye had told her about this, the time the dragon killed a Key and escaped the chapel. She hadn't thought to wonder about his other victims. "If Jake hadn't pulled me away . . ."

"Yes, we could have had another FitzRandolph Gate Tragedy on our hands," Grandpa said. "But thankfully, that didn't happen, so let's not dwell on it right now. Once you begin your training, we'll focus on avoiding reckless endangerment."

She didn't have a chance to reply. Surrounded by the half-dozen alums, she was herded toward Jake and the door. As she reached him, Jake blushed heavily before mumbling, "Congratulations, Lily."

She tried to think of something, anything, to say to him. No wonder he'd been so agitated at the chapel—he'd been in the presence of his parents' killer.

Jake looked as if he wanted to say more but he glanced at his grandfather instead.

Mr. Mayfair smiled warmly at her and said, "Well done, Lily Carter. And welcome." He shook Grandpa's hand. "Congratulations, Richard. You were right."

"Of course I was," Grandpa said. "I know my tigerlily." Beaming even more broadly than before, Grandpa ushered Lily inside.

Within the club, the weird radio static in her head faded beneath the hum of conversation. The club was packed with alums. They filled the leather couches and leaned against the mahogany walls. She hesitated just inside the doorway.

"Don't be nervous now," Grandpa whispered in her ear. "You passed! You're one of us!"

By the grand staircase, she saw a spread of cheese squares and a fondue fountain with skewers of fruit. Her stomach rumbled in response. *You can't be nervous in a place with fondue,* she told herself.

Placing his hands on her shoulders, Grandpa boomed to the assembly, "Allow me to present our newest member, my granddaughter, Lily, soon to be a Princeton freshman and our very own Key!"

All the Old Boys applauded. A few of the younger ones whistled and cheered. Others clapped politely and then swilled their whiskey and resumed their conversations.

As she and her grandfather ventured farther into the club, alums flocked to them. All the Old Boys that she remembered from her initial meeting—the man who'd held the book upside down, the heavyset woman with the ivory cane, the primly postured women—welcomed her. Others introduced themselves and shook her hand. She'd never had so many adults notice her before. Part of her wanted to bolt out of the club.

She spotted trays of pastry puffs. Someone offered her a shrimp. Grandpa accepted a drink. He clinked glasses with a nearby member and began to chat. A circle of alumni closed around her. Lily shifted her weight nervously as they studied her with a fascination that was more than a little bit alarming. She took a pastry puff and shoved it into her mouth. It was a good excuse for not saying anything. She hadn't the faintest idea how to start a conversation with these people. Plus she hadn't eaten since a rest stop on the New Jersey Turnpike that morning. She grabbed a second puff.

"Did you see any indication of military activity?" one man asked.

She nearly choked on the pastry. She swallowed. "Sorry?"

He wore an orange cravat and had eyebrows like woolly caterpillars. "Any large gatherings? Anything that could have been a training camp?" he asked.

Her appetite vanished. "It was a college campus," Lily said, "a lot like the real Princeton. But the students had more fur, feathers, and fangs."

"And what were those 'students' studying?" a woman asked. She was young, clearly a recent grad, and spoke with a Japanese accent. She regarded Lily intently, as if she were cataloging Lily's every breath.

"Please understand, we do trust the professors," said the man who had held the book upside down. "But the majority of them have not seen their home in a full century."

One of the prim women chimed in. "Exactly why we should seize this opportunity to convene a summit! Now that we'll have a Key we can trust, we can renew relations. We will be able to send envoys freely, perhaps resume scientific expeditions. We can end our isolationism!"

Ignoring her, the man with the orange cravat said,

"Numbers, weaponry, anything you learned about strategy or fighting styles. Any observations at all?"

The prim woman interrupted. "That is precisely the attitude—"

"We need to know—," the man began.

"You need lessons in diplomacy," the woman said. "Perhaps if you lessened your testosterone-laden xenophobia—"

"I am *realistic*, not xenophobic!"

All the Old Boys around her pressed in closer as the argument heated up. Lily wished she could sink against a wall and disappear. She glanced over at her grandfather for help, but he was engrossed in his own conversation.

"What sort of intelligence did the council glean from you?" a man in a striped blazer asked. "How much information did you volunteer?"

"Nothing!" Lily said. "They said to remind the 'knights' of Princeton that they don't condone Feeders, and they support you."

"See!" the prim woman said. "It's time to normalize relations! Refresh our treaties! Confirm our alliance!"

"Propaganda," the man with the orange cravat said. "This is useless. She's useless!"

Finally coming to her rescue, Grandpa put his hands on Lily's shoulders. "She hasn't been trained," he said. "She has zero background. You can't expect—"

"Trained or not, she could supply valuable intel, *if* she chooses to and *if* she hasn't already decided her loyalties lie against us." The man pounded his fist into his palm for emphasis.

Grandpa's face darkened. "Are you questioning my grand-daughter's integrity?" His voice was low, even, and clipped. Lily barely breathed. She'd heard him take that tone of voice only a few times before. Last time had been at a man who'd tried to corner Mom, mistaking her flightiness for flirting. Lily shrank back, again wishing she could disappear. "I have raised her as human," Grandpa said. "If you question her, then you question me." He thumped his chest for emphasis. "Are you questioning *me*?"

Had Grandpa really said "as human"? Lily wanted to ask him again about her father, but she was positive that this wasn't the right time or place. She'd be better off if she didn't speak at all. If she could shrink to mouse size and sneak away, that would be good, too.

Mr. Mayfair interrupted. "Gentlemen and ladies, if you don't mind, I need to steal our guest of honor for a moment." The orange-cravat man scowled as if he wanted to object. "Our sommelier has obtained a few bottles of high-quality Bordeaux. Please, it would be a crime to waste them." Encouraged by Mr. Mayfair, the knot of alumni around Lily dispersed.

Lily's knees felt as if they'd been jellied. Usually the scariest person in her day was her AP Chem teacher. She wasn't used to facing an inquisition over pastry puffs. "Thank you," she said to Mr. Mayfair. He inclined his head.

Grandpa was still fuming. "You're untrained! How any-one could expect—"

"Fear breeds impatience," Mr. Mayfair said. "And they have been afraid, ever since reports began trickling in about the Feeders uniting. . . . But that's not talk for today. This is a joyous occasion!" He smiled and winked at Lily, and she began to feel better. Mr. Mayfair exuded calmness. He was like a tree with wide, sheltering solid branches in the middle of a rainstorm. "Her approach to the truth was . . . unconventional, but she completed the Legacy Test in record time and demonstrated the necessary flexibility in her worldview. I have no doubt that she will be a great asset to us in our battles."

"Battles?" she asked.

"We defend the innocent against the evil they do not know exists," Mr. Mayfair said. Gesturing at all the people in the room, he spread his arms out wide. "We, the knights of Princeton, protect the world."

Knights of Princeton. She pictured Mr. Mayfair in a suit of armor. Surprisingly, the image didn't seem so strange. He'd look like King Arthur.

Mr. Mayfair laid a hand on her shoulder. "I know you must have many questions, but before anything else, we must drain you," he said. "I was remiss not to take care of that right away. Please accept my apologies."

"Drain me?" Lily squeaked.

"Don't worry. It will only take a few minutes and then

you'll feel like yourself again," Grandpa said. He kissed her on the forehead. "You can trust Mr. Mayfair."

Mr. Mayfair smiled reassuringly at her. "It's a safe procedure," he said. "I know precisely when to stop."

She felt as if she were in the doctor's office and the nurse was holding a giant needle and claiming, *This won't hurt a bit.* "What's the procedure?" Lily asked as Mr. Mayfair steered her through the reception crowd. She glanced back at Grandpa. He wasn't following them. Instead, he was weaving his way toward the fondue table.

"You'll be fine, my dear," Mr. Mayfair said as he guided her downstairs to the taproom.

He laid his hand on a wood-paneled wall beside the bar, and a panel slid open to reveal a hidden room. Lily peered inside. Shelves filled with unmarked bottles lined one of the walls. "What is all this stuff?" she asked.

"Please, have a seat." Mr. Mayfair selected an empty bottle and nodded at a heavy wooden chair. It had restraints on the arms and the front legs, not unlike an electrocution chair.

"I'd really rather not—," she began.

"Sit, Miss Carter," he said as he prepared an IV-like needle. He connected it to a tube that led to a tangle of beakers, glass tubes, and exposed electrical circuits. He flicked a switch, and the contraption began to whir softly.

"No offense meant," she said, "but don't you think that looks a little mad scientist–like?"

"We call it the drainer." He patted the heart of tangled tubes. "It's designed to extract the excess magic that now flows through your bloodstream due to your exposure to the atmosphere of the alternate world."

Lily backed away. "I feel fine."

He favored her with another reassuring smile. "Believe me, this is necessary and for your own good. You are currently a danger to yourself and others."

"Can't we just wait for the magic to leach out of me?" She couldn't take her eyes off the needle. "Seriously, 'drainer'?"

"You may have noticed that with your heritage, some of the members of Vineyard Club are having difficulty with your impending membership." He attached an empty bottle to the drainer and said in a mild voice, "It would be a shame to give them cause to doubt you, especially before admissions papers have been filed."

"But I passed the test!" Lily said.

"You might even be viewed as a threat, given the knowledge of us that you now possess." He patted the chair. "Lily, please trust us so we can trust you."

She wasn't trying to be ornery. She *did* trust him. He was her grandfather's oldest friend, and he had an air about him that seemed noble, honorable, even knightly. But . . . She pointed at the restraints. "Do I have to wear those?"

"Of course not," he said in a soothing voice. "You merely need to lay your arm on the armrest so that it remains steady for several minutes."

Gingerly, she sat down in the chair. "You've done this before?" she asked.

Nurselike, he rolled up her sleeve. "Many times." He selected a plastic tube from a drawer and tied it tightly around her bicep. He tapped the veins in her arm, and then he swabbed them with alcohol. She wondered if he was going to offer her Hello Kitty stickers and a lollipop when he finished. She turned her head as he readied the needle.

Footsteps thumped down the stairs.

Jake burst into the taproom. "Sir, Feeders are attacking Forbes!" He halted in the doorway to the hidden room. His eyes scanned the shelves, his grandfather, and Lily. "Whoa, what's all this?"

Mr. Mayfair laid the needle down. "Multiple Feeders?" he asked.

"At least a dozen," Jake said. "They never—"

"Has the area been secured?" Mr. Mayfair interrupted.

"Campus security is en route," Jake reported crisply. "Our alums are evacuating civilians." Mr. Mayfair strode out of the room. Jake followed him without even glancing at Lily. "Sir, it's a coordinated attack. No report of the new leader yet, but that's the only explanation for their behavior. . . ." His voice faded as they went up the stairs.

Lily wasn't sure if she was supposed to follow or not. She untied the tourniquet around her arm and waited for a moment to see if Jake or Mr. Mayfair returned for her. No one came. She listened to footsteps thump overhead. She bet she was the only one down here . . . in a hidden room . . . in an electrocution chair. . . .

She fled the room.

She halted at the top of the stairs. Wooden panels in the walls had been opened to reveal hidden compartments full of swords, knives, machetes, crossbows, vials of liquids, strings of garlic, packets of herbs . . . As Mr. Mayfair barked orders, weapons were passed out and tucked into pockets and underneath Reunions jackets.

Across the room, Grandpa strapped a sheathed sword onto his back and then hid it beneath his psychedelic zebra coat. Lily felt her jaw drop open. She tried to imagine her grandfather swinging a sword. She'd seen him wield pruning shears, slice up a chicken breast, and peel an apple, but that didn't seem the same. One of the prim ladies tucked a dismantled crossbow into an oversize purse. Nearby, Jake was adding a knife to a holster attached to his ankle underneath his khakis.

"Knives? Swords?" she asked Jake. Her voice sounded shrill to her ears.

"Part of protecting civilians is preserving normalcy," Jake said. He sounded as crisp and stiff as he had when he'd addressed his grandfather. "Gunfire is too difficult to disguise. Plus too many magic creatures are impervious to modern weaponry."

That wasn't what she'd meant to ask about. "What's happening?"

"It appears to be a coordinated attack on Forbes, one of the undergraduate dorms," Jake said. She noticed he was avoiding meeting her eyes. She guessed he didn't know how to talk to her after what had happened by the chapel. Or it could be that he didn't want to talk to her because she was a half breed. Maybe he was simply hiding his revulsion. She wished she knew how to bring back that look he'd worn in the gardens. "Feeders never used to unite like this. Feeders are suspicious of each other. Their strategy typically involves avoiding discovery by either knights or other magic creatures. They prefer to spread out and blend in as much as possible." From his tone, she guessed he was quoting a teacher, maybe even Professor Ape.

"Have you fought Feeders before?" she asked.

His face turned red. "I've had training."

Before she could ask another question, Grandpa strode across the room toward them. "Lily," he said, "you need to stay here."

Mr. Mayfair joined them. "She needs to see the enemy, Richard."

"This is not a typical engagement," Grandpa objected. "She'll have plenty of opportunities in a more controlled situation."

"With her magic level, we cannot leave her here unguarded and uninitiated." Mr. Mayfair's voice was pitched low so only Grandpa and Lily could hear. "You know how some feel. Think how it would look."

A vein pulsed in Grandpa's temple. "With her magic level, she'll be a tempting snack for any Feeder. If she must come, then I will guard her myself."

Mr. Mayfair shook his head. "I need my best on the front line." His voice was gentle, apologetic even. "You know that." To Jake, he said, "When we reach Forbes, you are to locate a safe vantage point for Miss Carter before you join the battle. She is to observe only."

"But Grandfather—," Jake began.

Mr. Mayfair raised his eyebrows.

"Yes, sir."

Mr. Mayfair laid a hand on his grandson's shoulder. "Good boy," he said. Lily wondered what Jake had intended to say, if he had been about to object to helping a monster. To Lily, Mr. Mayfair said, "Seek out Jake at Forbes. He'll ensure you're safe."

"Thank you, Joseph," Grandpa said. "She's the flower of my life."

Leaving them, Mr. Mayfair mounted the grand staircase. Bellowing to the Old Boys, Mr. Mayfair ordered, "Prep yourselves!"

On cue, all the knights, including Jake and Grandpa, withdrew flasks from their pockets. She heard soft pops as they were all unstopped at once. The flasks were raised up. In unison, everyone shouted, "To victory!"

All the knights drank.

Toast complete, Mr. Mayfair shouted again, "Move out,

people! This is not a drill. And remember, the campus is flush with civilians. Containment is paramount."

Grandpa kissed Lily on the forehead. "Don't draw attention to yourself," he said. "Find a place to hide and stay there." He then waded into the crowd of knights. "You, you, and you with me," he said, pointing at select men and women. With military precision, the men and women of Vineyard Club filed out the door.

Lily was swept along with them.

As soon as the Princeton knights crossed the threshold of the club, they snapped into Reunions mode: chattering, laughing, hamming it up. She saw Jake joke and horse around with the other students. One of them stumbled down the walk as if drunk. Others strolled. Some sauntered. One group of knights jogged down the street as if they were exercising. A few speed-walked with cell phones to their ears as if they were businessmen on calls. Lily followed the knights to the end of Prospect Avenue and through the 1879 Hall arch.

After the arch, the pack splintered. Some headed for the Gothic classrooms, others veered toward the student center, and a third group walked straight ahead. She lost sight of Grandpa almost immediately. She trailed Jake and his friends into Prospect Gardens, and the radio static hum in her head increased with each step.

"What the hell is that?" she asked.

Ahead of her, Jake's friends were caught up in their fake

chatter. She slowed, trying to pinpoint the source of the hum. It was almost like music.

As Lily entered the garden, the sound exploded into chimes that rang like a musical waterfall. She spun around in a circle, looking for the source. "Don't you hear that?" she asked. Not waiting for an answer, she followed the discordant music. It led her toward the flower beds.

Long shadows from the evergreens covered half the garden. The other half was bathed in low-angled light from the late afternoon sun. The tulips blazed. The music sounded as if it was rising up from the ground. Lily knelt beside a flower bed, and the chimes crescendoed.

It was the flowers. The tulips were *singing*.

"How very Disney," she murmured. She was proud that her voice only shook a little. After talking gargoyles, she wasn't going to let singing flowers freak her out, right? She reached her hands toward the tulips and brushed the petals with her palms. The blossoms leaned toward her as if her hands were the midday sun.

"They like you," a voice said behind her. She snatched her hands back, and the flowers lazily swung back to vertical. "They have good taste."

Lily jumped to her feet. "Tye! What are you doing here?"

"Stalking you, of course," Tye said with his lopsided grin. "And also, I noticed the knights in orange armor mobilizing and wanted to see what all the excitement was about."

Oh, no. She spun to look for Jake and his friends, but

they were gone. "Feeders are attacking Forbes," she said. "I'm supposed to follow and watch!"

Tye's grin vanished. He took her hand. She felt the tiny static shocks run up and down her arm. It felt as if her skin were carbonated. Now, after being in the other Princeton, she knew what it was: magic, his magic, touching her. "You shouldn't go," he said. "You could be hurt. Unless you have secret kung-fu skills in addition to the flowers-think-you're-swell vibe?"

"Plants have never acted like I'm a magnet before," Lily said. She tried to ignore the fact that he was holding her hand. "We own a flower shop; you'd think I'd have noticed."

"You must have never had enough magic in you," he said. He let go of her hand, and she instantly missed it. She resisted the urge to touch him and instead leaned over the flower bed and brushed the tulips again. And again, they danced under her touch.

"So weird," she said. On the scale of bizarre things she'd seen today, this wasn't overly high, but still . . .

"At least we now know what you are," Tye said.

She looked up sharply at him.

"You're the one who woke those vines and caught our wrinkly green friend. You're a dryad." He corrected himself. "Half dryad."

The tulips hummed. "I'm . . . what?"

"Tree spirit," he clarified.

She stared at him. "I'm part tree."

"Pretty much, yes," he said happily.

"You turn into a tiger, and I'm part *tree*?" She tried to sound flippant, but the plants betrayed her. As her hand tightened on the stem of a tulip, the flower shot into the air, stretching to twice its height. The blossom swayed back and forth like a cobra poised to strike. "Whoa!" She released the plant and stumbled backward.

Tye caught her as she tripped on the flagstones. Arms around her waist, he steadied her. She breathed in his rainforest scent. *Soul mates,* her memory whispered. The plants whispered, too, wordlessly murmuring in her head.

"Looks like plants respond to your emotions," he said. She looked up into his golden eyes. "Can you direct them?" he asked. For an instant, caught in his eyes, she had no idea what he was talking about. "The flowers," he clarified.

The tulip was still writhing like a snake.

Tentatively, she reached out her hand and touched the flower. Its petals curled around her fingers. "Shrink, please," she said. The flower quivered, and she heard a wobbly chime. She stroked its petals. "It's okay. I'm okay."

The tulip shrank.

Tye whistled. "Cool."

Kneeling in front of the flower bed again, she spread her fingers to touch several tulips. "Up," she said. Obediently, leaves lifted into the air. "Sideways," she said and tipped her hand to the right. All the flowers dipped their blossoms. "Other way." They reversed directions. "Braid." She twisted her fingers against the stems and imagined what she wanted them to do, and the flowers wrapped around one another.

Tye knelt next to her. "How do you feel?"

"Like I have a really lame superpower," Lily said, unbraiding the flower stems.

He laughed. "You did catch that goblin with the ivy."

"I guess so." She wasn't sure how. That had been *before* she'd crossed to the magic world and absorbed its magic. "What happened to him? Did he escape? Did you say 'goblin'?"

"I took him home," Tye said. "He's with his family now. He'll be all right, eventually."

She gawked at him. "You *helped* him? That monkey— goblin—thing gored you, remember?"

"He's a victim too," Tye said. He was watching her with an expression she couldn't read. "He's an addict, not a murderer. Deep down, he doesn't want to kill. I offered him a way to break his addiction."

Wow. That was . . . rather heroic. "You save Feeders?"

"You can too," he said. "We can do it together; we can offer Feeders a way out, a way home."

"I . . . I don't know." She'd just found out her father had been a tree spirit and she could hypnotize flowers. Now Tye wanted her to . . . what? Become some kind of superhero who saved vampiric monsters?

"Lily, I can't reach them all by myself."

"Can't the knights help?" She bet they'd be all over the

idea of returning Feeders to the magic world. It was a much better solution than knives and swords.

He flashed a wry grin, but the humor didn't touch his eyes. "The head knight and I . . . we have some philosophical differences."

Lily raised her eyebrows.

"I think he's an idiot, and he thinks I'm evil demon spawn."

"Oh," she said. "Are you?"

He tilted his head back and let out a mock evil laugh. "Mwa-ha-ha!"

Grinning, she swatted his arm. "Very funny. I'm serious. Why aren't you the knights' Key?"

"Latest reason? I accused the knights of trying to invent something to drain magic from Feeders." He made a face. "Even the gargoyles wouldn't side with me on that one."

"But they've already invented that—they call it a drainer," Lily said. "They were going to use it to drain my excess magic. We were interrupted by the attack on Forbes."

Tye stared at her as if she'd sprouted leaves (which, all things considered, she thought, wasn't impossible). "Say that again?"

"It's in this hidden room. I can show you."

"You can?" His face lit up in a smile. He looked as though she'd just offered him a mountain of chocolate. His smile was almost (though not quite) as brilliant as Jake's smile.

Lily nodded. "I think the door is still open."

"I am absolutely in love with you," Tye said.

CHAPTER *Eight*

One of the stone monkeys on the 1879 Hall arch scampered down the brick wall. Tye scooped him up, and the monkey wrapped its arms around his neck. He murmured to it, and then he replaced the monkey on the wall. It wormed itself back into the carving of monkeys and a lion. A second later, it was motionless stone again.

"Friend of yours?" Lily asked. She was pleased that her voice sounded light. A day ago, the sight of a monkey statue climbing off a wall would have sent her running for her medicine.

"I've known the professors my whole life," Tye said. He waved at them as he and Lily crossed through the arch toward Prospect Avenue. "After my mother died, the gargoyles pretty much adopted me."

"I'm sorry," she said. "I mean, about your mother."

He shrugged but didn't meet her eyes. "It was a long time ago."

She wanted to reach out and take Tye's hand. She didn't quite dare. Instead she walked silently beside him down the sidewalk. Whispers danced in her head, and she brushed the hedges in front of the eating clubs with her fingertips. The whispers spiked into a croon.

"Used to sneak into the classrooms to sleep near the gargoyles," he said. "And I ate a lot of picnics on rooftops. Endured a lot of sunburns. And rain. When your family is gargoyles, you get rained on a lot."

"You slept in classrooms?" Lily asked. "Why didn't the Old Boys take you in? They had to know you were here."

"After the dragon attacked . . . well, after that, the Old Boys had less enthusiasm for the magic world, yours truly included," Tye said. "As soon as I was old enough to understand, I kind of took it personally. And I did a few things I'm not proud of. Well, except for the time I nailed their shoes to the ceiling of Vineyard Club. That was rather awesome."

Lily slowed in front of the club. She'd never sneaked in anywhere, not even Grandpa's closet when she'd known it had held birthday presents. (Mom had peeked, reasoning that her brain hiccups would wipe out the memory anyway so it hardly counted.) This, however, was not like peeking at birthday presents, and Grandpa was likely to be much more pissed. "What if they didn't all go to Forbes?"

He trotted toward the door. "Just act like you belong," he said, "which you do."

Squashing down her nerves, she followed him inside.

Silence pressed down on her as the croon of the plants faded. She was shocked that she missed it. She was also acutely aware of the lack of direct sunlight on her skin. *Another dryad thing?* she wondered.

"Lily?" Tye said.

Standing in the foyer, she tried to adjust to being inside. "Sorry," she said. She pointed toward the stairwell behind the grand staircase. "Downstairs."

They crossed under an oil painting of monklike men at an ornate table. The austere group seemed to watch them pass. Lily felt her heart beat faster. Tye was wrong—she didn't officially belong yet. Her application hadn't been processed. All she had was a promise. She wouldn't really belong until she had that acceptance letter in her hand.

She nodded at the wood-paneled walls. "They keep their swords in there. Secret compartments."

Tye stopped and ran his hands over one of the walls.

"There's probably a hidden"—she heard a click—"latch."

He opened it and whistled low.

Lily peered in over his shoulder. Knives and swords filled every inch. She saw jeweled hilts and plain black serrated blades and sharp foils. Tye checked a second compartment. It held axes and throwing stars, plus more hooks and slots for blades—mostly empty. The third cabinet was packed with jars and packets. "Wolfsbane for werewolves." He pointed. "Garlic for vampires." He checked a silk packet. "Four-leaf clover?"

"For what? Leprechauns? Don't tell me there really are leprechauns."

He was frowning at the clover.

"Seriously? 'They're always after me Lucky Charms'? And did you just say 'werewolves' and 'vampires'?"

Tye replaced the packet and closed the cabinet door. "The four-leaf-clover thing is a myth—the gargoyles should have told the knights. Not a good sign if the knights have stopped listening to the gargoyles."

"Mmm," she said. "Never a good sign if people stop listening to gargoyles." She shot a look at the front door. "Can we move faster, please?"

He executed a mock bow. "After you, my lady."

She led him to the stairs. They tiptoed down past the black-and-white photos of former Vineyard classes. "I think the room's pretty secret," Lily said in a whisper. "Jake didn't seem to know it was here."

"Jake?"

"Mr. Mayfair's grandson," she said.

"Oh, right. Blond pretty-boy."

"He's not a 'pretty-boy,'" she said. "He's a knight." Tye raised both eyebrows so she changed the subject. "The drainer looks straight out of a cheesy mad-scientist movie. Tubes, needles, whirring noises . . . it's like a Rube Goldberg device made out of lab equipment." Reaching the taproom, she pointed. The door was ajar, exactly as she'd left it.

Beside her, Tye stopped.

"What is it?" she asked. She glanced at the stairs, half expecting an army of knights to burst into the taproom with swords flashing through the air.

Softly, he said, "I want to be wrong."

"Oh," she said.

Side by side, they stared at the door.

"You know," Lily said, "in a horror movie, this would be the point where the idiot teenagers get eaten by the monsters." She waited for Tye to make a witty reply. He didn't. She added, "I never really liked horror movies."

"Me neither," he said. He squared his shoulders and strode forward. She entered close behind him. Above, a single bulb swung on a string, sending shadows skittering around the room and over the shelves of bottles.

Lily watched Tye's face pale as he scanned the shelves. "This . . . it's bad?" she asked.

He swallowed and nodded. "Very bad," he said. "Do you know how many creatures had to die to make a collection this size?"

Die?

"The knights had to drain to death dozens of magic creatures to fill all these bottles," Tye said. He waved his hand at the shelves. "The knights are no different from the Feeders they fight! They've become another kind of Feeder."

Grandpa was *not* a Feeder. "Maybe no one died. Mr. Mayfair was only going to skim the excess from me." She pointed to the drainer with its knot of tubes. "It could be like a blood bank for magic."

He shook his head. "This . . . this is evil."

"Grandpa isn't evil! He'd never hurt anyone." He'd said the procedure was safe. He wouldn't have put her at risk. Lying to her about her heritage was one thing; endangering her life . . . He wouldn't do it.

Tye opened his mouth and then closed it.

Lily glared at him. "Grandpa is one of the good guys. They're *knights*." Grandpa was a florist—you couldn't ask for nicer than works-with-flowers. He was even kind to dandelions.

Tye lifted up a bottle and removed the stopper. He tipped the bottle over and spilled a drop of silver liquid. It beaded on the shelf like mercury. "Pure magic. There's no way the gargoyles know about this. And the council . . . I have to tell the council."

Lily felt her voice dry up in her throat as she stared at the silver dot. "That's magic?" she squeaked. It looked exactly like . . . She cut off the thought before she could complete it.

He nodded. "In its liquid form, yeah. This . . . this *thing* must produce some chemical reaction to keep the magic from evaporating into the air." He prodded at the glass tubes. "I should smash it."

She caught his arm. "Don't! They'll know someone was

in here. Besides, there must be an explanation for all of this."
Grandpa could explain. Yes, she just needed to talk to him.

"There's no explanation that could justify this," Tye said.
But he quit poking the drainer. Instead, he pocketed the
bottle of magic. "The council will want proof," he said. He
then wiped away the drop of magic on the shelf with his
sleeve. It smeared silver.

Lily tentatively touched the smudge. She studied the
silver that dotted her fingertips. She couldn't deny it: It
looked exactly like her and Mom's medicine.

Impossible, she thought.

Footsteps thumped from the top of the stairs. Tye swore
softly and colorfully. He spun around as if looking for a place
to hide. There wasn't one.

"Come on," he said, pulling her elbow.

They dashed out of the hidden room and wove among
tables, chairs, and the jukebox. The footsteps began to come
down the stairs. Lily thought of her mother on those stairs,
pausing to look at a photograph. She slowed. "You go," she
said to Tye.

Tye released her elbow. "What?"

Lily touched her hands together and felt the silver liquid
slide between her fingertips. She couldn't leave yet. "I'll delay
them," she said. "I belong, right? I'll be fine. Go." Without
waiting for a response, she darted across the taproom to the
stairs. She pounded her feet on the steps as loudly as she
could, hoping to hide any sound of Tye.

On the fourth step, she smacked into Jake. He grabbed her arms to keep her from falling backward. "Whoa, slow down!" Jake said.

He released her, and she gripped his wrists as if she needed him for balance. "Sorry," she said. Her eyes slid to the wall with all the photos.

Jake flipped his cell phone open. "Got her," he reported. "She's fine. She returned to the club." Closing the phone, he asked Lily, "Where have you been? Why didn't you follow us?"

"I . . . I chickened out," she said. "A few hours ago, I didn't know any of this was real, and now a battle? I've never even seen a fistfight. College is supposed to have professors and exams and roommates, not dragons and knights!" She waved her hand at the black-and-white photos of Princeton knights. She scanned the wall, looking for the picture that had caught her mother's eye earlier. Mom had stopped right about . . . Lily spotted it: a class photo with a familiar face. Smack-dab in the center of the photo was a young man in an oxford shirt and khakis who looked exactly like a younger version of Grandpa. He was surrounded by men and women . . . except there had been no women at Princeton when her grandfather had been a student, and the hair and outfits in this photo were from the wrong decade. That man couldn't have been her grandfather, though he looked almost identical to him.

Grandpa did have more secrets, she thought.

"Are you all right?" Jake asked.

Lily pointed at the photo. "That's my father," she said. "William Carter. He's Grandpa's son." Her voice sounded an octave too high, but she couldn't stop it.

Her father was Grandpa's son, which meant that Mom wasn't Grandpa's daughter. Her father was Grandpa's blood relation, which meant that Mom wasn't.

Her father was human, which meant that Mom . . . wasn't.

CHAPTER Nine

*M*om wasn't human.

Grandpa had lied to her. He'd lied about things so basic that Lily didn't even know how to process the information. She leaned heavily against the stairwell wall.

"Lily?" Jake said.

At least now she had an answer to how she'd survived: Grandpa hadn't fed her and Mom medicine; he'd fed them magic. Her stomach lurched. "I think I'm going to be sick." Lily clapped her hands over her mouth, and she barreled past Jake up the stairs. She ran under the eyes of the oil paintings and past the hidden compartments, the grand piano, and the marble fireplace. With Jake jogging behind her, she burst out the front door of the club.

Outside, she fell to her knees on the grass. Amber light from the setting sun poured over the back of her neck, and she heard the whispered voices of the lawn and the trees and the bushes. She buried her fingers in the grass. Green blades curled around her knuckles and crooned to her. Her chest loosened, and she could breathe again.

She heard Jake on the path behind her. "Lily, are you all right?" he asked.

"No, I'm not all right!" None of this was "all right." The woman she'd spent every day of her life with was a dryad, and her grandfather—the bedrock of her life—had intentionally lied to her about all of it. "I trusted him! Believed in him!"

"Who?" Jake asked.

"My grandfather, the liar," she said.

"Your grandfather is a noble man," Jake said. "A hero—"

Lily interrupted him. "You barely know him." She wondered how well she even knew him. Wrapped around her fingers, the grass squeezed tighter.

Jake squatted beside her. "Lily, are you okay?" He sounded concerned, as if he hadn't been the one to push her away on the chapel plaza. Since when did he care? She was the "monster," wasn't she?

"I'm not going to puke on you, if that's what you're worried about," Lily said.

"I'm not . . . I didn't mean . . . ," he said. He reminded her of a puppy who'd had his nose smacked. She felt a twinge of guilt. Jake wasn't the one who had turned her world inside out and upside down and then (for good measure) shaken it vigorously.

She unwound her fingers from the grass. The blades continued to rub against her like kittens that wanted to be petted. Lily thought of how Mom always treated the plants in the flower shop like pets. She'd coo and croon to the roses and daisies. Lily felt a hysterical laugh bubble up in her throat, and she choked it back.

"Do you . . . Are you feeling better?" Jake asked.

"My mom . . . ," she began. She stopped. "I need to talk to Grandpa. Is the battle over?"

He shot a look at the sidewalk. "Shh!"

After all the lies, for them to expect her to care about protecting their secrets . . . She saw Jake's expression, and she sighed. "Sorry," she said. "It's not your fault that my home life is even more messed up than I'd thought." She wondered how much of the truth Mom knew, or remembered.

"The fighting just started," he said in a low voice, checking to be sure he couldn't be overheard. "If we're quick, we won't miss much. But if you're too scared—"

"No, I'm fine now. Let's go to Forbes." She got to her feet. It occurred to her that she'd been stupid to come outside so quickly. She should have delayed in the stairwell until she'd been certain that Tye had had enough time to reach safety.

Jake trotted down the sidewalk, and Lily trailed behind. Street lamps flickered on up and down Prospect Avenue—the sky was beginning to darken to steel blue. She tried to subtly scan the area for Tye. She hoped he was long gone. As she followed Jake up the steps to the 1879 Hall arch, she wondered what would happen when the council saw the bottle of magic.

"You really didn't know about this, about who you are?" Jake said.

She felt tears prick her eyes. Blinking fast, she looked away from Jake and at the monkey gargoyles on the arch. They remained stone, but Lily imagined the blank gray eyes watching her. "Did you?" she asked. "When you met me, could you tell?"

"Not a hint," he said. "I mean, it's not as if you have a tail or scales . . . do you?"

She glared at him. "No!" Picking up her pace, she marched through the arch.

He caught her hand. "Listen, Lily. . . . Earlier, by the chapel, I shouldn't have pushed you away," he said. "That was wrong of me. I thought . . . I failed you, and I'm sorry."

She met his intensely blue eyes.

"You're not a . . . ," he said. "You're an extraordinary person."

"Extraordinarily freakish, you mean."

"Other people would hide or deny, but you want answers. That's extraordinary."

"Uh, thanks." With him looking at her like that, her legs felt like Jell-O. *He wouldn't be so nice,* she reminded herself, *if he knew you'd sneaked into the club with Tye.* "I ran from the battle."

"Don't blame yourself," he said. "You aren't trained yet. You'll be one of us in no time. You're a descendant of Richard

158

Carter. The fact that he raised you should compensate for any taint."

By "taint" he clearly meant Mom. Lily looked away from his angelic face. As they walked through Prospect Gardens, she kept to the center of the flagstone walk, as far as possible from the tulips and the rosebushes to avoid attracting their attention. Jake considered her tainted. Maybe she was.

Jake was struggling to piece together what sounded like an explanation. "I should not have let the . . . by the chapel . . . it was just . . ."

"Your parents?" she asked.

He nodded.

"I'm sorry," Lily said. They walked by a trio of women, young alums, whose eyes fixed on Jake admiringly. One of them whispered to her friends, and all three giggled. Jake either ignored them or didn't notice.

Changing the subject, he said, "The secrets are necessary."

She didn't reply. There was no point in arguing with him about that. Grandpa was the one who had hurt her with his secrets. As they passed the 40th Reunion tent, music poured out from the fenced-in area. She smelled cheeseburgers from their barbecue along with the omnipresent smell of beer, and she glimpsed orange-clad alums and their families chatting, laughing, and eating. No one seemed at all concerned that there was a battle with fantastical creatures occurring across campus. "How do you keep it a secret from all of them?" she asked.

"You'd be surprised what it's possible to hide if you have the resources," he said with pride in his voice. "We've had generations of practice at hiding this secret. See up ahead." He pointed.

Campus security cars and construction vehicles were arrayed across a street. She saw an ambulance and a fire truck in front of a Wawa market. Police cones and yellow do-not-cross tape blocked off an intersection.

"Water main broke," Jake explained as he ducked under the yellow tape and then held it up for her to duck underneath as well.

"It did? Because of the attack?"

He shook his head. "We have a special arrangement with campus security whenever a Feeder is spotted. Civilians are evacuated immediately, and campus security will help them 'remember' what they think they saw by providing a more plausible explanation and, if necessary, 'proof.' The area is then cordoned off. In this case, we needed a large explanation." She noticed that guards were posted along the yellow tape, plus there was a second layer of security guards closer to the dorm. "Containment is key." He flashed an ID at one of the campus police and said, "She's with me."

The security guard waved them both through.

"This happens a lot?" she asked, craning her neck to see more.

"Usually, Feeders stay as far from Princeton as possible, especially during Reunions when so many knights are in one place."

"You mentioned a new leader?"

"You shouldn't worry about it. My grandfather has made it his personal mission to hunt down this leader," Jake said. "And he does not accept failure. The new leader is as good as dead, especially if he's dared to come here."

"Oh," she said. She thought of the goblin and wondered what Tye would have said.

After they wove among all the police cars, Lily had her first good look at the dorm. The sprawling white building looked more like a country club than a battle site. Jake pulled her around the side of the building. "We've engaged the enemy behind the dorm on the golf course," he said.

"There's a golf course?"

He held up a hand to silence her. He poked his head around the corner and then beckoned her forward. She joined him. Cheerfully, he said, "Oh, yes, Forbes used to be a hotel. That's why it's used to house the oldest alumni during Reunions. Many of the rooms have private bathrooms."

"Um, nice," she said. She wasn't sure this was the appropriate time or place to discuss bathrooms.

Crouching, she followed him across a lawn toward a grove of trees. When they reached the first one, Jake drew his knife. It glittered even in the shadows. "Dorms are assigned at random," Jake said, "though the knights may step in to ensure you have a roommate who is also privy to the true purpose of Princeton."

"What exactly *is* the true purpose of Princeton?" she asked.

"Educating future leaders of the world," Jake said. "Also, protecting the world from . . . them." He pointed toward the golf course.

At first, all Lily saw was a picture-perfect sunset. The sky was stained rose red, and the clouds had deepened to dark ocean blue. Below, the golf course was blackened with dusk. But then she saw in the center, shadows circled and dodged one another in an elaborate dance. Lily picked out silhouettes: a man, a woman, a figure with angel-like wings, another with writhing tentacles, a lion with a woman's head . . . One dark shape even looked like a unicorn. Shadows blurred together and broke apart. She couldn't see faces.

"Stay here," Jake ordered. "Hide in these trees." Knife in hand, he crept across the lawn and jumped over a fence. He disappeared. She guessed that the hill sloped down to the golf course.

Following Jake's order, Lily stepped farther into the patch of trees. Leaves caressed her arms, and branches ran through her hair. Her bones vibrated with the hum of their tuneless music. She peered out between tree trunks at the golf course and tried to make sense of the dancing shadows. She didn't see Jake yet. Or Grandpa.

All of a sudden, the hum spiked into a shriek. She clapped her hands over her ears. "Stop it!" she hissed at the trees.

A nine-foot man with gray skin leaped over the fence. Lily screamed as he rushed toward her. The trees shrieked in concert with her. Jake vaulted over the fence after him, launching himself at the monster's back with his knife in his fist. As his feet crashed into the monster's shoulder blades, he swung at its neck. The monster toppled forward, and Jake's blade flashed in an impossibly fast blur.

The monster lay still only a foot from the grove of trees. Green oozed from its neck.

Flattened against a tree trunk, Lily stared. Her heart hammered so loudly that it drowned out the hum. The monster's eyes were open and sightless. It had all happened in less than thirty seconds.

"Sorry," Jake said. "I accidentally chased it toward you."

She swallowed hard, her mouth dry. "What is it?"

"Troll," he said. "You should be fine here now."

"Uh-huh," she said. Green blood soaked into the pine needles.

"Really," he said. "Just stay hidden."

"Uh-huh," she said.

"And try not to scream next time. You could lure more monsters."

Jake wiped his knife on the grass to clean off the green blood. Watching him, Lily asked, "How did you move so fast?" His knife arm had struck so quickly that she'd barely seen it. Even Olympic athletes didn't move that fast.

Ignoring her questions, Jake lifted the troll's wrist and checked its pulse. He grimaced. "Grandfather won't be happy that it was a kill instead of a capture. You saw it was unavoidable, didn't you?"

She nodded vigorously. "He wasn't coming to hug me."

Jake gave her a thousand-watt smile and then raced off to leap back over the fence. Alone again, Lily wished she had a big sparkly knife like Jake had. Not that she knew how to use one. As Jake had pointed out before, she wasn't trained. At Grandpa's insistence, she'd taken half a year of tae kwon do, but all that meant was that she knew how to break a board with her foot and could do fifty jumping jacks in rapid succession—she wasn't exactly "battle ready." She'd agreed to the class only because she'd wanted more extracurriculars on her college application. If he'd told her she'd need to worry about monsters . . . if he'd told her *anything* . . .

With one more look at the dead troll, Lily scooted deeper into the patch of trees. As if comforting her, the branches curled around her shoulders. She wished she'd thought to order the trees to help her. Maybe killing could have been avoided if she'd done something other than scream; for example, she could have had the branches hold the troll and then offered to help him like Tye had helped the goblin. If she'd been smarter, he might not have had to die.

On the darkening golf course, Lily saw blades spin as fast as jet plane propellers. If each blade was a knight . . . she counted thirty knights and six nonhumans. But she couldn't be sure. She wondered how many had already fallen, and she tried to scan the ground. But with the low light, it was impossible to distinguish shadows from bodies. From here, everything looked like a body and everyone looked like a monster.

She wished she could tell which shadow was Grandpa's. She couldn't imagine he was one of the swirling-dervish knights, but she refused to consider that he could be one of the shadows on the ground. *He shouldn't be out there fighting monsters,* she thought. He was an old man. He ran a flower shop. She wished there were some way she could help!

Her eyes were drawn to the dead troll. If she could catch the Feeders' attention for long enough to explain, she could offer them a way out—a way home. Everyone could put down his or her swords or knives or fangs, and no one else would be hurt.

She could be the key to ending this. Literally.

Skirting the fallen troll, Lily tiptoed out of the trees. She crept along the fence until she reached a knee-high stone wall, bordering the backyard of Forbes. It was the perfect podium.

Lily climbed onto the stone wall. Down on the golf course, the Feeders and Old Boys had drawn closer to Forbes. Before she could lose her nerve, she sucked in air and then shouted as loudly as she could, "Stop! You don't have to fight anymore! I'm a Key! I can take you home!"

Below her, from the base of the hill, she heard growls.

She looked down.

"Oh, crap," she said.

At least twenty goblins, trolls, werewolves, and fairies crouched in the shadows directly below her. And they did *not* look friendly.

"Lily!" She heard Grandpa yell. "Run!" Whirling and

slicing, he raced toward the hill, but the Feeders were between her and the knights.

She forced herself to stand her ground. *They won't hurt me*, she told herself. Tye had said that deep down they didn't want to kill. "I can help you!" Lily called to the Feeders. "You can go home! You can break free!"

A werewolf with red eyes stalked up the hill. "I *am* free, little Key." His fangs mangled his voice into a cross between words and a growl. "And your strength will help me stay free." He sprang toward her.

Jumping off the stone wall, she ran.

Behind her, she heard the Feeders charging up the hill and scrambling over the stone wall. She plunged into the grove of trees. "Help!" she cried. "Stop them!" She slapped the trunks. The branches knit around her like a barricade.

The wolf launched himself at the branches. They bent and strained under his weight. Lily dropped to her knees and plunged her hands into the underbrush. "Grow!" she shouted at the bushes. In response, the bushes swelled. "Slow them!" she commanded.

As other Feeders crashed into her woods, the underbrush writhed around their legs. Closest to her, the wolf snapped his jaws, breaking branches. Another gray-skinned troll sliced through the shrubs with a sword. A unicorn stabbed at the branches with a horn dark with blood. Lily retreated deeper into the grove. Sweat covered her forehead and dripped down her shirt. Her heart hammered in her chest. She backed up until she smacked against the fence on the other side of the trees. Saplings tried to close around her.

Suddenly, Grandpa was on the lawn.

Silver sword in one hand, knife in the other, he flew through the air. He spun among the Feeders, kicking and lunging so fast that he blurred like a film in fast-forward. The Feeders turned to face him and Grandpa whirled, his blades flashing in the dying sunlight.

"Help him!" Lily cried to the trees. Magic poured out of her and into the trees like blood flowing from a wound. She felt dizzy, as if the oxygen had thinned. Her legs buckled. Lily fell to her knees.

Around her, the trees surged forward. She heard the rip of roots as they strained against the ground. Through the branches, she saw the other knights join Grandpa. Jake tossed aside a svelte fairy as Grandpa charged at the wolf who had first chased Lily. Another knight slammed into the unicorn, and yet another leaped onto the second troll.

A faceless man stretched out his fingers. Fire burst into balls of red and orange on his fingertips.

"Grandpa!" Lily yelled.

Grandpa dove and rolled as the fireballs shot through the air. The flames slammed into the trees, and Lily heard screams. The sound felt like fingernails against the marrow of her bones. She collapsed into a ball as the trees' screams echoed and bounced inside her, drowning out all other sounds. Flames licked up the branches.

Through the red orange glare, she saw the Feeder shoot fire at her grandfather again. This time, a fireball grazed Grandpa's arm, and his sleeve burst into flame.

Lily tried to scream again, but her voice was a croak. She tasted smoke, and she tried to crawl from the trees. Her muscles quivered and gave way. Through the screen of leaves, she saw Grandpa drop to the ground. She had to help him! Lily thrust her fingers into the roots of the underbrush. "Smother the fire," she whispered. She saw leaves curl toward the flickers of flame. She saw the unicorn's horn slice down toward Grandpa. . . .

And then she blacked out.

CHAPTER  Ten

$\mathcal{L}$ily woke to her mother's singing. She blinked her eyes open as Mom planted a kiss on her forehead and sang, "Good morning, sleepyhead!"

"Morning," Lily mumbled. *What a bizarre dream,* she thought. She rolled onto her back and stretched. Above her, the ceiling was decorated with intricate swirls of vines and leaves and flowers.

She sat up quickly and faced the drawing of the Chained Dragon by the window, precise and elegant on the cratered plaster wall. It hadn't been a dream. She looked down at her hand. Someone had unbandaged it. The dragon bites were uneven bumps, closer to cat bites than the gashes they'd been just yesterday.

Yesterday.

An image flashed through her mind: Grandpa, falling

on the grass, flames licking his arm, a unicorn's horn about to stab . . . "Where's Grandpa?" she asked. She tried not to sound panicked.

"Grandpa's friend, that Mr. Mayweather or something, called to say they'd be breakfasting at his club," Mom said. She smiled brightly as she added, "We're to scavenge for ourselves. Like squirrels!"

Grandpa was alive. *Oh, thank God!* She felt her ribs release, and she could breathe again. Lily clasped her hands together so Mom wouldn't see they were shaking. If Mom had any idea what had happened last night . . . "You dyed your hair," Lily said. Mom's hair was neon orange.

"Like it?" Mom said, touching a few strands.

Lily peered closer. Mom's scalp was bright orange, and she had a streak of orange on her forehead. "That's not hair dye."

"Spray paint," Mom said.

Lily flopped back down on the bed. A spring poked into her back. "Ow." She wondered if hair-color obsession was Mom's own quirk or a dryad trait. She wondered how much of Mom's personality was her own and how much was due to her tree-ish-ness. She wondered how angry Grandpa was that Lily hadn't stayed hidden last night.

"I knew you wouldn't like it. Bought you a bribe to win your forgiveness." Mom yanked a shirt out of a bag and tossed it to Lily.

Lily caught it, sat up, and spread it out on her lap. It had an orange *P* and a tiger. She touched the tiger and thought of Tye. She hadn't realized how brave he was to try to bring Feeders home. They didn't *want* to break their addiction. "Thanks," she said belatedly. "Wait, you went shopping on your own?"

Mom patted Lily's shoulder. "You're such a worrier. I was fine."

Only because she'd been lucky. If she'd run into a Feeder . . . For an instant, Lily considered telling her mother the truth right then, without waiting for Grandpa. *You're not human,* she could say. *You're from an alternate world. Oh, and about the monsters from your nightmares? Yeah, they exist.* Mom would force-feed her medicine if Lily said any of that. "Did Mr. Mayfair say anything else when he called?" Lily asked.

"He certainly did," Mom said.

Lily felt her heart skip a beat. "What did he tell you?"

Mom threw her arms around Lily. "I am so proud of you, I could burst! Princeton girl! I'm sorry that I put pressure on you. But I knew you wouldn't fail. You never fail at anything."

Oh. That. "It's not official yet," Lily said. "It doesn't count until the letter is in my hand. Besides, I might still apply to schools near Philly."

"Absolutely not!" Mom gripped Lily's shoulders. "Now, you listen to me. I am not letting you sacrifice your future to take care of me. This place is your dream!"

Her dream had a few hidden nightmares in it. But Mom was right. Until the Old Boys changed their minds, she was a Princeton prefrosh. She'd wanted this forever. She should remember to be happy about it.

Mom handed her a Ziploc full of toiletries. "We'll buy you one of those bathroom caddies. And flip-flops. College girls shower in flip-flops. I'm not sure why."

"Remember the time we both refused to clean the apartment and waited to see who would break first?" Lily asked.

Mom grinned. "We wrote poems in the dust and grime."

"Bad poems."

"Some almost rhymed."

Lily said, "I'm guessing dorm showers are about that clean."

Mom wrinkled her nose. "We'll buy you flip-flops and Lysol."

At this rate, Mom would have her packed for college before Lily had finished junior year. "I'll be right back," Lily promised. And then she'd decide when and how to tell Mom the truth. Lily kissed her mother's cheek, fetched her towel, and headed down the hall to the bathroom. She didn't know how Grandpa had lived with such an enormous lie. It wasn't a love-the-new-hair-color kind of lie; it was a lie to top all lies.

Lily showered quickly and then tiptoed over the gritty and crusty hall carpet back to the dorm room. Still not sure what to say to Mom, she opened the door anyway. "Mom, did Grandpa ever . . ."

Mom wasn't there.

Lily froze, imagining goblins and trolls and faceless men

with fire at their fingertips. She noticed the window was open, but she couldn't remember if it had been open before. Mom did like fresh air, possibly a dryad thing. Lily crossed to the window and looked down at the 50th Reunion tent below. She lacked X-ray vision to see through the tent roof. Spinning back toward the room, she scanned for a clue or a note or anything.

She spotted a piece of paper taped to the ceiling. Her shoulders relaxed, and she grinned. Dryad or human, Mom was still Mom. Craning her neck, Lily read, *Gone to forage breakfast*. Mom had drawn a sketch of a squirrel with a pile of nuts.

Lily dressed quickly and wished she'd thought of a way to warn Mom about Feeders. She shouldn't be wandering around campus by herself. Lily tried Mom's cell phone. Voice mail. Standing on a chair, she added to her mom's note: *Gone to find you. Call me!* She headed out the door.

Chances were that the Feeders weren't a danger anymore. Someone had returned Lily to her bed and Mr. Mayfair had called Mom, so the battle had to be over and the Feeders taken care of. But still, this was Mom. Lily wasn't about to take any risks with her.

Across the courtyard, Lily spotted a table stocked with bagels and croissants—if Mom had wanted breakfast, she could have foraged there, but the volunteers at the table didn't recognize Mom's description. Chomping on a bagel, Lily tried the registration desk.

The same perfect-teeth elderly woman beamed at Lily as she approached. "Richard Carter's granddaughter, yes?" she asked.

"Um, yes," Lily said. She hadn't expected to be remembered. "I'm looking for my mother. She was wearing a Princeton shirt and has neon-bright orange hair. Did you see her leave the tent?"

"Oh, yes, she passed by here with Joseph Mayfair a few minutes ago," the woman said. "So lovely that your families stayed close after the tragedy."

"Um, yeah," Lily said. "Thanks."

The woman beamed with all her white teeth. "Happy to help!"

Lily hurried past her. She tried Mom's cell phone one more time and then Grandpa's. Mr. Mayfair should have fetched Lily as well as Mom. She should be there when Grandpa explained why he was bruised and burned. She should make sure Mom was told the truth. It was time.

On Prospect Avenue, Lily had to stop. She'd walked, not run, across campus, but she was panting anyway. She sucked in air, but it felt as if the oxygen had been leached out of the atmosphere. Her chest felt tight, and her muscles trembled.

She leaned against a maple tree to catch her breath. She felt the tree's bark against her arms, but she heard nothing. No static. No chimes. Just ordinary noises. She remembered how she'd felt with the trees at Forbes, as if the magic were pouring out of her. Maybe it had been. Maybe she should have taken a dose of medicine this morning instead of just a bagel.

Lily continued down Prospect Avenue, stumbling twice. She felt a headache pinch between her eyes as she entered Vineyard Club. She hoped Mom had remembered her medicine this morning. *No,* she corrected. *Not medicine. Magic.* She wondered how low Mom's magic levels were— she'd never caused the plants in the flower shop to dance. She had to be running on nearly empty every day.

One of the Old Boys lounging on a red leather couch rose as if to stop her, but a second one nodded. She recognized him from her first meeting with the Old Boys. "She's one of us," the man said. The first Old Boy sat down and picked up his newspaper. He continued to watch her, though, as the second man flipped open a cell phone and said, "Richard's granddaughter is here."

Almost immediately, Jake emerged from the stairwell to the taproom. "Jake, have you seen . . . ," she began. God, he looked terrible—or at least as terrible as a golden boy could look. His eyes were puffed and red, and his skin looked pale and waxy. "Are you okay?"

"First time helping with cleanup . . . ," he mumbled, and then he darted for a trash can in the corner of the room. Clutching the sides, he vomited into the can. He straightened after a moment and wiped his mouth with his sleeve. "Nice," he said, to either himself or the trash can. "Very manly."

"Do you want some water or . . . ?" she asked.

He flashed a weak smile at her. "I'm fine. Fine." And then he scowled. "What were you thinking last night? You were supposed to stay hidden."

She flushed bright red. "I thought I could help." Instead, she'd barely helped herself. She should have ordered the shrubs to stretch faster or the trees to seal bark around her and the knights. If she'd been more specific, maybe she could have been more effective. As it was, she'd only succeeded in getting people hurt. "Is everyone . . . all right? Is my grandfather here? Have you seen my mother?"

"Ask my grandfather," Jake said. "He's downstairs, running the clean—" His face contorted, and midsentence, he dove for the trash can again. She started to approach him, but he waved her away. "Don't watch."

She lingered another minute in case he needed help, and then she headed downstairs. She slowed as she got closer to the taproom. Odd noises drifted up the stairwell, groans and growls. Lily wondered what exactly had caused Jake to vomit. Maybe she should wait upstairs.

But Mom could be down there, too.

Fixing thoughts of Mom firmly in her mind, Lily reached the bottom of the stairs and halted. "Oh, my God," she breathed.

The taproom was crammed full of monsters. All of them were tied, blindfolded, and gagged. Most lay on the floor. A few were tied to chairs. To one side, three men in elbow-length gloves were stacking full trash bags. She vaguely recognized their faces from Forbes. Each of the men looked at her and then returned to his task.

"Mr. Mayfair?" she asked tentatively.

One of them pointed to the hidden room, now wide open. She stepped toward it and peered inside. Lying on the wood floor, with shackles from the chair stretched around his delicate legs, was a unicorn.

Between streaks of dirt and dried blood, his flank was mother-of-pearl. He was the kind of white that proved that white is composed of all colors. He shimmered beneath the grime like a pale rainbow about to disappear.

With a rasping breath, the unicorn lifted his head an inch off the floor and opened his eyes. They were so blue that they nearly glowed, but the lids were ringed with pus and blood. Shutting his eyes, he sagged his head back down on his silver hooves. The shackles clanged as they shifted.

Standing over him, Mr. Mayfair held steady a syringe that was plunged into the unicorn's hind leg. The drainer glugged and whirred. Silver liquid flowed through the tubes and into a bottle.

As the level in the bottle rose, the unicorn twitched. He flailed his head, cutting the air with his horn. His horn, which should have been luminescent gold, was black with blood. *Knights' blood,* Lily reminded herself. *Maybe even Grandpa's.*

Mr. Mayfair consulted his watch, and then with one hand still holding the syringe steady, he deftly replaced the full bottle with an empty one. Lily could see every vein in the unicorn's neck pulsing. The ragged breathing hurt to hear. He sounded as if his throat had been raked with nails.

She flinched as the unicorn spasmed. His head lolled forward onto the floor. Lily waited for Mr. Mayfair to stop. But he didn't. The unicorn's shakes lessened until his body merely vibrated. And then the beautiful beast was still.

He must be all right, she thought. Mr. Mayfair had said it was a safe procedure. He knew when to stop. The unicorn was only resting, right?

Mr. Mayfair squeezed the remaining drops from the tube, and then he removed the syringe from the unicorn's flank. He turned off the drainer, and then he discarded the needle. "Ready," he said.

The three men bustled past Lily into the room. She watched, glued in place, as they removed the shackles from the unicorn's legs. Released, he didn't move. Together, the three men hefted the unicorn up and carried him out into the taproom. They laid him down onto tarp-size black garbage bag.

Lily stared at the unicorn's chest, waiting for it to rise. It didn't.

The men closed the garbage bag around him, and then they heaved the unicorn's body onto the pile of other bags. Lily felt her knees shake. All those bags . . .

Stripping off his latex gloves, Mr. Mayfair joined Lily in the taproom. "You look pale," he said in his cultured voice. "Would you care to sit down?"

It was one thing to watch Jake kill the troll that had been about to kill her, but this . . . She kept thinking of the council unicorn, luminous in the sunlight. She forced herself to picture Grandpa prone on the lawn with the unicorn about to strike. "I was looking for my mother. And my grandpa." Her voice sounded thin to her ears.

"This is not a pretty sight, I know," Mr. Mayfair said. "But keep in mind that these are monsters, no matter what the storybooks say. They cannot be allowed to continue to prey on humanity. At least this way, their deaths serve a purpose."

Her eyes slid to the pile of garbage bags.

"Our only edge against them is the magic," he said. "It enhances our natural skills and enables us to hold our own in battle against supernatural beings. The death of these monsters . . . their magic will help us fight to keep humans safer."

The flasks, she remembered. They hadn't drunk a toast; they'd drunk magic. She bet Tye didn't know that. She wondered what he would say.

"We need to do this," Mr. Mayfair said. "We're fighting a war, and we are not winning." For the first time since she'd met him, he sounded troubled.

"Oh?" she said. She knew her response was inadequate, but she felt as if her mind was shrieking. She hadn't asked for this, not any of it. She didn't want to know about Feeders and wars and . . .

"Always before, Feeders were loners. We could hunt

them down one by one. But for the first time in generations, Feeders have united under a single leader, and the hunted are now the hunters. . . . But this is my problem, not yours." His eyes were full of sympathy. "I know all of this must be a terrible shock to you."

She nodded and thought that was the greatest understatement she'd ever heard.

"I'm afraid I have difficult news for you," he said.

Lily felt her heart freeze. "Mom?" she said. She scanned the taproom. This sight must have traumatized her mom beyond belief.

He shook his head. "Your mother is fine. She's upstairs."

Lily sighed in relief.

"It's your grandfather," Mr. Mayfair said. "His injuries were severe."

"Where is he? Will he be okay? What's wrong?" Her mind caught in a loop, repeating, *Oh no, oh no, oh no.*

"Come with me," Mr. Mayfair said.

He led her up the stairs to the main room and then up the grand staircase, past more oil paintings and more stained-glass windows. Her heart was pounding. *Please, be okay,* she thought.

At the end of a corridor, Mr. Mayfair opened a plain white door. Lily rushed inside. Grandpa was tucked into a hospital bed with an IV in his arm and an oxygen mask over his face. Bandages covered his left arm. His eyes were closed.

Beside him sat Mom. She turned when Lily entered the

room. Lily saw that her eyes were so pink and puffy that they looked bruised. "Oh, Lily," Mom said. She held out her hands.

Lily ran to her.

Mom wrapped her arms around Lily's waist and pressed her cheek against Lily's stomach. Lily stroked her orange hair.

Behind her, Mr. Mayfair said, "He slipped into a coma last night."

This is my fault, Lily thought. If she hadn't shown herself at Forbes . . . Lily drew in a shaky breath. She had to hold it together. She kept petting Mom's hair as she stared at Grandpa.

He looked frail. She'd never seen her grandfather look frail. "What's wrong with him?" Lily asked. "When will he wake?"

Mr. Mayfair hesitated. "Rose, will you stay with him? Watch him for any change? I'd like a few words with Lily."

Releasing Lily's waist, Mom laid her head on the edge of the hospital bed. Her fingers wove between Grandpa's fingers. She didn't speak.

"I'll be right back," Lily told her.

She followed Mr. Mayfair out of the room and into a study stuffed with antiques. Oriental rugs covered the hardwood floor, and a carved wooden fireplace filled one wall. Other walls held bookcases with gilded leather books. Mr. Mayfair gestured to a leather chair beside a Tiffany dragonfly lamp. He himself went to stand beside a window with his hands clasped behind his back. He looked out onto the street below.

Lily didn't sit. "I need the truth," she said. "Is he going to be okay?"

"The truth is that I don't know. He could wake in five minutes; he could wake in five years." His clasped hands, she noticed, had tightened so that his knuckles were as white as his oxford shirt. "We must brace ourselves for the possibility that he does not wake ever."

Lily felt as if the walls were leaning in. She sank into the chair. "Ever," she repeated. "But . . . it hasn't been that long. You can't have tried everything. He should be in a hospital! There should be doctors! Specialists!"

"Our facilities here are top-notch," Mr. Mayfair said. "But if we do not see significant improvement in the next twenty-four hours, then yes, we will transfer him to a hospital with specialists in combat injuries."

She couldn't think. Her brain felt like sludge. Lily sucked in a deep breath, willing herself to stay together. Mom and Grandpa needed her to not fall apart.

"However, there is a problem." Mr. Mayfair turned from the window. His eyes bored into hers. They were the same brilliant blue as Jake. "Your mother cannot go to a hospital. With her mental problems, it would be frighteningly easy for her to change from visitor to patient, and that would be disastrous. If a doctor examined her . . ."

"Mom's been to doctors before," Lily said. She'd accompanied her on lots of visits.

"Our doctors," Mr. Mayfair said. "Princeton knights."

Lily had never noticed. She tried to remember the degrees on the wall. She hadn't paid attention. It was possible. Grandpa had always picked the doctors and arranged the appointments. For a second, she thought about all those people in on the secret, all keeping everything from her and Mom, but she pushed the anger away to deal with later. "Then she's . . . different inside?"

"Very," Mr. Mayfair said gravely.

Lily tried to digest that, and then she pushed it away for later, too. "Can she . . . stay here?" she asked. She hated the idea of leaving her in a place that wasn't familiar, but Mom couldn't be left alone.

"There is another option," Mr. Mayfair said. "You could send her home."

"Home?" Lily repeated. She was certain that he didn't mean Philadelphia and their attic-floor nest of flowers and pillows and sunlight and pottery. He meant the other Princeton.

"It is what your grandfather wanted," Mr. Mayfair said. "It is why you are here this weekend. Your grandfather believed that your mother's problems are due to her heritage, and that her family might be able to help her, even cure her."

Lily had begun to think she was done being shocked, but this . . . Mr. Mayfair's words exploded like fireworks in her head. She remembered how Grandpa had said there was hope. This must have been what he'd meant.

"He had intended to explain it himself, but . . ." Mr.

Mayfair gestured toward the hall. "He wouldn't want you to wait. You must know that your mother is worsening. The magic doses aren't enough. If she doesn't have true help soon, she will lose herself entirely."

He left her to think. So she returned to Grandpa's room and curled up in a chair next to Mom. Mom lay where Lily had left her, cheek pressed against the hospital bedsheet and hands wrapped tightly around Grandpa's limp fingers. She didn't move or speak.

Lily studied the back of her mom's head, her orange hair splayed out like bright seaweed, the orange spray paint tinting her scalp. Mr. Mayfair was right; Mom was worsening. *Her rate of decline is worse than we expected,* Lily remembered Grandpa saying. *We must act now.*

Lily couldn't miss this chance. She had to do it. The steady *beep-beep-beep* of the heart monitor filled the room. Grandpa would have wanted her to, no matter how much she disliked the thought of entrusting Mom to strangers.

"Mom?" Lily said. "I have something to tell you. Grandpa had a secret. . . ."

Mom raised her head. She looked like a porcelain doll about to shatter. Her tears had left crisscrossing streaks on her cheeks like tiny fissures.

Taking a deep breath, Lily told her the truth.

As she talked, Mom's eyes widened and her mouth opened into an O. Her hands fell away from Grandpa's.

Finally, Lily ran out of words. Silently, Mom stared at her.

"Are you . . . okay?" Lily asked.

Mom looked back at Grandpa. She picked up his hand again and held it.

"This is why he bought us to Reunions," Lily said. "So that I could learn how to take you home."

Mom leaned over the hospital bed and kissed Grandpa's cheek. "No," she said softly and firmly.

Lily blinked. "What do you mean, no? No to which?"

"My place is here," Mom said, "with my father."

"Mom, he's not . . ." Lily faltered.

Mom smiled faintly. "Of course he is," she said. "He is my family, even if we don't share blood. Or chlorophyll."

Lily winced. For the first time, she couldn't read Mom. She couldn't tell if she was bitter or amused. She merely sounded calm and certain. "But you've said it yourself: Every day, you slip away more."

"I won't leave him," Mom said.

Shaking her head, Lily opened her mouth to object again.

Mom laid a light hand on her arm. "No, Lily."

Lily thought of a dozen arguments and discarded each one. Mom wasn't stubborn often, but when she was . . . Grandpa had once compared her to a tree, happily bending whenever the breeze wanted her to but sticking in place when it mattered. Lily wished she could hate him for saying things like that. "You don't even seem surprised," Lily said.

Mom cocked her head and looked as if she was considering

her level of surprise. "It makes sense," she said finally.

Lily gaped at her. She was joking, right?

"Once, I took extra medicine," Mom said. "Not intentionally. I forgot that I'd already taken it. Every flower in our apartment bloomed. The roses, they danced." Her eyes began to shine. "The morning glories, they sang as beautifully as their name. And the herbs border . . . the apartment smelled of basil and rosemary for days. You asked me what I'd cooked; I said that I couldn't remember. I thought I had imagined it all."

Lily didn't know what to say.

Mom almost smiled. "It is nice to know that I'm not quite as crazy as you thought, isn't it? I think it's nice." She turned back to Grandpa and patted his hand. "You had your reasons for your secrets, I'm sure. You can tell me when you wake. I'll be here."

"Mom . . ."

She repeated, this time to Lily, "I'll be here."

*I*n the club cafeteria, Lily fetched a cup and filled it with Sprite. She watched the bubbles froth and tried not to think too hard about Grandpa upstairs hooked up to IVs and monitors. Jake approached her. He handed her a lid and straw.

"I heard," Jake said. "I'm sorry."

"He'll wake up," Lily said. "He's strong. He runs half marathons on weekends. For fun. With no one chasing him." She tried to fit the lid over her cup. It popped up, and soda spilled over her hand. She stared at it and suddenly felt like crying. She blinked hard. "He'll wake up, and he'll ask me why I didn't help my mother." She watched a tear drop into the soda. "The dryads could help her. They may have some kind of cure. But she won't go with me, even if it's what Grandpa would want. . . ." She sucked in air and blinked faster, forcing herself to quit crying before she really started. It wouldn't help Grandpa for her to fall apart. She met Jake's eyes. "I can't force her to go. She's my mother. But I can't wait here while she gets worse and while Grandpa . . . I can't do nothing."

Jake looked as if he was considering how to answer. Or how to flee. He probably hadn't expected her to unload when all he'd done was hand her a straw. "Does she need to go herself?" he asked. "I mean, if there's a cure, maybe it's something you can bring back to her?"

Lily gawked at him. Of course! That was perfect! "Brilliant," she said.

His cheeks tinted pink. "I could go with you," he said. "I . . . owe you."

"You don't owe me," she said. "I understand. Your parents . . ."

". . . were heroes," he finished. "They fought the dragon when they could have run. They saved a woman and her baby when they could have saved themselves. Least I can do is behave like a knight."

She studied him for a moment. "Okay. Let's go."

He nodded and straightened his shoulders, looking like a soldier about to march. "Are you ready now, or do you want to tell your mother?"

"Fifty percent odds that she won't remember," Lily said. "And if she does, she'll only worry. Or hope. Better to go now, find the dryads, ask for their help, and then be back with whatever brain-hiccup cure they have before Grandpa opens his eyes."

Jake nodded.

Lily set the full soda on the table, and they walked out of the club cafeteria and through the main room. The Old Boys positioned on the couches watched them, but no one seemed interested in stopping them. They walked out the door and down the path to the sidewalk. Lily looked back at the second-floor windows. Mom and Grandpa were safe for now. Being with them wouldn't change anything; returning with a cure could change everything. And maybe it would make up for her idiocy at Forbes. *I'll be right back,* she thought.

Lily picked up her pace, and Jake matched her. By the third street lamp, her knees buckled. She grabbed Jake's elbow as the sidewalk undulated in front of her.

He propped her up. "Lily, are you all right?"

She knew this feeling. "I think . . . I need the gate."

Jake wrapped an arm around her waist. "Lean on me," he instructed. Together, they walked to Nassau Hall. They stopped in front of FitzRandolph Gate. Looking up at the stone eagles, Jake said, "This will work, right?"

"Sure," she said. She had no idea. But they'd know in a few seconds.

"So many times I've walked past this gate. . . . Now, to stand here, about to cross through . . . Intellectually, I know what waits for us, but to actually experience it . . ."

How nice, she thought. She felt like death warmed over, and he was having a special moment. She didn't let him finish rhapsodizing. Pulling him with her, she hobbled through the gate. White light flashed, and then she faced a forest instead of Nassau Street.

"Whoa," Jake breathed. He spun in a circle, looking in every direction. "Even the air feels different. Heavy, like it's about to rain."

She took a deep breath. The air tasted wonderful. As she continued to breathe in, she felt tingling on her skin like light fingernails dancing over goose bumps—the now familiar feel of magic.

"You bring a human here," a metallic voice said above them.

Jake tensed. "Run," he instructed Lily.

"You must see the council," the eagle said.

The second eagle pushed off his pillar and soared into the air. Jake yanked Lily toward the forest. "Go," Jake said. "I'll cover you." With a screech, the eagle dove straight toward them. Jake tensed, ready to lunge at the bird.

"Stop!" Lily said. "We want to see the council!"

The eagle veered away.

"We do?" Jake asked.

"Do you know how to find Mom's family?" she asked him.

"No, but . . ."

"They're good guys too," Lily said. "Remember?" Taking Jake's hand, she led him through the side gate and across the yard. On his pillar, the first eagle preened his wings. His feathers clinked like metal.

Crossing the yard, she brushed her hand against the bark of an oak tree and was comforted by a faint, wordless whisper. She'd feel better soon; she'd already absorbed some magic. She wished she'd made sure that Mom had taken her dose.

She wondered how soon Jake would feel the effects of the magic.

Firmly she reminded herself that she'd be back at Vineyard before it was an issue for either of them. She'd talk to the council, find the dryads, and return to Mom. Quick errand.

As they approached, the double doors to Nassau Hall swung open, and the stone man filled the doorway. Beside her, Jake tensed again. Lily's mouth felt dry. She'd forgotten how very inhuman the stone creature looked. She tried (and failed) to find eyes in the mass of pebbles that rattled across his face. "I . . . we'd like to talk to the council," she said.

"You return, and not alone," the stone man said. She shuddered at the sound of his voice, like bones being ground in a mixer. He beckoned to them, and Lily and Jake climbed the steps and walked into the marble-walled foyer of Nassau Hall.

He whispered in her ear, "Are you sure about this?"

Lily whispered back, "No."

Before Jake could reply, the rock man shifted, the stones in his body tumbling as if in an avalanche. A sharp rock pointed like an index finger at the marble floor. "You will leave your weapons here," he said.

"I don't have—," Lily began.

"Him," the rock man said.

Jake hesitated, but then he reached under his shirt and removed a knife.

"All of your weapons."

Out came two more knives. "I'll need them back," Jake said.

The stone man didn't answer. He led Lily and Jake into the sun-dappled council room. Only three council members were present: Tye's father, the elven woman, and the unicorn. Tye's father and the elf occupied two of the thronelike chairs, while the unicorn stood by the window in a shaft of sunlight. He shone with a soft glow.

Jake swore under his breath. Out of the corner of her eye, she saw him touch his belt where a knife used to be. "Good guys," she said softly to him.

"So you say," he whispered back.

The tiger man curled his lips back as soon as he saw Jake. "Why are *you* here?" He turned to the other council members. "This is an insult—"

"He's with me," Lily said quickly.

Tye's father fixed his orange cat eyes on her.

She shrank back. "I didn't know I shouldn't bring him. I thought . . . You guys are allies."

He snorted. "Have you come to drain our magic, *ally*? Go directly to the source?"

"Allow them to speak," the unicorn said. His voice was just

as beautiful as Lily remembered, like listening to a waterfall. "Perhaps they have come to explain."

The elf raised her delicate eyebrows. "They are quite young for ambassadors. But please, do speak. I for one would love an explanation as to why the knights feel it is not morally reprehensible to murder for magic."

Jake bristled. "We're knights, not murderers."

"I see," the elf said. With her elbows on the chair's arms, the elf propped her chin on her hands. "So you deny that you drain magic from your prisoners of war?"

Lily winced. She hadn't thought about the fact that Tye had already come here with that bottle of magic. She jumped in. "This isn't why we're here."

"It should be," the tiger man growled. "You, Lily Carter—you survived by *drinking* this stolen magic. Like a Feeder."

Feeling her face flush bright red, she thought of the unicorn that Mr. Mayfair had drained. "I didn't know," she said.

"You were an 'innocent' Feeder," he mocked. "You had no idea of the cost of your survival. You were blithely living your days unaware of everything around you." He pointed a clawed hand at her. "Perhaps you have fooled my son, but whatever game you play will not fool me."

Jake's hands clenched into fists. "She *is* innocent."

"And you, my dear boy?" the elf said. "Have you never tasted magic drawn from the veins of a dying addict?"

"We do what we must," Jake said. "We're at war."

Sorrow in his beautiful voice, the unicorn said, "Then you admit it. You not only drain the magic but you consume it."

"Vile," the elf said.

The tiger man growled, "Instead of fighting the Feeders, you have chosen to become Feeders."

"We have not!" Jake said. "Grandfather was right about you. You'd rather see humanity suffer and die than harm a single monster. Feeders are the bane of humankind and must be stopped at all cost."

"Or perhaps it is the knights who should be stopped," the tiger man said.

Lily wanted to scream. "Please," she said. "I'm here for my mother. She's a dryad, and I need—"

The elf rose from her chair, cutting Lily off. "We do not condone Feeders of any kind. We must summon the full council, and we must declare the alliance void."

Jake and the tiger man paid no attention to her.

"You want to stop us?" Jake said to the tiger man. He crouched as if preparing to fight. "It's our duty to defend humanity from the likes of you."

"You'd challenge me, boy?"

"Just try me." Reaching behind his back, he drew a hidden knife.

Lily shouted, "No!" as the tiger man leaped off his throne and transformed midair. A massive Bengal tiger slammed into Jake's chest, knocked him backward, and then reared above Jake. Shielding his face with one arm, Jake stabbed up at the tiger's chest. The tiger batted the knife away, and it clattered across the marble floor.

Everyone stared at it in silence. Jake's breathing echoed, fast and ragged.

"Enough," the unicorn said. "You have better control than this. Attacking children in the council chambers. What has gotten into you? Release him."

The tiger shifted back to almost a man. His clawed hands continued to pin Jake to the floor. "You have your mother's eyes," he said. "It is a shame you do not possess her heart. Or her intellect." He released Jake.

"Child," the unicorn said to Lily. "Tell us why you have come."

"For my mother," Lily said. Quickly—before they could fight again—Lily told the council about her mother's brain hiccups and how her grandfather believed there was hope. She asked for their help in finding the dryads.

"Lies," the tiger man said. "Or truth mixed with lies. We don't know how deep the corruption runs. The knights could plot against us. These children could be pawns, sent to distract us before an invasion."

The unicorn tossed his mane. It reflected light in a spray of colors, like a burst of water droplets in sunlight. "We've heard nothing that suggests an invasion. You are letting your personal biases blind you," he said. "You look at this boy, and he reminds you—"

The tiger man roared. "We will not discuss this in front of *them.*"

The elf nodded at the stone man. "Take them to a waiting room, please, and convene the council. We must vote on the future of our alliance with the knights. This evil cannot be ignored."

The stone man clamped his hand on Jake's shoulder. Jake tried to twist away, but the stone man dragged him toward the door. Jake shouted, "You can't do this! I'm a knight of Princeton!"

As the stone man passed Lily, he snagged her arm.

"Wait!" Lily said. "All I want is to help my mom. I'm not part of your battles."

Silent, the stone man pulled them both out of the council room.

As he dragged them downstairs, Lily clutched at the railing. Her feet slipped on the worn steps. "Please, you have to listen," she begged the stone man.

Jake punched the stone arm that held him. "I demand you release me!"

"If you won't help me find the dryads, at least help me go home," Lily said. "I can't stay here. My mother needs me."

Unimpressed with both of them, the rock man deposited them in a small, gray room and shut the door. Lily tugged on the door handle. "Please! Let us out!"

"Stand back," Jake said. He rammed his shoulder against the door. It didn't budge. He tried again. Nothing. A third time.

"Why did you attack Tye's father?" Lily asked. "What

were you thinking? This wasn't supposed to be about your stupid war with Feeders; this was about my mother!"

Jake stopped and blinked at her. "I . . . oh, whoa . . . I just . . ."

Lily sighed and let him off the hook. "You were baited. Tye's father went after you as soon as he saw you. I don't know why. He wasn't *that* unreasonable when I met him before. Scary, yes. Irrational, no." Changing the subject, Lily waved her hand at the cell. "I don't suppose you had a training exercise on this?" She tried to sound light, but her voice cracked.

"Several," Jake said. He picked up a chair and smashed it against the wall. He selected a chair leg out of the wreckage and brandished it like a sword.

"What—," Lily began.

The door clicked and opened. Jake lunged forward, swinging the chair leg at the figure in the doorway. The figure leaped backward and said in a mild voice, "I rather liked that chair."

Lily grabbed Jake's arm. "Jake, don't!"

Tye poked his head into the room. "Coast clear, or is Pretty Boy still playing baseball?"

Jake continued to hold the chair leg like a bat. "Stay behind me, Lily."

"It's okay, Jake," Lily said, squeezing past Jake. She threw her arms around Tye's neck. He wrapped his arms around her waist. "You found us! How did you find us?"

"He's a clever little tiger boy," Jake said behind her.

She released Tye's neck. He was slower to withdraw his

arms. Lily felt a blush creep onto her cheeks and was glad that her back was to Jake. Maybe she shouldn't have jumped into Tye's arms quite so enthusiastically. She barely knew him, after all. The tingle she felt every time they touched—that was just the feel of magic or very enthusiastic static cling, not a sign of destiny.

Ignoring Jake, Tye answered Lily. "Father likes to stick me in here whenever the council debates whether or not I behaved appropriately on my latest trip to the human world. Not a fan of waiting, so I borrowed a spare key." He shrugged. "We Keys are supposed to open doors, after all."

"Your council's security is lax," Jake said disapprovingly.

"You're welcome to stay and lodge your complaint," Tye said. He nodded at the room. "This isn't a cell, though; it's just a waiting room. If the council believed you were a threat, then your lodgings would have been much more secure. Guess you were voted harmless, Pretty Boy. Congratulations."

"I could show you 'harmless.' . . ."

Lily shot a look at the staircase. Any second, the stone man could thump down those steps and throw them into a real cell. "Guys, can we chat about this *after* we escape?"

Tye executed a courtly bow. "As my lady wishes." He crooked his arm and looped her hand through as if escorting her to a dance. He then strode down the hallway. She had to half jog to keep pace. His arm muscles, she noticed, were tense under her fingers. He wasn't nearly as cool and collected as he sounded.

Jake trailed behind them. "Why are you helping us?"

"I'm helping *Lily*," Tye clarified. "Who are you?"

"Her guard," Jake said.

"Nice job on that," Tye said.

"You can't trust him," Jake said to Lily. "He refused to swear allegiance to Vineyard. He hasn't been through our training. All the trainees are told to keep our distance. He's a wild card. For all we know, he could be leading us into a trap."

Considering they'd just come from what was essentially a cell, Lily found it hard to get worked up about that idea. "He's only lied to me once or twice," she said.

"That you know of," Tye added cheerfully. He shoved his shoulder against a door, and it popped open. He ducked through it.

"Tell us why you're switching sides," Jake said. He clamped his hand down on Lily's shoulder before she could follow. "Or we go no farther. I won't let you endanger Lily."

Lily stared at him, her wannabe knight in shining armor. He'd come a long way from calling her a monster.

"Your pretty boy seems to have some trust issues," Tye commented to Lily. To Jake, he said, "I'm a Key. We don't have sides. If we pick a side, we die. One of the many perks. Besides, aren't we supposed to be allies?"

"Please, Jake," Lily said. She touched his arm lightly. "I don't have a better plan. Do you?"

Jake opened and then shut his mouth. He released her shoulder.

She followed Tye through the door, and Jake followed her. He shut the door behind him, and the three of them hurried down a hall that looked like a stretch of basement: pipes on the ceiling, concrete floor, gray walls.

"So how did you piss off my esteemed paternal figure?" Tye asked.

She hesitated, not quite ready to admit that they might have nailed the coffin shut on a centuries-old alliance. "I'd guess it was Jake's knife."

Jake agreed with her. "He did take exception to the knife."

"You sneaked a weapon into council?" Tye whistled. "And they only put you in a waiting room? Wow, you must be really bad with a blade."

Lily winced.

"Nearly sliced open that monster you call Father," Jake said.

To her surprise, Tye laughed. "Wish I could've seen the look on his face."

"You dislike your father that much?" Lily asked.

"Pretty Boy never would have nicked his fur," Tye said. "But it's been a long time since anyone has done anything but cower in front of my father."

"Including you, I assume," Jake said, disgust dripping from his voice.

"Absolutely," Tye said. "I'm not suicidal."

They turned the corner and faced more corridor. The

dull gray hall looked as if it stretched on for the length of a football field. It ended in shadows and a red EXIT sign.

When they reached the exit, Tye put his finger to his lips. He pushed open the door and led them into a carpeted hall. Office doors lined either side. At the end of the hall was a wooden door with a window. Daylight shone through—it was a door to the outside.

"Where are we?" Lily asked.

"Shh," Tye said.

Jake answered, "Stanhope Hall, next building over from Nassau."

Tye glared at him. "What part of 'shh' was unclear?" he hissed. He peered into one of the offices. "Lucky that no one is here," he said. "We should have been intercepted by now."

"You *expected* to get caught?" Jake asked.

Tye shrugged. "It was more than likely. Usually, these buildings don't empty out."

"You still trust him?" Jake said to Lily.

"Yes," she said simply.

Lily walked toward the sunlight that poured through the window in the door. Both boys blocked her before she could go farther.

"You scout; I'll guard," Jake said.

"Logical," Tye agreed. He darted out the door before Lily could even voice an opinion. In a few seconds, he was back. "Garden clear."

Lily stepped outside with Jake close behind her. She tilted her face up to the sun. Plants around her crooned and hummed. "Jake, how do you feel?"

He flashed his dazzling smile. "Ready for anything."

"Any headache? Spots in your vision? Trouble catching a full breath?"

He frowned. "I—"

Tye clapped him on the back. "He's a knight. Feels no pain."

Lily thought of Grandpa in the hospital bed and frowned. She felt Jake's eyes on her. "We'll be back before he wakes," Jake promised. He pointed to oak trees rising behind a brick wall. "That's the yard. Gate is there."

A green door led through the brick wall to the yard. Motioning for Jake and Lily to stay back, Tye crossed the garden, cracked open the door, and peeked through. Lily leaned against the brick. Moss tickled her shoulder. Absently, she petted it. It cooed back at her.

"Clear," Tye whispered as he tiptoed back to them. "But we'll want to run."

Jake nodded.

Lily stepped away from the wall, and the moss that had curled around her ripped as she moved. She heard it shriek as it tore. She looked at the moss and then at the door. "I can't leave yet," she said. "I have to find the dryads." She told Tye about her mother, the brain hiccups, and Grandpa's plan. "All my life, Grandpa and I have taken care of her.

And now I have to do this. I have to find out if the dryads can help her. Grandpa would never forgive me if . . . Do you understand? There's no guarantee I'll ever get another chance at this."

Tye nodded. "Knew you were no fragile flower."

She exhaled a half snort, half laugh. "Really? Plant jokes? Now?"

"We can find the dryads in the forest," Tye said.

Jake snorted. "Brilliant deduction, Tiger Boy."

"You don't have to come," Tye said. "Gate's right there."

Jake merely glared at him. "Lead on, kitty cat."

Tye crossed the garden in the opposite direction from the gate, and Lily and Jake followed. Stepping onto a stump, Tye vaulted onto the brick wall and balanced catlike on the top. He held a hand down to Lily. She grabbed it and climbed up next to him. Hand in hand, she and Tye hopped down to the other side. They landed in a bed of ivy.

Tye didn't release her hand. "We'll make them help your mom. Don't worry."

She felt her throat close up. She nodded.

"You're not alone in this," he said. He leaned closer. His eyes bored into hers. His lips were so close that she could feel the flutter of his breath. "You never have to be alone again." She wondered if he was still talking about her.

Jake landed beside them, and Tye let go of her hand. She remembered how to breathe. "Everything all right?" Jake asked.

"Fine," Tye said.

Lily avoided Jake's eyes. "Let's go." She set off at a run. The boys followed her. Together, all three of them plunged into the woods beyond campus.

CHAPTER Twelve

As Lily ran through the forest, roots flattened under her feet. Branches drooped out of her way as she brushed against them. Leaves caressed her as she passed. Behind her, Jake and Tye swore as they stumbled over roots and were swatted by branches. Lily barely heard them. She was surrounded by the hushed hum of the forest. For the first time since this had all begun, she felt safe.

"Lily, wait!" Tye called.

Stopping, she looked back. She hadn't noticed, but the boys had fallen behind. She jogged back to them. Jake was sagging against a tree trunk. "Are you all right?"

He straightened. "Fine."

"Not used to the extra magic," Tye said. "No offense, Pretty Boy, but you shouldn't have come." He shook his head. "You shouldn't be feeling it so fast."

Lily answered, "He downed a flask of magic with all the other knights last night. Jake, you can go back if—"

Tye swore. "You're *drinking* the magic? Does the council know this?"

Jake scowled at both of them and began walking. "It was necessary."

"Necessary to become a Feeder to fight the Feeders?" Tye said, matching his pace.

"It's not the same," Jake objected. "Magic from a bottle isn't addictive. Only feeding from humans causes the addiction. What we do is perfectly safe and—"

Tye snorted. "Safe for your victims?"

"Our victims are monsters," Jake said.

"Do you bother to check that?" Tye asked.

Jake clapped his hand on Tye's arm, stopping him. "Never accuse the knights of—"

Orange fur suddenly sprouted on Tye's hands and cheeks. "Never put your hand on me." He wrenched his arm away.

"Guys?" Lily said. It felt as if they were about to launch into each other like rival frat boys at a bar—except one of them had warrior training and the other sometimes grew claws. Stepping between them, she put a hand on each of their chests. "This isn't the time or place for this. Isn't it bad enough what happened with the council? Do we really need to fight amongst ourselves too?"

"You're certain everything you do is right," Tye said to Jake. "Do you even listen to the gargoyles anymore?"

Jake clenched his fists. "You have no idea what it's like on the front lines."

"I *live* on the front lines," Tye said, with an edge to his voice that Lily had never heard.

"And how do I know *you* haven't killed to do that living?" Jake said. He stepped around Lily to stand inches in front of Tye.

"Stop it, both of you!" Lily said.

"Go ahead and try me, kitty cat." Jake said. "I'm trained to take down monsters like you. Like father, like son."

"I don't need training to know which of us is the monster who needs taking down," Tye said. Claws poked through Tye's fingertips. "And I believe my father already kicked your ass."

Jake lunged at Tye.

"Stop!" Lily said.

She was knocked back as the two boys wrestled, slamming each other against the trees.

Lily dove for the nearest one. "Stop them," she ordered the tree. "Hold their arms."

Branches curled around Tye's and Jake's arms, coiling tighter and tighter. Both Tye and Jake yelped as their arms were pinned back. They struggled.

"Don't hurt them," she told the tree. "Just hold them." She put her hands on her hips and scowled at both of them. "You. Are. Not. Helping."

Tye and Jake glared at each other.

"He's everything that's wrong with the knights," Tye said. "He can't tell the difference between allies and enemies."

"I know a monster when I see one," Jake said. "Lily, we can't trust him."

For an instant, she contemplated leaving them both there, trussed up in branches. "Do you trust me?" she asked Jake. "Or do you still see a monster when you see me? And how about my mother? Is she a monster? Worst crime she ever committed was eating an apple from a supermarket without paying for it." Jake lowered his eyes. She turned on Tye. "And you . . . It's not like Feeders are innocent victims waiting to be freed from their debilitating addiction." She told him about what she'd tried at Forbes. "They weren't exactly embracing me as their savior."

"A lot of them don't know any different," Tye said. "Most were born in the human world after the gate closed, the children of the trapped. It's been kill or die their whole lives. But if we could reach them and show them another way . . ." Loosening his hand from the branches, he reached out to her. "You and me. We could save them."

Jake cut in, "How many have you 'saved'? Come on, tell us how well your plan works."

Tye kept his eyes on Lily. "Yes, it takes time to rehabilitate, but—"

"Feeders are incurable," Jake said. "The only good Feeder is a dead Feeder."

Glaring at Jake, Tye said, "It's not so great a leap from

there to 'the only good magic creature is a dead one.' You want to make us all your enemies."

"Your council is dissolving the alliance, not us."

Lily threw her hands into the air. "That's it. Stay there. I have dryads to find." She turned her back on them and began to tromp over the underbrush. It spread to let her pass.

She heard Tye swear behind her. "Lily, wait!" he said.

Lily stopped but she didn't turn. She crossed her arms. Behind her, she heard Jake and Tye speaking softly to each other.

Tye spoke up again. "We have a compromise. First, we'll help you find the dryads. And *then* we'll beat the crap out of each other."

Jake began, "That's not what—"

"Come on, Lily," Tye said. "You need us."

Lily considered it. "Not really." So far, Jake's picking a fight with Tye's father had landed her locked up, and Tye's picking a fight with Jake had slowed her down. "I'll find the dryads myself, thanks."

"But they might not cooperate," Jake said. "You might want backup." He struggled against the branches. Twigs snapped, but the tree didn't budge.

"And you might need help reaching the gate afterward," Tye said. "The council will be looking for you now. My father can be . . . a bit of a grouch."

Lily looked back at them. Bark had closed around their legs, and branches had curled tightly over their forearms.

"I can sneak by. We snuck out without a problem."

"Sneaked," Jake said.

"Sorry?" Lily said.

"Past tense of 'sneak' is 'sneaked,'" Jake said. "Technically, 'snuck' isn't a real word."

"Way to focus on the important details," Lily said.

"He is right," Tye said. "It's 'sneaked.'"

How nice they agreed on something, she thought. "If I let you out, will you promise to quit trying to pummel each other?"

Both boys nodded—half nods, since branches were entwined in their hair.

"And will you promise to help me find the dryads as quickly as possible?" Lily asked.

Tye's eyes flickered away from her. He focused on something in the distance. "I can do better than that," he said. "I can find them right now." Following his gaze, Lily turned around.

A slender figure stepped out from between two tree trunks. His skin was wrinkled bark, and his features were carved wood. His hair looked like woven leaves, and soft moss covered his body like clothes. On either side of him, green and brown men and women emerged from the forest.

Lily began to back toward Jake and Tye.

As the tree people drew closer, Lily saw they were changing. The bark on their faces was smoothing into pink and brown skin. Their mossy clothes spread into green dresses and tunics. Leaves and twigs on their heads split into fine strands, forming pale brown and green hair. Soon, they looked human.

"Guess we got their attention," Tye murmured.

Lily noticed that the hum of the trees had faded to a whir. It felt as if the whole forest had focused its attention on them and was waiting to see what would happen next. She placed her hands on the tree that engulfed Tye and Jake and whispered, "Release them. Please."

The tree retreated. Tye and Jake stumbled forward. Immediately, they each moved to either side of her, Tye on the right and Jake on the left. Shoulder to shoulder, the three of them faced the dryads.

"We mean you no harm," Tye said loudly.

"Sorry for the, um . . ." Jake pointed at the broken twigs that littered the forest floor.

As expressionless as the wood around them, the tree people studied them without speaking. The hum of the plants and trees coalesced into a rhythmic thrum. Slowly, it crescendoed. "Someone's coming," Lily said. She, Jake, and Tye pressed closer together.

Beyond the semicircle of dryads, a voice rose. "Who has been changing my trees?"

The dryads widened the circle to allow the speaker inside, and a woman walked out between the trees. Seeing her, Lily felt her jaw drop. "Mom?"

It wasn't her.

She looked like an older version of Mom: same arched eyebrows, same sky blue eyes, same bone-thin body. She even had the pale green hair that Mom preferred (before her latest spray-paint experiment), but this woman's cheeks were lined with concentric wrinkles like the rings in a tree trunk.

Lily swallowed. Her throat felt as dry as bark. "Grandmother?"

The woman drifted closer, her bare feet soundless on the forest floor. "How very unexpected," she murmured. Inches from Lily, she stopped. She lifted one hand and touched Lily lightly on the cheek. Her fingers were as cool as leaves. "You have his hair and eyes, but I think my lips and cheeks." Her voice was detached, as if observing nothing more important than the color of the sky.

Lily stared into her grandmother's eyes. She tried to see Mom in her, but the woman who looked back had none of Mom's mix of silly and sweet. This woman—this dryad—looked as if she'd never laughed in her life. "Are you . . ." Lily's voice cracked.

Beside her, Tye said softly, "She's the queen of the dryads."

"Queen?" Jake said. "Lily, you're royalty?"

Lily continued to stare at the dryad queen, trying to wrap her mind around the idea that she'd found family, never mind royalty. It had always been just her, Mom, and Grandpa. Now here was a grandmother, albeit not welcoming her with hugs and cookies, but still here in the flesh. Or bark. Or whatever.

"Interesting," the queen said. "Why are you here?"

"My mother . . ." She licked her lips and tried again. "I think you can help her. She needs your help." She wondered if she had aunts, uncles, or cousins.

The dryads whispered to one another, a sound like watery wind. The trees swayed. Branches slapped together in the air.

"My daughter died years ago," the queen said, her voice harsh.

The twelve dryads drew closer together. Leaves and vines curled out from their fingers. Their arms hardened into wood.

Under his breath, Tye said to Lily, "Don't piss off the foliage. Kind of surrounded here." He and Jake continued to flank her, one on each side like bodyguards. Lily saw that the dryads had fanned into a circle, hemming them in on all sides.

"I told her not to consort with humans," the dryad queen said. "Stay with your tree. Root in our soil. Sing with our wind. But he wooed her with sweet compliments. He lured her from her home, and he led her to her death." Above, the leaves knotted together, blocking the sun. The forest fell into shadows. Underbrush writhed like snakes.

"She's not dead," Lily said.

"Impossible," the queen said. "She has not returned to her trees. Without our trees, we lose ourselves. We lose our memories."

That's it, Lily thought. Without any fanfare, without

even asking, she had her answer, the reason for Mom's brain hiccups. Lily thought of all the times she had mentioned something—a birthday present, a TV show, a funny thing a customer had said—and how much it had hurt to see that those memories had slipped out of Mom's mind like sand through her fingers. It was all due to . . . to a weird homesickness?

But the queen wasn't done speaking. "If she lived, she would return. She would never voluntarily be parted from this place. You must lie."

"Mom doesn't remember," Lily said. "She thinks she's human. Or thought she was. Until this weekend, I thought she was too."

The dryad queen's skin began to bubble with leaves. Vines sprouted on her arms and twisted around her wrists and shoulders. "*He* has done this to her!" She was shaking with rage. The trees began to howl.

Lily clapped her hands over her ears. "Stop it! He didn't do anything to her! He died in an accident sixteen years ago."

"Yet she did not return!" The trees swayed as if they were in a storm. Vines writhed around the queen like snakes. They reared back from her and then dove back into her skin, causing bulges to rise and fall up her arms and neck. "Why? There must be more to this 'accident.' Someone has kept her from us! Someone keeps her from us now. Why is she not here with you? Where is my daughter?"

"She's fine," Lily said. "She's safe. She doesn't remember you—"

"Return her to me," the queen said. "We will restore her memory."

"Right now, she doesn't want to—"

"Then you must make her," the queen said. "If she cannot see the trap for herself, then you must free her from it."

Acorns pelted the forest floor like hail. Lily covered her head as leaves and twigs rained from the trees. "She's not trapped!"

Without warning, Jake sagged.

"Whoa, Pretty Boy." Tye went over to his side and propped him up.

Lily caught his other arm. "Jake?" She felt his arm muscles shake.

"Fine. I'm fine." He waved them back and then he sank down onto his knees. "Just need to . . . gotta catch my breath."

Above, the leaves calmed, and the forest stilled as if it were drawing a breath. The dryad queen focused on Jake for the first time. "Young knight, I knew your mother."

Jake's head shot up.

"She visited our world often," the dryad queen said. "She was one of several knights who wanted to build friendships between humans and our kind, led by the man who stole my Rose's heart."

Jake gaped at her. "My mother . . . she came here?"

"At first, they were brought by a Key who was also a

knight. Later, your brother and Lily were their Keys."

"I don't have a brother," Jake said.

"Half brother," the queen corrected.

"My grandfather never mentioned a half brother," Jake said. "He would have told me. We have no secrets. You must have mistaken me for someone else."

The queen's eyes slid across the trees, as if seeing a memory. "One day, Rose and the knights crossed through the gate. She had her baby in her arms. And she simply . . . did not return. None of them did. We believed that they had all died." She fixed her eyes on Lily. "If she'd lived, she would have returned. If she'd lived, you would have brought her back. The knights must have prevented it. They kept her in the human world until her memory faded, and they kept you in ignorance of it all."

Lily shook her head. "No." Grandpa wouldn't have done that.

"Where is she now?" the queen asked.

"In Vineyard Club," Lily said. "Safe. Waiting for me."

"So, they hold her even now," the queen said. Once again, the trees began to tremble and shake. Branches creaked and snapped.

"I told you, she *chose* to stay!" Lily said. "My grandfather is sick—"

The queen touched Lily's face again, a gentle stroke. "I do not blame you, my dear," she said. "You have been used—you are being used—to keep Rose from her home."

"No one's using me." Lily said. "My world is her home now."

"Help her return," the queen said. "Give her back her memories. And then let her choose. If you truly love her, you will give her the chance to choose with full knowledge of what she has lost."

Lily opened her mouth to reply, but she couldn't think of what to say. The queen was right. Mom deserved the chance to choose. But what would happen to her when she regained her memories? Would she still be Mom, or would she change into one of these distant and inhuman creatures?

"She must return," the queen said. "You know this, or you wouldn't be here. She slips away a little more from you every day, doesn't she? If she doesn't return, she will continue to lose herself bit by bit until you have lost her, too."

Unable to speak, Lily nodded.

"Good," the queen said. "To ensure that the knights do not interfere, we will keep the head knight's grandson with us until my Rose is home." She smiled as if pleased with herself.

"You can't!" Lily clutched Jake's arm. "He can't stay in this world. He's already feeling the effects. He has to return!" The dryads shifted closer, tightening the circle around Lily, Jake, and Tye.

"I will not risk a refusal," the queen said. "My daughter is alive! But do not trouble yourself. We will treat your beloved human with every kindness. If you'd like, his half brother may remain with him to ensure his good treatment." She nodded at Tye.

Tye jumped. "I'm not his . . ." His voice trailed off. His eyes widened as he studied Jake. In a strained voice, Tye said, "You know, I always wanted a brother. Kind of pictured him less bigoted and with more of a sense of humor, though."

"I have a sense of humor," Jake said, "and I think the idea that you're my brother is laughable."

"You aren't laughing," Tye pointed out. "Tell me your mother's name."

"Anne," Jake said. "Anne Mayfair, born Anne Norton. She died when I was little."

Tye's voice was a whisper. "She used to sing a lullaby about horses, and she always smelled of apples."

"She did," Jake said, his voice a croak.

"And she liked to read. I remember lots of books."

"We still have her books," Jake said.

Tye and Jake stared at each other as if they'd both grown wings and a tail.

Again, silence. And then Tye flashed his lopsided grin at Lily. "You seem to have quite a knack for uncovering secrets," he said.

"She's a Key," her grandmother said with a wintery smile. "She does as she was born to do. She unlocks us all." The dryad queen then flicked her wrist. Branches swooped down, wrapped around Lily, and snapped her up into the air.

CHAPTER *Thirteen*

Snared in branches, Lily was yanked into the treetops. Screaming, she burst through the leaves into the sunlight above the forest, and then the branches coiled around her. "Tye! Jake!" Whirring as loudly as a windmill, the leaves rushed to form a cylinder around Lily. She screamed again, and then she was sliding through a shaft of solid green. She tried to grab at leaves and branches as they rushed by. Suddenly she plummeted, held in a falling net of branches, vines, and leaves. And then the trees withdrew, leaving her lying on pine needles next to FitzRandolph Gate.

On their pillars, the gold eagles shrieked.

She could not afford to be sent back to the council. Lily scrambled to her feet and dove toward the gate. She saw a flash of white, and then she was skidding down the slate flagstones that led to Nassau Hall.

Her throat raw from screaming, Lily lay panting on the walkway. Her skin still fizzled with magic, but behind her, she heard the whiz of cars mixed with the hum of trees. She turned her head to see the shops of Nassau Street.

One of the stone eagles spoke. "Welcome home, little Key."

"Thanks," she said automatically. Looking up at the twin eagles, she asked, "You see everything that happens here, don't you?"

"Of course," the same eagle said.

Lily got to her feet. "Do you remember my mother? Rose Carter? The last time she crossed through the gate . . . did anything unusual happen?"

Both eagles were silent.

She started to think that they weren't going to answer her.

"You were a baby in her arms the last time she crossed," the first eagle said. "Your father was with you, as was Jake Mayfair's mother. Jake's father met them here. He was a surprise, I remember."

"Yes," the second eagle said. "There had been animosity between him and his former wife, but he had come to reconcile."

Lily remembered what Grandpa had said, that Jake's parents had been "only beginning to find peace." She felt her stomach clench. Half of her didn't want to hear what happened next; the other half was pretty sure she already knew. "Then what?"

The stone eagles fell silent again.

"Please, I need the truth," she said.

"Humans call it the FitzRandolph Gate Tragedy," the first eagle said.

"It's not our place to tell you this," the second eagle said. The first eagle agreed. "It is not. Ask your grandfather."

"He's hurt," Lily said. "You have to tell me. Mom doesn't remember. And I have to know—why didn't she go back?"

But the eagles didn't speak again.

She hugged her arms. Even though it wasn't cold, she couldn't stop shaking. The dryad queen had been right about one thing: The last time Mom had walked through that gate, something had happened that changed everything. Lily had a very good guess about what that "something" was. If she was right, then her parents, Jake's parents, and the eagles hadn't been the only ones at the gate that day.

Lily started walking without telling her feet to move. Around her, the oak trees whispered and hummed. She walked faster. As she passed through East Pyne, the ivy hissed and buzzed. She began to run.

Crossing the plaza, she fixed her eyes on the Chained Dragon, still swollen from their earlier encounter. The stone serpent dominated half of the arch. His tail curled among the carvings of grapes, leaves, birds, and foxes, and his stone face with the sad puppy eyes hung low, just above the door.

She halted underneath him. "I'm back," she called up to him. "Wake up!"

Above, the stone tail flicked. It clattered against the stone leaves that surrounded the dragon. Bits of dust rose into the air and caught the sunlight.

"I want all the truth this time," she said.

"Come closer," the dragon said.

Lily snorted. "Do you think I'm an idiot?"

"You returned. That means you are either foolish or desperate." His voice slid around her, and despite expecting it, Lily shuddered. *"Do you not yet know what I am capable of?"*

"I think I do," she said. "I think you killed my father."

The Chained Dragon smiled. *"Oh, yes. Yes, I did."*

Lily rocked back on her heels. She couldn't speak. Sixteen years ago, her father hadn't died in a car accident. He'd been killed by a dragon.

So that was the event that had changed everything.

The dragon was not done speaking. *"Killing him was of course not my intent."*

"Oh?" So she was supposed to believe it had just been an accident after all? Oops, the dragon accidentally attacked? She'd lost her father. Jake had lost both his parents, including the woman who was both his and Tye's mother. . . .

"My intent," the dragon said, *"was to kill you."*

Unable to think, unable to breathe, Lily ran into the chapel. Her footsteps echoed on the stone floor. She ran between the pews. Blue light from the stained-glass windows tinted the shadows. The silence closed around her.

Inside, she couldn't hear the horrible laugh of the stone dragon. She couldn't hear the hum and buzz of the trees and ivy. Inside, she could breathe again. She sank down into one of the pews and dropped her face into her hands.

Behind her, Lily heard footsteps. She didn't turn. She didn't want to face some random alum who wanted to tour the chapel or a priest who didn't realize that his sacred church was a prison for a murderer.

A hand landed on her shoulder, and Lily jumped up and spun around.

"Calm," Mr. Mayfair said. He spread his hands to show he meant no harm. "I didn't intend to startle you."

She wanted to leap up and hug him, but in his starched Brooks Brothers shirt, he wasn't the sort of man that one hugged. "How did you . . ."

"Know you were here?" he said. "The eagles reported that you'd returned. I saw you outside the chapel on my way to the gate to meet you."

In a whisper, she asked, "Grandpa?"

Mr. Mayfair patted her shoulder. "Same. Unresponsive but still stable."

She sank her head into her hands again.

"You were talking to the dragon," Mr. Mayfair said. "He upset you."

"Is it true?" she asked, looking up at him. "Did he really kill . . ." At his pained expression, Lily remembered that Jake's father was Mr. Mayfair's son. "I'm sorry," she said. "The

223

dragon said . . . he said he was trying to kill *me*."

Mr. Mayfair sighed. His shoulders dipped, and he suddenly looked old and tired, as if the weight of the cathedral roof had settled onto his back. "I knew you would eventually discover that."

"My mother . . . she could have continued to carry me back and forth. She could have kept her memory, her sanity. But she didn't return to the magic world."

"She thought you would be safest if you had a normal life, away from the gate," Mr. Mayfair said. "She convinced your grandfather that it was worth the cost to herself. She allowed her family to believe she was dead, and she let herself decline."

For a minute, Lily was silent, digesting that. "But . . . but once the dragon was imprisoned again, why didn't she return then? Was I still in danger?"

Mr. Mayfair studied her. "You are a bright thing, aren't you? It's little wonder that Richard is so proud of you."

Lily felt a lump in her throat. Grandpa always told her how proud he was. She pictured his face after he'd met her at the gate. He'd been beaming. "The Key guy . . . he would have known better than to go too close to the dragon," she said. "How did the dragon catch him? He couldn't have done it alone."

"Come," Mr. Mayfair said. "There's someone here who can answer your questions. She waits for us in the choir box."

Lily twisted in her pew to look up at the choir box. She

saw a balcony of pews beneath organ pipes and a stained-glass window shaped like a blue rose. The window shed a gentle light over the box. In the front, she saw a shimmer in the air like heat over hot pavement. She squinted at it and saw a figure. Someone knelt in one of the pews. "Who is it?"

"Come upstairs with me," he said. "I will introduce you."

He led the way back to the antechamber. At the white marble staircase, he unhooked the red velvet rope with the sign that read BALCONY CLOSED. He gestured for Lily to walk in front of him.

She climbed the stairs. At the top, Mr. Mayfair opened the door to the choir box. Six rows of wooden pews overlooked the chapel. Brass organ pipes protruded from the back wall.

A woman knelt in the pew closest to the railing.

As Mr. Mayfair closed the door behind him and Lily, the woman rose in a single fluid motion and faced them. She was as beautiful as a doll, with plastic-smooth skin and shimmering blonde hair. She wore a simple white summer dress that showed off her flawless skin . . . and her gossamer wings. An iridescent pair framed her head like twin halos and then swept down to the floor like a bride's train. Lily stared at the wings and wondered what the hell was going on.

The fairy asked, "A present for me? Oh, you shouldn't have."

"She's a Key," Mr. Mayfair said.

The fairy laughed, a tinkling sound like crystal shattering. "Splendid! So this must be the dryad's daughter."

Lily took a step backward. Mr. Mayfair laid a hand on her shoulder, halting her retreat. "Mr. Mayfair, who is she?" Lily asked. She tried to keep her voice even. There was no cause for alarm, she told herself. This was Joseph Mayfair, leader of Vineyard Club, a knight in shining armor, and Grandpa's oldest friend.

In a kindly voice, Mr. Mayfair said to Lily, "I hope you understand that this is nothing personal. I admire your intelligence and resourcefulness. But so long as travel between worlds is possible, the war between humanity and Feeders cannot end."

Please, Lily thought, *let me be hearing this wrong.* She looked into his earnest blue eyes. "What are you saying?"

"All magic creatures are potential Feeders." He was patient, grandfatherly. "The only way to truly protect humanity is to eliminate all access between the worlds."

The fairy laughed again. "Lock the door and throw away the key," she said. "Pun intended, of course."

Lily yanked away from Mr. Mayfair and lunged toward the door. With ease, he darted in front of her. He caught her wrist in his iron grip.

"I am deeply sorry for how this has turned out," he said. She twisted, trying to pull away from him. "Your grandfather insisted that you take the Legacy Test for your mother's sake. I did my best to convince him to keep you safely in ignorance. Indeed, when persuasion failed, I set the goblin on you to frighten you, but you persisted."

She felt her mouth drop open. "You sent the goblin?"

"*My* goblin," the fairy chimed in behind her.

Mr. Mayfair ignored the fairy. "You see, I didn't want it to come to this," he said to Lily. "For the last sixteen years, I tried to avoid extreme measures. The tiger boy was easy enough to discredit with the knights. He was no threat to my plans. But you, the daughter of a highly respected knight . . . Already the knights accept you as our new Key. Already they talk about new alliances and renewed relations. This cannot be. Our worlds must be separate. It is now clear to me that I have no choice. Your death is the only way to protect mankind. Do you understand, my dear?"

She kicked at his knee and swung her free fist. He caught her hand easily and evaded her kicks. "You're supposed to be good. You're supposed to be a goddamn knight!"

Behind her, so close that Lily could feel her soft breath in her hair, the fairy said, "You shouldn't blaspheme in a church."

Tears poured down Lily's cheeks. "My grandfather trusted you."

"Your grandfather is a good man, blinded by idealism," Mr. Mayfair said. "Your death by a Feeder will convince him at long last that the war with the Feeders *must* end. This is a necessary and regrettable sacrifice for the cause of a greater good."

Oh, God, this couldn't be happening. He couldn't do this. She tried to think of something to convince him, anything to stop him. "But your grandson . . . Jake will die!"

Mr. Mayfair froze. "Explain." His voice was low. It shot through her.

"The dryads have him," Lily said. "They'll exchange him for my mother. Tye is with them, so that means I'm the only one who can save your grandson. You have to let me go!"

Mr. Mayfair turned away from her. "And let you reveal what we have discussed here? There is too much at stake. There is the world at stake." His voice was flat.

"You can't let Jake die!" she cried. "He trusts you. He believes in you. He loves you."

"And I will mourn him," Mr. Mayfair said simply.

Tears poured down Lily's cheeks. "Please!"

To the fairy, he said, "For Jake . . . make it hurt."

Lily spun around to see the Feeder smile at her as beatifically as one of the angels in the stained-glass window that rose gloriously behind her. Her wings fluttered, and her feet hovered six inches above the floor. Lily felt a breeze in her face, and it smelled of lilacs and lavender. She backed toward the door and kept backing up until she realized Mr. Mayfair was gone.

Run, she thought. She turned and—

The fairy was there.

CHAPTER Fourteen

The fairy laid a delicate finger on Lily's lips. "Shh," she said.

Lily's heart beat as fast as a hummingbird's wings. *Oh, God.* "Please," she said. "Please, don't kill me. Don't listen to Mr. Mayfair. He's not on your side. But I can help you. I can take you home. I'm a Key."

The fairy looked amused.

"Just think—you'd never be hunted by knights again," Lily said. "You'd be safe."

The fairy's iridescent wings fluttered. Bits of sunlight flashed off them. "But I *am* safe," she said. "I have assurances from the leader of the Princeton knights himself: in exchange for my cooperation, he will ensure my survival."

"He doesn't mean it." Lily said. "You heard him. He's willing to sacrifice his own grandson to keep his secret. There's no way he'll let you live. Even if he didn't hate Feeders, you know too much."

"Oh, but he is a noble knight," the fairy said. "Virtue personified." She let out a happy bubble of a sigh. "Don't you feel elevated simply from his presence?"

Slowly, Lily inched backward. "He makes me sick."

The fairy pressed her hands to her cheeks in mock horror, and then she careened backward with peals of laughter that bounced off the cathedral ceiling. "Of course I know he plans to kill me, silly."

"You do?"

Swooping close to Lily, the fairy smiled conspiratorially, as if she planned to tell her best friend her most secret dream. "But before Joseph Mayfair double-crosses me, I shall double-cross him. You, my dear darling dove of delight, will open the gate for me."

"Oh!" Lily said. "Oh, wow—you want to go home!" Relief rushed through her so fast and strong that she swayed. She felt her muscles turn to puddles.

The fairy scooped up a cloak from the coatrack by the door. Her wings flattened back as she swirled the cloak over her shoulders. It settled on her back, and she draped it artfully over her wings until the delicate appendages were lost in the shadows of black cloth. "I have been waiting for this moment for many years." The fairy linked her arm through Lily's. Cloak sweeping the marble floor, she descended the staircase arm in arm with Lily. "It is high time that I end my association with Joseph Mayfair, as entertaining as it has been. Tell me, my dear, how did you come to keep such unsavory company as the Princeton knights?"

"I just wanted to get into college," she said. A few days ago, it had all seemed so simple: take a campus tour, complete an application, cross her fingers, and that was it. "And then things got complicated."

The fairy patted her hand. "They always do." She waved up at the Chained Dragon as they passed under him. "Off to claim my freedom, old friend. Pity you can't join me."

Above, the dragon hissed. *"Set me free. Give me the Key."*

The fairy cooed in sympathy. "Wish I could for old times' sake, but I'm afraid I can't part with this Key. If you'll pardon the pun, she's the key to my dream come true!"

He thrashed in the stone. Dust plumed around him.

"Temper, temper." The fairy tsk-tsked.

"Let us finish what we began," the dragon pleaded. His voice slid down Lily's back like a worm inside her spine. *"This time, I will not fail."*

On the steps, Lily froze. "This time?" she repeated. She began to put two and two together. "Years ago, when the dragon escaped . . . He couldn't have caught that Key alone." The fairy blushed prettily and curtsied. "You helped him. You're the one responsible for my father's death. And Tye and Jake's mother. And Jake's father."

"Oh, don't be mad, kitten," the fairy said. "I was the hired help. Just following orders."

"Whose orders?" Lily asked.

On the arch above, the dragon rumbled.

"Think it through, cupcake," the fairy said. "You were close to the truth down there in the nave." She giggled. "Literally."

"Mr. Mayfair?" Lily asked.

Above them, the Chained Dragon hissed and lashed his stone tail hard against the chapel arch. Rock dust sprayed down. *"Explain!"* he demanded.

The fairy laughed louder, a sound like church bells. "Oh, this is fun! I really ought to double-cross my allies more often." To the dragon, she said, "I was merely the messenger. Yes, my scaly friend, it was he who offered you freedom in exchange for the death of this Key and then he who revoked your freedom. He betrayed you."

"Traitor!" the dragon cried. *"I will rend his flesh from his bones!"*

Lily felt as if her head were swirling. "But . . . but the dragon killed Jake's parents. His own son."

"Oh, the son was the whole problem," the fairy said merrily. "He wasn't supposed to forgive Jake's mother. She'd left him, you see, for some furry man. Joseph's son was not supposed to meet her at the gate on that day. When Joseph learned that his son was there . . . well, he rushed to save him, and that's when the plan went awry. The knights followed Joseph and interrupted all the festivities, arriving in time to save you and your silly mother but too late for the other humans. After that failure, Joseph reimprisoned the dragon and swore to avoid any more 'extreme measures.' Until now, of course."

"*I will crush his body!*" the dragon cried. "*I will flay him with fire!*"

The fairy smiled sunnily at Lily and hugged her shoulders. "Oh, my sweet, I am so happy that the plan went awry. If it hadn't, today wouldn't be possible. I would never have had this opportunity." She swept Lily down the steps and across the plaza as the dragon continued to rage on the front of the chapel. "Your world has been a place of a thousand delights, but I miss my family. I miss my friends." As they passed through East Pyne courtyard, the fairy waved at the indent where the vines had held the goblin. "I even miss the little goblin that your tiger boy so kindly returned, pest though he was. He was like a puppy to me. Always so obedient."

Still trying to wrap her head around these new revelations, Lily nodded in response. They passed through East Pyne, circled Nassau Hall, and crossed the yard.

The fairy squeezed Lily's hand. "Thanks to you, we will never be hunted again."

Lily couldn't wait to be rid of the fairy. "Ready to go?"

"One sec, pudding pie." She flashed a smile at Lily and held up a finger.

Two goblins skittered across the yard and scrambled up the stone pillars. "What are they doing?" Lily cried. The fairy held tightly to Lily's hand and waited with a pleasant smile on her face as the goblins attacked the eagles. In seconds, they'd wrapped their green bodies snugly around the stone eagles, pressing their wings together so they couldn't fly. "Stop them!"

Amused, the fairy said, "After I went through all the trouble of recruiting them? I think not. Besides, we can't have our pesky bird friends alerting Vineyard Club, can we?" The goblins squeezed the eagles' beaks shut to prevent their cries and tossed cloths over their heads to hood their eyes.

On the street, pedestrians halted and gawked.

"But why—," Lily began.

"Now I am ready," the fairy said, and she shoved Lily against the wrought-iron gate. Some of the pedestrians shouted. A few whipped out cell phones.

"Ow," Lily said. "Stop. Let go of me!"

The fairy drew a rope from the folds of her cloak and lashed Lily to the iron gate. She touched Lily's lips. "Shh."

Various onlookers called out, "Hey, what are you doing? Let her go!"

With a smile to her audience, the fairy pushed Lily halfway across the threshold of the gate. Half of Lily's body vanished.

En masse, the pedestrians gasped and withdrew. A few ran in the opposite direction. One applauded as if it were a show. The fairy winked at the crowd and then kissed Lily on the cheek and walked through the gate.

The fairy vanished.

Lily struggled against the rope. "Help me, please!" Several yards away, the onlookers still gawked. One person snapped photos. Lily tried to pull her arm and leg back into the human world. "Please, someone, help!"

A middle-aged man with nondescript brown hair and plump cheeks broke out of the circle of onlookers. He inched toward her with his hands spread wide. "Don't worry," he said. "Stay calm." Slowly, as if reaching toward a rabid raccoon, he touched the knots in the rope.

In that instant, the fairy returned.

Hand on the rope, the man froze.

"Tut-tut, none of that," the fairy said. She'd lost her cloak. As the man gaped, the fairy extended her glorious wings and then folded them around him. She pulled him close to her, and nuzzled against his neck. Pink shot through her wings like streaks of lightning, radiating out until they shone. The fairy pressed her body against her victim's body. She moaned in pleasure.

The man twitched.

Seconds later, he crumpled to the ground. Blood leaked from delicate bite marks on his neck. His eyes were open and sightless. The fairy wiped a streak of red from her cheek with the back of her hand. She smiled at the crowd and laughed in a voice so high that it sounded like shattering glass. Her teeth were stained pink.

The crowd screamed and ran.

"Do you really think I want to give *that* up?" the fairy said to Lily. "Drinking straight from a human . . . nothing can compare. You would have me trade fine wine for water. Less than water. For air." She glowed as if she were lit from within. "Oh, I feel like I could fly." She giggled at her own joke.

"You can't do this!" Lily shouted. "Let me go!"

From the other side of the gate, claws grasped Lily's invisible arm. She screamed and tried to yank herself away, but the rope held tight. A goblin emerged into the human world. On the street, a car slammed into the rear of a truck.

Smiling brightly, the fairy scooped the goblin up in her arms and swung him in a circle as if he were a toddler. "Well done, my pet!"

He was followed by others. Elves, gorgons, fairies, and trolls crossed. A snake woman slithered past Lily so close that she felt the scales against her skin. On Nassau Street, cars screeched and crashed into one another as the creatures ran down the road. Lily struggled harder against the rope as more creatures slipped into the human world.

Suddenly, a blur of orange and black shot through the gate. It slammed into the fairy, knocking her backward. Pivoting, the tiger slashed at Lily. The ropes split away from her.

As the fairy flew toward them, Lily swung herself onto the tiger's back and wrapped her arms around his neck. The tiger, with Lily clinging to him, ran.

• • •

The tiger raced across campus. Holding tightly to his fur, Lily felt the muscles in his back shift as he leaped over stone benches and bounded down marble stairs. She buried her cheek in his neck as she held on. He smelled like summer-warmed leaves, like grass after rain, like Tye.

He slowed to a walk, and she lifted her head. She saw the manicured flower beds of Prospect Gardens as the tiger padded across the grass to the fountain at the center of the tulips. He lapped up water as Lily slid off his back. Grass curled around her feet and cooed at her. Late afternoon shadows covered the garden.

"You came for me," she said.

The tiger's fur rippled, and the air smudged around him like summer heat. The orange and black tiger fur melted away, and Tye in jeans and a black T-shirt crouched in front of her. "Always," he said, rising to his feet.

Lily threw her arms around his neck and pressed her face against his shoulder. His arms curled around her back. After a second, he stroked her hair.

"I screwed up," she said into his shirt. "Really screwed up." She shouldn't have trusted Mr. Mayfair. She should have gone directly to Vineyard Club and . . . then what? She should have quit the Legacy Test. She should have picked another damn college.

Tye didn't reply with a platitude like "it will be okay" or "it's not your fault." He simply held her and continued to stroke her hair. She tilted her face up to look into his tawny eyes. His lips were inches from hers.

Lily pressed her lips against his. His eyes fluttered wide for a moment, and then he kissed her back. When they drew breath, Lily noticed that the petals of the closest buds had opened and exposed their hearts to the sky. Her lips tingled.

She began to pull away, but he kept his arms around her. "Did the Feeder hurt you?" he asked.

Lily thought of the man who'd been drained, and she shuddered. "Not me," she said. "Tye, what are we going to do?"

Tye smiled.

"What?" she asked.

"You said 'we,'" he said. "I didn't think you knew that word."

"I studied it for the SATs," she said. "I don't understand how there were so many creatures. It was like they were waiting on the other side of the gate."

"I saw it happen," he said. "The dryad queen had us all wait at the forest edge, watching the gate for your return." He tangled his fingers in her hair. "As soon as the fairy appeared, two trolls disabled the eagles, and the Feeders guarded one another as they crossed. They were ready."

"But how?" Lily asked. "It's not like she could have called ahead to warn them. . . ." She remembered how the fairy had greeted the goblin. "She sent word with the goblin?"

Closing his eyes, he said, "See, you're not the only one who screwed up. I took the goblin through. He used the time to contact criminals, former addicts, and anyone so unhappy with their lives that they'd be willing to leave their world and live in the human one, to feed. Once the fairy appeared, dozens were able to pass before anyone could react."

"You reacted," she said, lifting her head to look at him. Her knight in shining fur.

This time, he kissed her first. Her fingers wove up into his soft hair, and his arms held her against him. For an instant, she stopped thinking about her mother, about the Feeders, about the knights.

"Clearly, I should rescue you more often," he said when they broke apart.

"Clearly," she agreed.

He rested his forehead on hers. For an instant more, she tried to keep from thinking about everything that had gone wrong. But she couldn't. Fifty or so wannabe serial killers were spreading across campus and beyond, dispersing and vanishing into her world, and it was her fault. "How do we send the Feeders home?" she asked.

"We can't convince them to leave; they'll have to be stopped by force," he said. "This is what the knights are for."

"The knights . . ." She told him about Mr. Mayfair.

He was silent for a moment, and then he said, "At least now I know why the knights never accepted me. Mr. Mayfair has been poisoning them against me from the start. Because of my mother. Because of his son. Because I'm a Key." He shook his head. "Jake won't take this well."

Funny that Tye thought of Jake's feelings. That was a switch. "Is Jake okay?" She wondered what they'd talked about in the dryads' forest. She wondered what it felt like to discover a sibling, to suddenly be less alone than you thought you were. She thought of Mom's family and wished she'd gone straight to Vineyard Club.

Tye hesitated. "He's conscious. And he's an idiot. He should never have come when he knew he was already full of magic."

"Mr. Mayfair is willing to let Jake die to protect his secret," Lily said. "He'll never let us close enough to the knights to warn them about the new Feeders." If she could just tell someone what she'd learned about him! She'd uncovered the kind of secret that should be broadcast by CNN, shouted from the tops of towers across alpine mountains, taught to every child. . . .

"The more time that passes, the harder it will be to find and catch the Feeders," Tye said. "We need someone the knights will listen to, someone they won't automatically skewer on sight."

Lily realized whom he meant. "The gargoyles."

Tye nodded and took her hand.

Together, they ran out of Prospect Gardens toward Dillon Gym.

On the street in front of Dillon Gym, orange-and-black-clad alumni cheered for P-rade. As the Class of 1985 marched by, the younger alums on either side of the street chanted, "Hip-hip, tiger-tiger-tiger, sis-sis-sis, boom-boom-boom, bah! Eighty-five! Eighty-five! Eighty-five!"

Lily clutched Tye's hand, determined not to be separated from him. "Excuse me, excuse me," she repeated as they wove among alums.

Breaking through, they darted into the street. A band bore down on them, and they dodged trumpeters and tuba players. Reaching the opposite sidewalk, they squeezed through the crowd and then ran hand in hand to the entrance of Dillon Gym.

"Professor Ape!" Tye called.

"Literate Ape, please, wake up! We need you!" Lily shouted.

Tye cupped his hands around his mouth and shouted over the trumpets, "It's an emergency!" Behind them, the crowd cheered as drummers marched past.

She turned to Tye. "Can you lift—"

Before she finished the sentence, Tye dropped to one knee, wrapped his arms around her legs, and hefted her up into the air. She reached up and knocked on the gargoyle's chin. "Feeders are here."

In a soft voice, the gargoyle said, "Feeders are always here. Call the knights."

"Can't," she said. Quickly, she explained about Mr. Mayfair and the fairy.

With the sound of shifting gravel, Professor Ape tilted his

head to look down at Lily and Tye. "Grave accusations," he said disapprovingly. "You cannot be serious."

"Come to Vineyard Club." Tye said. "See how serious we are. Make them show you the hidden room. Ask Mr. Mayfair where his grandson is. But first, warn them about the Feeders."

Without altering a single stone feature, the ape looked appalled. "Leave my post?"

"If the knights don't rally fast, the Feeders will disappear into the world," Tye said. "You want to be responsible for that?"

"Joseph Mayfair cannot be a traitor," the ape said. "I trained him myself. He has passion, yes, but he would never—"

"Remember when you asked me to skip the I-can't-believe-it speech?" Lily said. "Can we skip it now? We have to warn the knights!"

"You can ride me," Tye said. "We'll blend in with all the P-rade costumes." He lowered Lily onto the sidewalk, and then he stepped back, shook out his shoulders and arms, and changed into a tiger. Lily could hear the crowd cheer as a new class marched past.

"Tye!" The ape's stone eyes bulged. Uttering a string of curses, only a third of which Lily recognized, he pried himself away from the wall. Legs, paws, and a tail emerged from the stone. He scurried down the arch. "Unprecedented," he muttered. "Rash." He grasped Tye's fur with his paws and clambered onto his back. "You had best be correct, prefrosh. If all you saw was a pack of squirrels—"

"I wish they were squirrels," Lily said. She climbed onto the tiger's back behind the gargoyle and wrapped her arms around his stone waist. It felt like hugging a rock.

"Wave like you're in the parade," the ape instructed.

Plastering a smile on her face, Lily waved like Miss America. Tye bounded across the sidewalk and then joined the parade. The alumni clapped and cheered.

Tye broke through the crowds on the other side of the street. Lily continued to wave until they were safely up the hill and into the gardens. In seconds, they were on the other side of the garden and heading for 1879 Hall.

As they ran through the arch, the monkey gargoyles swiveled their heads to watch them pass. A few skittered down from their perches. But Tye didn't slow. He raced onto Prospect Avenue.

Professor Ape cried, "Hold! Fall back!"

"Oh, no," Lily breathed.

Emerging from behind one of the clubs, a troll crept along the stone wall in front of Vineyard Club. Lily spotted pixies perched on the telephone wire. A dead bird lay on the street beneath them. Goblins skittered across the roof of Vineyard Club.

The Feeders hadn't disappeared into the world.

The Feeders were here.

Tye pivoted and raced back toward 1879 Hall. Lily clung to the stone ape as they bounded up the steps. At the top, Lily looked back over her shoulder. Nothing had chased them. The Feeders were closing in on Vineyard Club.

"Hold here!" the ape instructed. He leaped off Tye's back and then scrambled up the brick wall to the campus security phone under the arch. As Lily slid off the tiger boy's back, Professor Ape stabbed the red emergency button with a stone finger. "Code forty-four. Prospect Avenue. Vineyard Club is focus."

Monkey gargoyles scurried over the bricks as Tye transformed back to human. The monkeys crawled over him and wrapped their stone arms around his neck, arms, and legs. He patted them.

"What's a code forty-four?" Lily asked.

"Lockdown," Tye said. "Campus security will blockade the street to protect civilians."

"It won't be enough," the Literate Ape said.

Now that she was looking for them, Lily could see Feeders everywhere: slipping between parked cars, slinking along the hedges, climbing over stone walls. She counted far more than fifty rogue magic creatures streaming toward the club.

"There must be hundreds," Tye said, staring at the street.

"She didn't want to be hunted anymore," Lily said. "*This* was her plan."

"Forbes . . . they were testing the knights in preparation for this." He shook his head. "She must have gathered every Feeder for hundreds of miles. I didn't even know there were so many."

The Literate Ape was grim. "Over the years, criminals

have sneaked into this world when Keys crossed, but most are simply the children and the children's children of all the magic creatures who were trapped here when the gate closed."

"But this is why the knights exist, right?" Lily said. "It's not like they're defenseless." She thought of the cabinets full of knives and swords.

"It won't be easy or quiet," Tye said.

"But they'll be okay," Lily insisted. She thought of Mom and Grandpa inside, helpless.

Tye looked pale. He stroked one of the monkeys that clung to his shirt. "If the battle isn't quick, campus security won't be able to contain it. It won't stay secret. Not with a campus full of alums."

"Gather all the gargoyles," Professor Ape said to the monkey gargoyles. "Tell them the unimaginable has happened. Tell them our secret is in jeopardy. Tell them war has come to the warriors."

Chittering, the monkeys scampered away. Lily watched them swarm over 1879 Hall. Stone tigers, goblins, and dwarves peeled away from the stone. Lions climbed down from their pedestals. As the gargoyles marched toward Prospect Avenue, the monkeys scattered and spread across campus to rouse more.

"Will it be enough?" Lily asked.

"I don't know," the ape said quietly.

Together, the three of them watched as the knights poured out the front door of Vineyard Club. Shrieking and screaming, the Feeders charged toward them.

There had to be something more they could do. *Think, Lily!* she ordered herself. "Tye, if we ask . . . ," she began.

"It won't work," Tye said.

"How do you know—"

He flashed her a lopsided grin, but the smile didn't reach his eyes. "Soul mates think alike." And then he shook his head. "The council will never agree to help. Not now."

Professor Ape drew himself up tall. "They must," he said. "Suit up in your fur, boy. It's time for me to go home."

Squeezing her eyes shut, Lily clung to the Literate Ape as Tye carried them across campus. He paid zero respect to paths or obstacles, barreling through bushes and leaping over bike racks. Lily felt her teeth bash together. She opened her eyes in time to see the gate speeding toward them, and then she saw the white flash as they crossed.

Tye skidded to a stop in front of the forest.

The Literate Ape leaped off the tiger boy's back. "We will speak to the council," he announced to the gold eagles. Lily noticed that the eagles were covered in scrapes and scratches. The ape didn't wait for their response. Leading the way, he marched to Nassau Hall.

The stone man had only an instant to throw open the door to the council chamber as the Literate Ape plowed forward without pause.

Inside, the council was in session. The tiger man, the

unicorn, the centaur, the tiny man, and the elf all broke off conversation as the ape, Lily, and Tye barged in. Lily buried her fingers in Tye's tiger fur to hide how much they were shaking.

Rising to his feet, Tye's father bowed. "Welcome home, Ambassador."

Others echoed his welcome. Lily noticed that no one welcomed her or Tye.

With no preamble, Professor Ape said, "The Princeton knights are under attack. You must summon every available warrior, pass through the gate, and join the battle."

The unicorn spoke. "With all due respect, Ambassador, we will not."

The ape's eyes bulged.

Had he really expected them to leap to their feet, wave their swords in the air, and charge to the defense of the knights? *Yes,* Lily thought, *he had.* Beside her, Tye shifted from tiger to human. Like Lily, he stayed silent behind the ape.

"You cannot turn your backs on the knights." Professor Ape said. "They're your allies."

"Our alliance with the humans is void," the centaur said.

Professor Ape punched the air with his fists as if he wanted to knock sense into all of them. "This university was founded to promote understanding and cooperation between our worlds. It is the purpose of your existence here. You *cannot* turn your backs on the humans."

"Our responsibility is to our people," the elf said, rising to her feet, "as well as to our principles. We do not and will not condone Feeders of any kind."

"I know these knights. I know each man and each woman, and I know they are not Feeders." The ape thumped his chest for emphasis.

The tiger man snorted. "Oh? You know? With all due respect, Ambassador, you have been stone for most of your tenure."

Lily noticed that the ape's gray stone flesh had darkened to brown fur. His angular face had softened into more lifelike curves, and his eyes were now milky white, instead of stone. He was shedding his gargoyle traits, albeit slowly. Now he vibrated in very unstonelike fury.

He's going to fail, she thought. She had to say something.

The tiger man wasn't finished. "Show me one knight who is worth the risk to our people. Show me one that's worth saving."

"Jake," Lily said. "He's here right now, held by the dryad queen."

Tye leaned close to her and said under his breath, "Lily, you know my father hates him. Jake reminds him of losing my mother."

"That's what makes Jake perfect," Lily said, loudly enough for Tye's father and the council to hear. "If he can find something to save in Jake, then he has to save them all!"

"So be it," the tiger man said. He strode out of the chamber. The other council members filed out behind him. He threw open the door to Nassau Hall and roared across the yard, "Bring me the boy held by the dryad queen!"

With a caw, the gold eagles pushed off their pillars and soared toward the sky. Lily saw the eagles circle once over the yard and then spiral down into the forest beyond the gate. As she watched them, the Literate Ape joined her.

In a quiet voice, he said, "You are bold. I admire that."

Moments later, the trees thrummed and branches quivered. Soon, the leaves shook as if in a high-speed wind, and the dryads emerged. Lily spotted her grandmother. Her pale green hair was curled on her head and decorated with leaves in the shape of a jeweled crown. Her dress swept around her in green strands like weeping willow branches.

Behind her, two green-skinned men carried Jake. The other dryads flanked them. They moved closer, then lowered Jake to his feet. "Oh, no," Lily whispered. He looked even worse than she'd feared. His face was pale and covered in slick sweat. His hair clung to his forehead.

Standing in front of the council, Jake swayed. Lily started forward, but the ape clamped a stone-cold but fur-covered paw on her arm. "He must speak for himself."

Jake's eyes widened as he focused on the monkey gargoyle. "Professor Ape, you left your post!" He took a step toward the Literate Ape, but one leg caved. He rested his hands on his knees for a second and then straightened. "Why are you here? What's going on?"

"First, we must ask you questions," the centaur said.

Fanning out in front of him, the council began to question Jake. They grilled him on his childhood, his training, his knowledge of their world, his opinion of the other knights. . . . Lily watched him shake and tremble as if every sentence were a stab to his lungs.

Finally, Lily couldn't stand it anymore. "Stop it! You don't need to know his favorite breakfast cereal or how often he clips his toenails. Can't you see he's a good person? He's worth saving."

Everyone looked at her. Jake flashed her a smile, but it was a weak smile that trembled at the corners. Lily felt her face flush bright red and wished she'd kept her mouth shut.

"Are you our enemy?" the tiger man asked Jake bluntly.

"Depends," Jake said. "Am I going to die today?" He straightened his shoulders and looked directly into the eyes of each of the council members. The council members exchanged looks, and Lily couldn't read their expressions.

Oh, God, she thought, *it's not going to work.* She pictured Mom trapped in the club, not leaving Grandpa's side as the Feeders closed in, and Lily felt sick.

Beside her, Tye cleared his throat. "Council, you're asking the wrong questions." He took a deep breath as his father fixed his cat eyes on him. "It doesn't matter if he's a good ally or not. It doesn't even matter if we like him or not. If we don't aid the humans, we will become their enemies. We can't afford that. We *have* to keep peace between the human and the magic worlds."

The tiger man stared at his son, as if stunned that Tye had had the audacity to speak. Beside her, Lily felt Tye shrink back. She covered his hand with hers.

Jake frowned. "Aid them in what? Lily?"

"Feeders are attacking Vineyard Club," Lily said.

He jerked as if struck. "I have to help them. Take me back!"

Professor Ape stepped forward. "It is clear from this young man's testimony that we gargoyles have failed our purpose. The new generation of knights has doubts and fears about the magic world that we alone were not enough to assuage. You must make a gesture of goodwill if relations are to be repaired."

The elf spoke. "Of course the half breed wants relations repaired, but *we* don't travel between worlds. We have no need—"

Speaking up again, Tye said, "If you don't help the knights, then the battle will become public and everyone will see magic creatures as the enemy. If that happens . . . the humans will come here. They'll force a Key to open the gate, and they'll send their armies. Count on it."

The tiger man flexed his claws. "We are not defenseless."

The ape snorted. "It won't be enough. There will be retaliation on a scale that you cannot imagine. Humans outnumber us by the millions. Casualties of a war would be catastrophic. Princeton . . . *both* Princetons were founded to prevent such an occurrence."

The centaur leveled his gaze at Jake. "Young knight, do you concur?"

"Yeah, we'll kick your ass," Jake said. "And right now, that's fine with me." He doubled over in a fit of coughing.

Tye held up two fingers. "Only two ways to avoid humans pouring through that gate and raining death, destruction, and unprecedented mayhem on our world. One, you help the knights now. Or two . . ." He looked directly at his father. "You shut the door. You kill Lily and me."

Silence spread across the yard.

Jake doubled over again in another fit of coughing. Tye went to his side and wrapped his arm around Jake's waist. "Lean on me."

Raising his head, Jake stared at him.

Lily held her breath. It felt as if everyone, including the trees, was holding his or her breath, too, waiting to see how Jake would react.

"Thank you," Jake said, and leaned on him.

Both of them looked at the council.

The tiger man sighed gustily. "You have made your point." He turned to the council. "I will lead our warriors into the human world. Summon them here."

CHAPTER *Fifteen*

$\mathcal{L}$ily waited by the gate as dreams and nightmares trickled into the yard. Looking out over the warriors, she saw wings and tentacles, scales and fur. She saw skin of emerald and ruby and sapphire, as well as moonless-night black and earth brown. A few warriors were as tall as the oak trees. Others no larger than moths darted through the air.

"Follow me," the tiger man boomed. He strode toward the gate.

Hastily, Tye stepped against a pillar. His left arm and foot vanished. Lily mirrored him and leaned against the other pillar. She stuck her arm into the human world.

Without pause or even a glance at his son, the tiger man strode through the gate and disappeared. Others followed: a lion with feathers instead of fur, an eight-foot troll, a lady centaur, three unicorns. Soon, a steady stream of creatures flowed through the gate.

As the stream slowed to a trickle, Jake begged the dryad queen, "Let me fight."

"Our daughter is not yet returned to us," the queen said. She leveled a finger at the two dryads who flanked Jake. "Keep him here."

"No! Let me go!" Jake cried. The two dryads held his arms tight.

Lily's grandmother swept toward the gate with her entourage. "Mom's inside Vineyard Club, second floor," Lily said.

Leaning forward, the dryad queen brushed her lips against Lily's cheek. The gesture felt as soft and cool as a leaf. "She will be brought home." Before Lily could respond, the dryads disappeared through the gate.

Jake continued to thrash in the grip of his captors. Lily crossed to him. "Jake," she said. She touched his shoulder. "Jake, it's okay. We'll come back for you. I promise."

He sagged against one of the dryads. "Just . . . help the knights, okay?"

She opened her mouth to tell him about his grandfather, but he was trembling so violently that she couldn't do it. If she told him, he'd shatter. She'd tell him as soon as he was well. "Hang in there," she said as she hugged him.

Tilting his head, he leaned toward her and pressed his lips against hers. He held the kiss as if breathing her in. Stunned, she stared at him wide-eyed. He smiled at her as he drew back. As racked with pain as he was, his smile still had the power to melt icicles. Lily cast around for something to say.

"Go," he said. "I'll see you soon." The dryads led him away. She watched as he stumbled and then disappeared into the forest. Barely able to walk in a straight line, she stumbled back to the gate.

Silent, Tye waited for her.

She stopped in front of him.

He still didn't speak.

"Look, you don't know I'm your soul mate," Lily said. "You barely know me at all. I have terrible habits. I swallow toothpaste. My socks don't always match. I'm not good at small talk. I'm just about the most unpopular kid in my class, a close third behind the guy who doesn't shower and the girl who's a compulsive liar. Besides, it's not like Jake and me . . . He was just being nice."

"You are my soul mate, even if you don't know it yet," Tye said.

She had to look away from the fierceness in his golden eyes.

"But we have a battle to win first." Without waiting for her to reply, he walked through the gate, vanishing as he crossed the threshold.

She followed him.

On Nassau Street, a crowd of pedestrians clustered on the sidewalk. Drivers had climbed out of their vehicles. Several stood on car roofs and hoods. Everyone was staring at the stream of creatures that flowed toward East Pyne. A few were taking photos. *Uh-oh,* Lily thought. *So much for secrecy.*

"New part of P-rade!" Tye called to the crowd. A few cheered.

"You really think that will do it?" Lily asked.

"Humans believe what they want to believe," Tye said. "Of course, all bets are off if they see any violence, especially if humans start dying. Screams, blood, and death are not very paradelike."

"Not so much," she agreed. She tried to keep her voice as light as his, but her heart was pounding fast in her rib cage and her palms felt sticky with sweat.

"The faster this ends, the better," Tye said grimly.

Jogging, they caught up with the tail of their small army as it flowed through the courtyard. She noticed that the Unseeing Reader was missing from her arch. Alone on the chapel, the Chained Dragon lashed his tail against the stone vines.

Passing by a set of Gothic classrooms, Lily heard music blasting in the distance. As they neared Prospect Avenue, the music grew louder until the bass thumped against her skin.

"Clever," Tye commented.

Lily looked at him.

"It's to drown out the sounds of the fighting."

Ahead of them, campus security guards had cordoned off the intersection of Washington and Prospect. Police cruisers lined the street, and guards manned the barricade. They had widened a gap between two police cars for the magic creatures to funnel through. Professor Ape stood with the guards, shepherding in the army.

"Ride on me," Tye said. Dropping to his hands and knees, he transformed into a tiger. She climbed onto his back and rode toward the blockade.

When they got closer, Lily saw that some of the guards were clutching their guns so hard that their knuckle bones showed white against their skin. She tried to give them a reassuring smile, but they didn't even focus on her. They'd seen too much in the past five minutes to even notice a girl riding a tiger. She and Tye passed through the police barricade.

Down the street, in front of Vineyard, she saw a snarl of colors. She couldn't identify individual figures. It was more of a mélange of shapes, as if a parade had exploded and left behind a pile of colorful living decorations. It didn't look like a battle, and with the music overpowering everything, it didn't sound like a battle, either, which she guessed was the point.

It was only when they were halfway down the street that Lily began to hear the screams.

One car lay upside down. Up ahead, a centaur fought a fairy. He raised his front hooves and struck at the winged woman's stomach. She sailed backward and then dove forward again. The fairy swung a sword at the centaur's neck. He ducked.

Lily was acutely aware she didn't have a sword or any fighting ability. Tye had his claws, but what did she have? She could befriend plants, that was all. She didn't belong here.

A massive wolf leaped on top of a car and howled. Lily saw a fireball shoot into a hedge. The bush burst into flames, and Lily heard the plant cry. A unicorn clattered past on the sidewalk, a streak of iridescent white, and a scorpion man scuttled across the street.

As she and Tye padded closer to the battle, Lily saw figures slumped in the street and on the sidewalk. Ahead, a griffin launched himself into the air and then slammed down hard in the yard of a cloister-style eating club. A man in orange and black was tossed like a doll over a stone wall. He thudded onto the pavement and didn't move.

Lily clutched the fur on Tye's tiger neck so hard that her nails dug into her palms. *Run!* her mind screamed at her. She'd never make it through the tangle of monsters between them and Vineyard Club. She couldn't even see the front door.

Three goblins charged toward them. One snarled and raised a sword. Another was drenched in blood so red that it looked like paint. He bared needle-sharp teeth.

"Tye!" she screamed.

Beneath her, the tiger boy tensed, ready to spring forward.

Suddenly, a streak of orange and black slammed into the goblins. Roaring, Tye's father knocked the creatures back. They skittered across the street. He lunged toward them, jaws wide, and the three goblins scrambled to their feet and ran.

Tye's father transformed from tiger to man. He strode toward them and clamped his hand hard onto Tye's neck fur. He steered them back down the street toward the blockade. At the line of police cars, Tye's father ordered, "Dismount."

Lily slid off Tye's back.

"Transform."

Tye changed into his human self. "Father . . ."

"You need to leave now," Tye's father said.

"I want to help." Tye said. "This is my world, too."

"If we lose you, we'll all be trapped here. We'll be forced to feed or die." The tiger man glared at Lily. "You let the new Feeders into this world. Don't compound your mistake by creating even more."

Lily felt her face burning red. Tears pricked the corners of her eyes.

Tye leaped to her defense. "It's not her fault—"

"You must split up," Tye's father said. "Two targets are safer than one. Blend in with humans, or simply hide. But leave this area."

Lily began, "My mom and grandpa—"

"You can't help anyone if you're dead," the tiger man said, and then, to Tye's obvious shock, he wrapped his arms around his son's shoulders and pulled him into a rough embrace. "I will fight better if I know you are safe." Releasing Tye, he transformed back into a massive tiger and loped down the street toward Vineyard Club.

Openmouthed, Tye stared after him.

"You okay?" Lily touched his sleeve.

Tye squeezed her hand. "Keep away from the monsters," he said. He reached toward her with his other hand, cradled the back of her head, and then kissed her. "And don't kiss any more knights."

Before she could think of a response, he strode toward the barricade. The security guards intercepted him, and Lily heard the Literate Ape say, "He's safe to pass."

The guards nodded him through.

She glanced back at Vineyard Club. Mom was in there and so was Grandpa, helpless as the battle raged over the street. Lily told herself she was being smart, not cowardly. Both Mom and Grandpa would have wanted her to run.

Beyond the blockade, Tye disappeared through the 1879 Hall arch. With the approval of the Literate Ape, Lily passed through the line of security guards and climbed the steps to the arch.

She looked back again and saw a column of fire shoot up from the center of the street. A red orange figure ran toward the barricade. Lily saw flames running up and down his arms. He pitched forward as he was tackled from behind by a woman with tentacles that writhed on her back.

"Hold the line!" one of the security guards barked.

Lily fled.

She ran for the gardens, but once there, she kept running. As much as she wanted to bury herself in the comfort of the petals and leaves, she didn't dare. Tulips and roses couldn't keep her safe from monsters. Continuing through, she heard the chants and cheers of P-rade.

Lily joined the fringes of the crowd as they shouted, "Hip-hip, tiger-tiger-tiger, sis-sis-sis, boom-boom-boom, bah! Oh-six! Oh-six! Oh-six!" A fire truck passed with its lights flashing. Alums threw candy from the ladders. A real tiger paced in a cage on the bed of the truck. Cheering with the crowd, she summoned up a fake smile.

Only a day ago, she'd planned to be here at P-rade with Grandpa and Mom. She'd intended to walk with him down the street when it was his class's turn.

She should have found a way to reach Grandpa and Mom. She could have used the chaos of the battle somehow. She could have hidden in the hedges or commanded the trees to hide her. *And if you'd been killed?* she asked herself. Tye's father was right. She had to stay safe. Once the Old Boys and the magic army defeated the Feeders, she could return and save her family. She just had to be patient and it would all be over soon.

She continued to clap and shout with the crowd, learning the P-rade locomotive. The marching classes shouted, "Hip-hip, tiger-tiger-tiger, sis-sis-sis, boom-boom-boom, bah! Oh-nine! Oh-nine! Oh-nine!" and she chanted back.

As the end of the parade passed in front of her, the crowd surged off the sidewalk. She was swept forward with the alums from the Class of 2009. Some alums linked arms and spun in a circle. Others sang loudly and badly. "In praise of

Old Nassau we sing; hurrah, hurrah, hurrah! Our hearts will give while we shall live; three cheers for Old Nassau!"

As they marched down the street, other alums peeled off the sidewalks to join P-rade, until the road between the Gothic dorms and the brilliant green lawns was filled with people laughing, dancing, and cheering.

Soon, she told herself, *everything will be okay*. Soon, the knights and the magic creatures would defeat the Feeders; Grandpa would wake and stop Mr. Mayfair; Mom would regain her memories; and Jake would return to the human world. She simply had to wait and march. In unison with the Class of '09, she punched her fist into the air and shouted, "Hip-hip, tiger-tiger-tiger!"

"Hello, little Key," a bell-like voice said behind her.

Lily spun around.

The fairy smiled at her and laid a perfectly tanned finger against Lily's lips. "Shh," she said cheerfully. "One scream, and I'll snap your neck."

"You wouldn't dare." Lily couldn't stop the quiver in her voice. "We're in a crowd."

"Ahh, but I have wings," the fairy said.

She's right, Lily thought. The fairy could kill Lily, flash her wings, and then fly away in the confusion that followed. They might as well be in an empty alley.

"Come walk with me, sweet cakes." The fairy wrapped her arm around Lily's shoulders.

"I'm too valuable to kill," Lily said. "I'm rare."

"Oh, sweetie, don't overvalue your importance," the fairy said, half hugging her shoulders. "My allies are already here, and as for my enemies . . . If you die, either they become my allies or they die. Either way suits me. You *might* be useful to me, sugar, but only if you cooperate." The fairy beamed at her. "Now, smile, lovey-dove. Show these nice people that we're friends."

Lily plastered on a fake smile as the fairy guided her up the street, in the opposite direction from the parade. She tried to think of a plan. If they veered closer to the trees, Lily could touch a branch or leaf . . . but the fairy kept them to the center of the paved road and wove among the marching alums. Smiling like a deranged mannequin, Lily avoided catching anyone's eye. Last thing she wanted to do was cause another innocent's death. The fairy waved at the thinning crowds and cooed at the babies until at last they were beyond the end of the parade.

The fairy led her past Nassau Hall. With all the alums marching in the parade, the heart of campus was deserted. "Please, tell me what you want," Lily said. "Maybe we can compromise. I know you aren't really evil. We just want different things."

"Aw, you're so sweet," the fairy said. "But really, honey, I am evil." She smiled prettily as she dragged Lily up the chapel steps, beneath the sleeping dragon, and into the chapel foyer.

"What do you want?" Lily asked, her voice a high squeak. The fairy didn't need the solitude of the chapel to kill her. As she'd pointed out, she could kill Lily anywhere and no one would stop her. So why bring her here?

"I want what everyone wants, of course: To be safe. To be free to pursue that which makes me happy without fear of persecution or a messy, icky death. And you, my dear, will ensure that safety for me."

The fairy propelled her to the marble steps and unhooked the rope. Lily dragged her feet, trying to delay reaching their destination until she had a plan. Any plan! But the fairy simply tugged harder, and Lily stumbled up the stairs behind her. At the top of the steps, the fairy opened the door to the choir box and thrust Lily in before her.

A man knelt in one of the pews, his hands clasped in front of him in prayer.

"I have brought you a gift," the fairy said.

The man turned his head.

It was Mr. Mayfair.

CHAPTER *Sixteen*

"She isn't dead," Mr. Mayfair said. Raising his eyebrows, he regarded Lily as if she were a specimen in a lab that had survived a dip in formaldehyde. "Very curious." His voice was so calm and urbane. Lily shrank back and felt herself start to shake.

"She can be," the fairy said, "but I thought perhaps you'd wish for a way to return that pesky magic army to its home before she dies."

"How thoughtful of you," he said blandly.

"Accept her as my apology to you," the fairy said. "I hope you will not count my one small instance of disobedience as a breach of our arrangement."

Oh, God, Lily thought. *I'm going to die.*

"Indeed, it was not in our agreement for me to lose warriors at Vineyard today," he said. Lounging against a pew, he continued to sound as if he were pleasantly discussing the weather.

Lily felt herself start to cry. She choked back tears and told herself it wasn't over yet. She could still escape. The fairy patted Lily's cheek fondly as she said to Mr. Mayfair, "I bring you this gift to show I wish to continue our old arrangement: I will be at your beck and call if you will ensure I am not hunted."

"Your numbers have swelled considerably," Mr. Mayfair said.

"If you wish to guarantee their safety too, those Feeders will be loyal to you," the fairy said. "Think of it: a whole army at your disposal. A few civilians may fall to pay for your army, but isn't your noble goal worth a few sacrifices?"

"Noble!" Lily shouted. "You—"

The fairy clamped a hand over Lily's mouth. "Hush, child, the grown-ups are talking."

"After today, many of my knights again will view magic creatures as allies," Mr. Mayfair said. "Separating the worlds will now be even more difficult. You have set me back a decade's worth of careful work."

"Please accept my apology," the fairy said, "with this gift." Removing her hand from Lily's mouth, she laid both hands on Lily's shoulders.

Mr. Mayfair rose from the pew. "Your apology and gift are appreciated." In one hand, he held a sword.

He's going to kill me, Lily thought. "You need me alive,"

she said. Mr. Mayfair crossed the choir box. His expression was still casual. He might as well have been approaching to merely shake her hand. "The magic army . . . they'll return peacefully to their world if they can. But if you kill me, they'll be trapped, and you'll have new enemies." She tried to back away, but the fairy held her firmly in place.

Mr. Mayfair raised his sword.

Lily tried to throw herself to the side, but the fairy's hands were like shackles. Lily kicked and flailed, but the fairy held on without budging.

As the sword sliced through the air, the blade caught the blue light of the stained glass. It flashed on the stone walls of the chapel. Lily felt wind in her hair. She heard a wet *thunk*.

The hands on her shoulders loosened and then slipped away.

Behind her, the fairy fell to the floor.

"Our alliance is ended," Mr. Mayfair said in his gentlemanly voice. He wiped his sword, now red, on a black choir robe that hung from the coatrack. He selected a second robe and lifted the fairy's head up by her blood-soaked platinum blonde hair. He wrapped the head in the robe as if it were a Christmas present.

Blood seeped around Lily's shoes. It soaked into her sneakers, and it stained the white marble floor. She heard roaring in her ears, and her vision swam with black spots.

Mr. Mayfair spread a third robe across the body. Only the tips of the fairy's wings remained visible. They looked like broken cobwebs. "Sit, my dear," he said to Lily. "You look pale, and we may have a long wait." He sounded as concerned as an ordinary grandfather.

She wet her lips and tried to ask, "Wait for what?"

Despite her cracking voice, he understood her. "For the battle to end."

"Are you"—she couldn't stop her voice from shaking—"going to k-kill me?"

He sighed. "Eventually, I probably will. You are a danger to mankind, as well as an abomination in the eyes of God, though perhaps less of one than she was." He nodded at the fairy's wrapped-up head. It lay on a pew. A tendril of blonde hair had escaped the binding.

Lily bolted for the door. She slipped in blood, but she threw herself forward anyway. Moving faster than any ordinary human being could, Mr. Mayfair sprinted in front of her. He leveled the sword at her chest. "I said, *sit*." He gestured with the point toward a pew, and she retreated until a pew bumped the back of her legs. She sat with a thump.

Mr. Mayfair fetched some ropes from a pile of what looked to be more choir robes. Returning, he wrapped them around her, encasing her like a fly in a web. The ropes bit into her skin, and she yelped.

A streak of orange and black fur dashed behind the coatrack. *Tye!*

He'd come to rescue her, again her knight in shining fur. Lily felt her heart soar, but she kept her eyes focused on Mr.

Mayfair. She had to keep him from noticing Tye. "You're psychotic," she said. "You're an egomaniacal psychopath with delusions of heroism."

Mr. Mayfair secured the last knot. "You should take a few psychology classes once you enroll here," he said. He coiled the remainder of the ropes beside Lily. "You'll find them beneficial, regardless of your major. Have you given any thought to your major?"

Speechless, she stared at him. A corpse lay three feet from her, her sneakers were soaked in blood, she was hog-tied to a pew, and he wanted to talk about her *major*?

"Perhaps economics?" he suggested. "Your grandfather claims you have a knack for business. I believe you assist with the accounts for the florist shop?"

"I'm going to live long enough to have a major?" she asked.

"The situation has changed, and I'm capable of flexibility," he said. "So long as your life benefits humanity more than your death, you will continue to live. Of course, I need to be certain that I can trust you."

"You can trust me," Lily said. "I am totally trustworthy."

As she finished speaking, a tiger sprang from behind a pew and launched into the air directly at Mr. Mayfair's back. As smoothly as if he'd known the attack was coming, Mr. Mayfair spun with his sword raised.

"Sword!" Lily screamed.

Midleap, Tye veered, contorting his tiger body above the pews to avoid the blade. The sword grazed his fur, and Lily saw specks of red blood fly. She screamed again and strained against the ropes.

Tye landed, paws forward, against a pew. Under his weight, the pew tipped and crashed into the next pew. Sword arcing through the air, Mr. Mayfair advanced on the tiger boy. Tye twisted aside and swiped at Mr. Mayfair with his claws. Mr. Mayfair dodged, and the sword blade flashed again. Tye crouched, and the sword nicked his shoulder.

Rearing up on his hind paws, Tye swatted at Mr. Mayfair's sword arm. His paw impacted, and Mr. Mayfair staggered backward and the tiger boy hurled himself at the knight. Mr. Mayfair dodged again. His sword flashed toward Tye's flank. Tye jumped up onto the stone railing, narrowly avoiding the blade.

For an instant, the tiger boy perched on the railing. Behind him, the chapel stretched soundless and beautiful. He crouched, ready to spring again.

Mr. Mayfair lunged across the choir box and thrust his sword at Lily's neck. She didn't have time to scream. He halted an inch from her throat. In a calm voice, he said, "That's enough, kitty." The tip of the sword touched Lily's throat. She sucked in air shallowly.

Balanced on the stone, the tiger boy froze with muscles poised for another leap.

Everything was silent.

"Change yourself and join us," Mr. Mayfair said, as civilly as if inviting Tye to join him for a cocktail party.

The tiger boy hesitated. *He could escape,* she thought. One leap and he'd be down on the chapel floor. "Go!" Lily shouted.

"She'll be dead before your paws hit the ground," Mr. Mayfair warned. He pressed the tip of the blade against her neck, and Lily felt a prick. Involuntarily, she gasped.

Tye didn't move.

"Don't trust him," she said, barely a whisper. "Remember, he freed the Chained Dragon. He was responsible for our parents' deaths. He was responsible for the death of his own son. He's willing to sacrifice his grandson. He won't hesitate to kill us."

"I never hesitate when the cause is right," Mr. Mayfair said. "It is a burden that I bear, and do not think that I bear it lightly. But you don't need to die today, Tiger Boy."

Tiger fur shimmered. In seconds, Tye crouched on the stone railing as himself. He rose, balancing. "Tye, please, jump! Run!" Lily said. "I need you free. You have to take my mother through the gate. You have to take your father and my grandmother and all of them."

Tye climbed off the railing. "Sorry, Lily, but I'm not losing you."

Her heart sank. With both of them caught, the Fitz-Randolph Gate was sealed.

"Wise choice, young man," Mr. Mayfair said. "Come here and sit beside your overly melodramatic young friend."

Without a word, Tye sat next to Lily.

Mr. Mayfair wrapped the remaining ropes around Tye.

"What a rare opportunity," he said. "For once, you are not under the watchful eye of your gargoyle friends. None of them were here to see you enter this chapel, were they?"

"Please don't hurt him." Lily struggled against the ropes. "If you hurt him, I'll . . ." She tried to think of a suitable threat and failed. "Don't you dare."

"You, my dear," Mr. Mayfair said to Lily, "have an alarming tendency toward heroics. You are quite a bit like your father, you know. If he had merely run instead of staying to protect you and that creature you call 'Mother,' the dragon would have spared him." He rose and crossed to the opposite side of the choir box. "How fortunate for me that I have appropriate leverage."

Out of the corner of her eye, Lily saw Tye sprout claws on his left hand. He began to saw through one of the ropes as Mr. Mayfair bent over the pile of robes next to the coatrack.

He returned with the mass of robes draped over his arms. Lily saw spray-paint orange hair amid the robes and suddenly she couldn't breathe. *Mom.* He laid her mother on a pew and removed the robe from her face. Mom's head lolled to the side.

"She's breathing, Lily," Tye said quickly. "It's okay. She's alive."

Lily gulped in air. He was right. Mom was alive. Her chest rose, shuddered, and then fell. Her eyelids fluttered but didn't open. "What have you done to her?"

"She was . . . resistant to leaving your grandfather's side, and so I was forced to drain her to ensure complacency," he said. "Such devotion from a monster. So unexpected."

"She's not a monster! She's a good person." Lily's eyes were glued to her mother's face. Mom looked so pale. Her cheeks were sunken. Every wrinkle stood out like a sharp black line.

"She isn't a person at all," Mr. Mayfair said. He shook his head. "My son was lost as well, but unlike Richard, I did not choose to shelter an abomination. I treat monsters as they deserve to be treated." She noticed he didn't mention Tye and Jake's mother.

Tye detected the omission as well. "My mother was 'lost,' too."

"She was a traitor to humanity," Mr. Mayfair said, "as your very existence proves."

Mom's breathing sounded so strained, as if each inhalation were squeezing her lungs. "If you're such a paragon of virtue," Lily said, "then why didn't you ever tell your grandson what you did, that you were responsible for his parents' deaths? Bet he would have called *you* the abomination."

For an instant, a shadow of pain crossed Mr. Mayfair's face. It was the first time she'd seen any emotion but unruffled calm. "Jake is young and idealistic," he said. "Someday he will understand that I serve a greater good."

"He won't understand if he's dead," Lily said. "Please, what 'greater good' do you serve by keeping my mother? You have me. You have Tye. You can let her go. She's not a threat to you."

"She isn't a threat," he agreed. "She's insurance." He pulled a flask from his pocket, propped Mom up, and poured silver liquid into her mouth. In an instant, Mom spit and coughed. Her eyes snapped open.

"Mom!" Lily said. "Are you okay?"

Mom looked at Lily, at the ropes, and at Mr. Mayfair, and then she began to scream. He clapped a hand over her mouth. She whimpered. "Perhaps I should have left you drained for longer," he commented. Mom's eyes flickered everywhere.

"Calm down, Mom, please," Lily said. "Everything's all right." The lie rolled easily off her lips. "Take a deep breath. Now exhale."

Mom obeyed.

In a minute, Mr. Mayfair removed his hand.

"Now," he said, "listen to me carefully. You want your daughter safe, yes?"

Mom nodded. Her eyes were wide.

"She inexplicably wants you safe as well," Mr. Mayfair said. "So this is what we will do: When the battle ends, you will both accompany me to the gate. Lily will return the army of potential Feeders, *and* she will help me repair the damage she's done to my reputation with the knights and the gargoyles. You will walk through the gate, and the dryad queen will return my grandson. Do you understand?"

Mom's eyes were like a storm. "If you harm my daughter—"

"Good," he said. "We understand each other. If you

disobey me, I will kill her. If Lily disobeys, I will kill you. Are we clear?"

Wordless, shaking with fear and fury, Mom nodded.

"And you?" Mr. Mayfair asked Lily.

Eyes glued on Mom, Lily nodded, too.

Mr. Mayfair took a call as calmly as if he were in an office. "Splendid!" Lily heard him say. "Send the army and the prisoners to the gate. We'll meet them there. Begin damage control." He paused. "Wonderful. Thank you." He slid the phone back into his pocket. "Excellent news," he said. "We won."

He untied the ropes around Lily, and then he pulled her and Rose to their feet. Smiling at them, he picked up the fairy's head wrapped in the choir robe.

As Mr. Mayfair led them toward the door, Lily glanced at Tye. He had nearly sliced through his ropes. If she could distract Mr. Mayfair for only a second . . . Trying to send a hint with just a look, she met Tye's eyes.

I love you, he mouthed.

He *what?*

Startled, she slipped in the fairy blood. Mr. Mayfair caught her arm. That was all the distraction Tye needed. He cut through the last frayed rope and sprang from the pew.

But Mr. Mayfair was faster. Drawing his sword, he lunged forward. In a move so fast that Lily could barely see it, he slammed the hilt down on Tye's head.

Tye crumpled onto the marble floor.

Mom screamed and screamed and screamed.

"Foolish boy," Mr. Mayfair said. He leveled the sword at Mom. "Silence."

Mom stopped.

"Is he . . . ," Lily began. She saw Tye's chest rise and fall. He was alive.

Without another word, Mr. Mayfair fetched the ropes and retied him. This time, he lashed Tye's fingers together. He left him cocooned in rope, unconscious on the floor. Then he slid his sword into a scabbard under his coat.

"You are a monster," Mom said.

He blinked at her. "That is almost amusing, coming from you."

Scooping up the robe with the fairy's head, he propelled both Lily and Mom out of the choir box, down the stairs, and out of the chapel.

Outside, the sky had darkened. The sun had sunk below towers and turrets, leaving behind streaks of bruised rose. As they descended the chapel steps, Lily noticed that her footprints were rust red smudges on the stone—the fairy's blood.

"Lily?" Mom's voice was strained. "That dragon . . . I know him. . . ."

Lily looked up at the Chained Dragon. He was silent, sleeping to conserve his magic. "How can I trust that you won't just get rid of me, Mom, and Tye after we've helped you?" Lily asked Mr. Mayfair.

"You have little choice but to trust me, my dear," he said.

She didn't think that was a comforting response.

Looping his arm around hers, he escorted her across the plaza. In his other hand, he held the robe with the severed head. Looking dazed, Mom walked beside them. She kept shooting glances back at the stone dragon; he continued to sleep.

Stay calm, Lily told herself, *and think.* There had to be something she could do, but what? Overwhelm him with her fantastic power over lawns? She'd seen him fight. He was stronger and faster than a tiger. Her best hope was the ivy vines in East Pyne courtyard.

But Mr. Mayfair bypassed East Pyne. Instead, he marched them straight toward Nassau Street, exiting campus via a service driveway and keeping to the center of the road, away from any greenery.

Lit by street lamps and lights from storefronts, Nassau Street was as silent and empty as a vacant lot. Cars had been diverted to side streets, and campus police warded off pedestrians. Yellow tape cordoned off the entire Nassau Hall yard. Recognizing Mr. Mayfair, one of the guards waved them through the blockade. As they passed, Lily tried and failed to catch the security guard's eyes.

Using the side entrance, Mr. Mayfair propelled them onto the lawn. Grass shivered as it touched Lily's bloody shoes, but the trees didn't hear her silent yells.

Mr. Mayfair halted in front of the gate and said to Lily,

"You are to think of your mother and follow my lead. No heroics. Are we clear?"

Lily swallowed. "Crystal."

He pulled Mom closer to him, and they waited.

Coming from beyond Nassau Hall, creatures marched, limped, slithered, flew, crawled, and walked across the shadowed yard. A few were carried. Others winced in pain with each step. Lily saw blood and dirt streaks on faces and exposed skin. In the distance, she spotted her grandmother, tall and unearthly, surrounded by the usual entourage of dryads. Lily also saw a flock of unicorns, sweat stained and dirt covered. The Literate Ape and the other gargoyles marched with them. The Princeton knights were interspersed among centaurs, medusas, elves, goblins, and trolls.

"Friends!" Mr. Mayfair called. "Congratulations on an important victory!"

As the creatures fanned out across the darkened lawn, Professor Ape crossed to Lily and Mr. Mayfair. "We missed you at the battle, Joseph," the ape said.

"I had a task to complete," Mr. Mayfair said. "Believe me, it was vital."

"Grave accusations have been made against you."

"Yes, I am aware," he said. He smiled fondly at Lily. "The young are easily confused, but we have sorted it out now, haven't we, Lily?"

She had a chance to shout the truth. Here was an audience, primed to listen. He'd skipped the battle, and the ape was suspicious. But Mom stood as straight and still as an oak tree, and Lily imagined a knife pressed against Mom's back. "I was wrong," Lily said softly.

Mr. Mayfair flourished the choir robe. It fell to the ground in a puddle of cloth, and he held up the fairy's head. "Behold, the leader of the Feeders!" he cried. "I have been hunting her, and at last I was victorious! This girl was a witness, as her shoes can testify."

Everyone looked at the blood on Lily's sneakers.

Mr. Mayfair addressed Professor Ape. "I owe you an apology. I doubted your kind. I believed you were all like this fairy." He lifted the severed head higher into the air. "Today I have been proven wrong, and I am more grateful than you will ever know. I hope this is the start of a new era of cooperation between our peoples."

As the ape beamed, the knights and magic creatures burst into tremendous applause. Lily scanned the faces in dismay. Tye had said that people believed what they wanted to believe. The knights and creatures *wanted* to believe Mr. Mayfair was a hero. Only the Feeders snarled and glared. A few strained at the ropes that held them. Others were perfectly still, swords at their necks or knives at their backs. One of the goblins cried.

Pushing to the front, Tye's father scowled at Mr. Mayfair. "A very pretty speech," the tiger man said. "But we will need your assurance that your people will cease the Feeder-like behavior of draining and drinking magic creatures."

"After a victory such as this, we will not need to. The practice shall cease," Mr. Mayfair said. "You have my word." Lily had never heard anyone lie so smoothly or with such sincerity. Truth throbbed through his voice. "I know we have drifted apart and that much work remains to rebuild relations between our worlds, but perhaps a start can be made through this child." He placed a hand on the back of Lily's neck—a casual gesture, but she was aware of how fragile her neck was and how hard he could grip. "She will send you home!"

Cheering, the army surged forward, pushing the prisoners before them.

Lily was driven back toward the gate.

"Slowly!" Tye's father shouted. He drew his sword and positioned himself between Lily and the creatures. She glanced at Mr. Mayfair, and he nodded. She leaned against the pillar and straddled the threshold. Half of her body disappeared into the magic world.

"Very well. Begin," Mr. Mayfair said.

Prodded by knights and gargoyles, the Feeders filed toward the gate. The line of monsters was flanked by the council's army. She saw elves, trolls, goblins, satyrs, winged lions, snake women . . . A few times she wasn't certain if some creatures were actually Feeders, but their eyes gave them away. The Feeders shot her looks that ranged from sullen to so full of hatred that she felt as if her skin would blister from the stare. Sometimes she had to look away—and when she did, she saw Mr. Mayfair, with his hand on Mom's shoulder, watching her.

Once the Feeders had passed, the Literate Ape led the gargoyles to the gate. "We wish to assist our brethren," the ape announced to Mr. Mayfair. "Please care for the knights in our absence."

Mr. Mayfair bowed. "Of course."

One by one, the gargoyles crossed through the gate. Lily saw chips and scratches on the stone monkeys as they scurried by her. The Unseeing Reader limped past with help from a stone lion. Even the stone eagles flew through. Lily wanted to scream, *Don't leave!*

As the last gargoyle left the human world, the knights dispersed from the yard. *Oh, no,* she thought. *Stay! Please!* Soon, only Tye's father and the dryads remained.

The tiger man sheathed his sword. "I must assist on the other side as well," he said. "My son . . ."

"Will be with you soon," Mr. Mayfair finished smoothly. "He wished to remain at the club to assist the injured knights. He's a good boy."

"Yes," Tye's father said. "Yes, he is."

The words were in Lily's throat. If anyone could take on Mr. Mayfair, it was Tye's father. All she needed was a word or a phrase. Just a clue. One sentence. But then her mother made a small chirp: "Oh!" Lily noticed that Mr. Mayfair's hand was behind Mom's back. Mr. Mayfair smiled at Lily.

She let Tye's father leave.

At last, only the dryads remained. The yard was empty shadows. Oak trees whispered wordlessly, a steady hum, as the dryads walked to the gate.

The dryad queen approached Mom. "My daughter," she said, as if tasting the word. "Rose, my child, you live!" She clasped Mom's hands in hers as Mr. Mayfair shifted to stand behind Lily. In the small of her back, Lily felt a cool, sharp point press against her.

Mom's eyes filled with tears. "I don't . . . I don't remember you."

The queen touched Mom's cheek. "You will, my Rose." And then she frowned. "Child, what did you do to your hair?"

Now Lily believed that this woman was Mom's mother.

"Come," the queen said. "We will take you home."

Mr. Mayfair interrupted. "Return my grandson first."

Looking at her entourage, the queen snapped her fingers. "Fetch him." Several of the dryads filed through the gate. To Mom, the queen said, "You will love our home. You may not remember it, but you had your own grove and garden. You had orchids and irises that were the envy of us all. You had roses that defied winter. And your lilies . . . your lilies were your delight and glory."

"My lily now is my delight and glory," Mom said. "She must come with me."

Mr. Mayfair's smile was like winter. "She has work here. Her friend Tye is expecting her back. He will be very disappointed if she doesn't return."

"You should go," Lily said. She tried to put into her eyes that she meant it. If Mom was safe . . . She had to know that Mom was safe. "I'll be there soon."

Mr. Mayfair held up his hand. "First, my grandson."

In seconds, Jake popped through the gate. His knees buckled, and he collapsed on the slate sidewalk. Mr. Mayfair didn't move. He kept the blade on Lily's back.

Beckoning to her entourage, the dryad queen said, "Now we leave."

"Lily!" Mom's voice was shrill.

Lily felt tears wet her cheeks. "Go. I love you." On the other side, Mom could tell the dryad queen the truth. The council and their warriors would charge back through. They'd stop Mr. Mayfair.

"I never forgot that I love you," Mom said to Lily.

And then the queen led Mom and the dryads through the gate. They vanished as they crossed. Instantly, Mr. Mayfair pulled Lily away from the pillar. Lily pretended to stumble as she reached for a tree, her mind screaming to the oak—

Grabbing her shirt, Mr. Mayfair yanked her back to the sidewalk. "You have been doing so well. Don't fail me now," he said softly. "It's nearly done."

He's right, she realized. It was nearly done. He had what he wanted: The bulk of the Feeders were returned, the magic army and the gargoyles were on the other side, and he had two Keys under his control. He had no more reason to keep her alive.

On the sidewalk, Jake moaned.

Releasing Lily, Mr. Mayfair knelt by his grandson. He gripped Jake's shoulder. "I don't know what I would have done if I'd lost you. Can you stand?"

"Yes, sir." Jake struggled to his feet. His hair was plastered to the sweat on his forehead, and his face was waxy and pale.

"Get yourself to Vineyard Club and see the doctor immediately," Mr. Mayfair said.

"Thank you, sir." Jake dredged up a smile for Lily. "I hung in there like you said. Knew you'd be back for me. You truly deserve to be a knight."

She had to speak. If he left, she'd be alone with Mr. Mayfair. She'd wasted all her other chances. Lily began, "Jake—"

"Tell the doctor to wait for my orders before transferring Richard Carter to the hospital," Mr. Mayfair said. "I'd like to be there to ensure that he's in good hands." He smiled at Lily. "Was there something you wanted to say, my dear?"

Numbly, she shook her head.

She watched Jake limp across the yard.

As Jake rounded Nassau Hall, Mr. Mayfair patted her on the shoulder. "One item left on the list: the humans." He steered her back through the side entrance and through the blockade of security. As they passed the guards, Mr. Mayfair nodded to them. "Tell your men that they can stand down. The threat is over. Humanity is safe."

The nearest guard saluted. "Sir, what are your orders for the civilians?"

Keeping Lily close to his side, Mr. Mayfair detailed plans for what to tell the people who had seen more than they should have. He barked orders, and campus security sprang into action. The battle at Forbes was to be explained as a maintenance issue. Prospect Avenue was closed for "renovations." They were to contact the media to begin damage control, monitor the Web for photos and other incriminating evidence, and compile a list of all potential leaks. Vineyard Club would be bringing all of their considerable resources to the cover-up, but security had to plant the seeds now. It took Mr. Mayfair fifteen minutes at most to disperse the guards. While he talked, Lily tried to form a plan. There had to be a way to escape, save Tye, and protect Grandpa. She just had to think of it. She was supposed to be smart, Ivy League smart. *Think, Lily!* she ordered herself.

But Mr. Mayfair was stronger and faster, and he held all the cards. She discarded every plan that sprang into her head. None of them would work. She couldn't do this alone.

As the guards dispersed, Mr. Mayfair said to Lily, "Let's check on your friend in the chapel, shall we?" Leading her away, he seemed as pleased as a cat in sunshine. *Of course he is,* she thought. *He's won.* He was whistling as he ushered her toward the chapel. With each step, she became more convinced that she was going to die.

I need a miracle, she thought.

Staring up at the chapel spires, she prayed for one. But

instead of avenging angels coming to save her, all she saw was the dragon writhing on the stone facade. Tears rolled down her cheeks. "Please . . . ," she began.

And then, across the plaza, she saw her miracle: her grandfather, hobbling toward them, with Jake at his side. Jake waved to them.

"Grandpa!" Lily cried. *Oh, thank you.* She was saved. She started to laugh and cry at the same time. When they met in front of the chapel, Lily threw herself at Grandpa and wrapped her arms around his neck. He was awake. He was alive. He was here. Everything was going to be okay. Grandpa would fix everything.

Jake was beaming. His cheeks were a healthier pink, she saw, and he wasn't swaying as he stood anymore. "I went to talk to the doctor, as you said, and Mr. Carter was there. Pulled out his own IV and insisted on coming once I brought him up to speed."

Grandpa staggered under the force of Lily's hug and then patted her back. "I'm all right, my tigerlily. Everything's all right."

"Richard," Mr. Mayfair admonished, "you should be resting."

Lily noticed that Grandpa's muscles were trembling.

Grandpa frowned at Mr. Mayfair. "Joseph, we need to talk. Is it true that you returned my Rose to the magic world?"

"Your daughter is fine," Mr. Mayfair said soothingly. "She's with family."

"I was supposed to accompany her. She was supposed to be reintroduced gradually and carefully," Grandpa said. "She has no memory of who she was. She'll be frightened."

Mr. Mayfair's voice dripped with concern. "Don't upset yourself, Richard. Your health is fragile. I did what was best for everyone. You were not available to consult, and it was my place to decide."

His health *was* fragile. Taking a step back, Lily studied him. One arm was bandaged from shoulder to wrist. His face was a sunken mask of wrinkles. He wasn't Superman, she realized, and he was in no condition to save the day. In fact, by coming here, he had put himself at risk. "You should be back in bed," Lily said. "I'll take you." Looping her arm around him, she began to walk fast, pulling Grandpa with her.

"Lily, not yet," Grandpa said. He dug his heels against the stone. Even weakened, he stopped her. "There's something that I've come to say to Joseph, and it isn't right for me to delay." He turned to face Mr. Mayfair.

"Grandpa, whatever it is, I'm sure it can wait. . . ."

"Joseph, you know I have the utmost respect for what you've done for Princeton, indeed for humanity, over the years," Grandpa said.

Mr. Mayfair executed a half bow. "Thank you. I appreciate your—"

Grandpa held up a hand. Lily noticed his fingers shook. "Lately I have watched you, and I have been disturbed by what I've seen. There has been no new research added to the library in decades. There have been no trips to the magic world, no summits with their leaders. The gargoyles have been marginalized. But worse, you have shown lapses in ethics that are alarming. I am sorry, Joseph, but when the knights convene tonight, I must call for a vote of no confidence."

Stunned, Mr. Mayfair stood as still as the statues on the chapel.

Jake stammered, "B-b-but . . ."

Lily thought that she had never been more proud of her grandfather. He'd seen the clues to Mr. Mayfair's corruption, even if he had no idea how truly evil his friend was. In as calm a voice as she could manage, she said, "Grandpa, we need to run now."

Grandpa, Jake, and Mr. Mayfair all looked at her.

"He'll kill you," she said. "He'll kill anyone who stands in his way. He killed Jake's parents. He killed your son." She tugged on his arm, the one not in bandages. "Please, Grandpa!"

Throwing his head back, Mr. Mayfair laughed. "Oh, my dear. You have had a rough day, haven't you?" To Grandpa, he said, "Your granddaughter is a lovely girl, but she has had so much happen to her in the past twenty-four hours that she's obviously misunderstood much of what she's learned."

"He had an alliance with the leader of the Feeders," she said.

Sputtering, Jake said, "H-how can you say that? My grandfather is a hero!"

"Your grandfather was going to let you die," she said.

Jake shook his head. "You're wrong," he said firmly. "Tell her she's wrong."

Mr. Mayfair's smile was tight. "Of course she is," he said. "She's imagining plots and conspiracies where none exist."

"He wants to close the gate between worlds permanently," Lily said. "Grandpa, he plans to kill me."

Grandpa patted her hand. "Lily . . ."

He had to believe her. "Dragon! Chained Dragon, wake up!" she called. "Tell them how he used the fairy to make a deal with you. He promised you freedom in exchange for killing a baby half dryad by FitzRandolph Gate. He was responsible for all those deaths."

The dragon lashed his tail. *"Free me, and I will avenge myself on the traitor!"* His voice made her feel as if she'd swallowed a snake. It twisted and writhed inside her.

Grandpa was pale. "Rose always suspected a knight."

"Death to the betrayer!" The dragon screeched and scraped stone. Bits of the facade crumbled under his claws, but the chain held tight. *"I will see you suffer as I have suffered! Your blood will paint the stones!"*

Mr. Mayfair's smile vanished. "Richard, you cannot seriously believe—"

Lily said to her grandfather, "He's lied to you. All these years."

"There have been too many secrets, too many lies," Grandpa said. He touched Lily's cheek, and Lily realized he was apologizing to her. She'd have preferred a better apology, but if this one saved her life, she'd accept it. "We will bring the matter before all the knights tonight. Present the evidence and let the full Vineyard Club judge. Everything out in the open. How does that sound, my tigerlily?"

She opened her mouth to say that it sounded great.

Jake sputtered. "B-but ... but there *is* no evidence! You can't take the word of that ... that killer." He pointed to the Chained Dragon. "I'm sorry, Lily, but I stand with my grandfather."

"Of course you do," Mr. Mayfair said. "Richard, drop this crazy idea. You cannot bring this for discussion with the knights. It will undermine my authority needlessly."

Above, the dragon thrashed as he hurled threats and insults down at Mr. Mayfair. "*I will dine on your flesh. I will feast on your entrails. False knight!*"

"You want proof?" Lily asked. She pointed to the chapel doors. "Right now, Tye is inside, bound in ropes. Mr. Mayfair did that to him. And my mother ... we can bring her back from the dryads. She can testify that he drained her and threatened her. And what about the goblin? He sent a goblin to attack me. We can find the goblin."

Jake was gawking at the chapel entrance. "Tye is in there?" He began to climb the steps.

Mr. Mayfair held out a hand and stopped him, saying, "You can't possibly be listening to this drivel."

Gently, Grandpa said, "If it's drivel, what do you fear? Let him go."

"*Yes, yes, see the betrayal!*" the dragon cried. "*Feel my pain!*"

"Jake, I order you to step down," Mr. Mayfair said.

Lily heard a hint of desperation creep into his voice. Jake heard it, too. His eyes locked on to Lily's. "Your brother needs you," she said.

Jake's face twisted. "Forgive me for doubting you," he whispered to his grandfather, and then he took a step toward the chapel antechamber.

Before Jake could react, Mr. Mayfair brought the sword hilt up and slammed it against his head. Jake crumpled to the ground. "You will understand when you're older," Mr. Mayfair said, and then he turned toward Grandpa.

"No, don't!" Lily screamed.

Mr. Mayfair sprang toward Grandpa. Grandpa dodged backward, and his knees caved. He collapsed on the plaza flagstones. Mr. Mayfair leveled his sword. Grandpa fought to stand as Mr. Mayfair advanced, but his legs again folded under him. Bringing up his arm, he turned his head as Mr. Mayfair raised his sword. Sunlight flashed over the blade.

Lily did the only thing she could think of doing. She jumped as high as she could and grabbed the ribbon of stone beneath the dragon. "Stop him!" she cried. "Avenge yourself!"

The dragon's head darted down, and his jaws latched on to her arm. He sucked, and she felt the world spin. It only lasted a few seconds—the dragon was half-free already. All he needed was a taste of magic. With a cry, the beast snapped the chain and burst off the arch.

The Chained Dragon soared free.

CHAPTER *Seventeen*

With every breath, the dragon stretched and swelled. Lily sagged onto the chapel steps and stared upward as the stone gray scales shimmered with flecks of emerald and gold. The dragon's tail extended into a curl, and his wings expanded until they blocked the evening sky.

Mr. Mayfair's face twisted and reddened. "Foolish girl, what have you done?"

Lily tried to stand, but her knees folded under her. Silence roared in her ears. She could see her grandfather was shouting, but she couldn't hear him.

Above, the dragon jackknifed. He flattened his wings against his now full-size body and dived toward Mr. Mayfair. The aged knight sliced up at the sky with his sword. Landing on the plaza, the dragon wrapped his front talons around Mr. Mayfair. *"You tricked me,"* the dragon said. His voice punctured the white noise that filled Lily's head. *"You will pay with pain."*

"You failed me!" Mr. Mayfair shouted. "You killed my son, not the girl!"

The dragon pushed off his hind claws, and the concrete flagstones cracked beneath him. As the dragon lifted him into the air, the old man hacked with his sword at the dragon's scales. The ring of steel on stone echoed across the plaza.

"Our alliance is ended," the dragon said. He bit into Mr. Mayfair's shoulder, and Mr. Mayfair screamed as the dragon drained him.

Grandpa struggled to his feet.

Lily watched without understanding. She wanted so badly to sink into the stones and rest. But the tiny part of her brain that was still able to think told her that she couldn't. Tye still needed her.

Gritting her teeth, she dragged herself up the steps and then stumbled into the chapel. She crawled up the marble stairs to the choir box.

Tye lay at the edge of the fairy's dried blood. Lily knelt beside him and untied the ropes around him with shaking hands. "Wake up," she said. It hurt to talk. Her head throbbed. Her lungs ached with every breath. "Please, Tye." She leaned against his chest and laid her head on his shoulder. "Please."

"Lily?" Tye's arms wrapped around her.

"Please. I need you to be okay," she whispered.

Tye opened his eyes. "You're drained. What the hell happened?"

She felt like crying, but she couldn't summon the strength. Her muscles felt like stone. Everything hurt. She felt bruised from the inside out. "I released the dragon."

He swore.

"Lily, hold on," he said. "I'll take you through the gate. But you have to stay awake."

She tried, but her eyelids fluttered closed.

"Lily!" He shook her. "Open your eyes. There's a good girl. Come on, I'll carry you." She sucked in magic-less air and tried to focus on Tye. "Look at me—that's right."

Her vision tilted and darkened.

A second later Tye lifted her up. She laid her head against his chest and felt his heartbeat through her cheek. "I like you," she said.

"Very nice," Tye said. "Don't die, and I'll take you out for ice cream."

"I like ice cream," she said.

And then she screamed as every bone in her body felt as if it were shattering. Lightning lanced over her eyes. She heard voices around her shouting, and she felt her body spasm. *"She won't make it!" "Put her down!" "There, right there!" "Open her mouth!"* She felt cool, thick sweet liquid pour into her mouth and hit her throat. She coughed and gagged. *"More! Make her drink it! Lily, baby, please, you have to drink this!"*

She heard Jake's voice. "Take mine!"

And more was forced down her throat. She swallowed and swallowed. The magic spread like fire in a forest. It coursed through her. Her blood blazed. Her skin sparked. She opened her eyes and saw pure light.

"Lily, my Lily!" Grandpa cradled her against him.

High above, the dragon circled, a dark shadow against the starry sky.

Lily felt arms around her. She breathed in the smell of earth after rain, and she knew it was Tye who held her this time. Her cheek rested against his chest. She must have blacked out again. She tilted her head to see his chin. Above them was the East Pyne arch. They were tucked under it. Tye was looking out at the plaza, so she followed his gaze.

The knights were spread across the flagstones, and the dragon spiraled above them. Flattening his wings, he dove. His empty talons stretched toward the knights, and they fought back with swords and knives and spears.

It wasn't enough for him to have had his revenge on Mr. Mayfair. He seemed determined to punish all of the knights.

Over the sounds of the battle, Lily heard the music of the plants, louder and clearer than ever before. The notes tumbled over her like a waterfall. She thought of Mom's piano playing in the lobby of Vineyard Club. Mom had been playing *this* music, she realized. Lily hadn't heard the plants clearly enough before to recognize it.

"Tye?" she whispered. Her throat hurt, as if she had swallowed flames.

"He's toying with them," Tye said grimly.

The swords ricocheted off the dragon's scales. He breathed fire, and a knight screamed as orange flames engulfed him. He dropped to the ground, and other knights piled on top of him, trying to smother the fire. The dragon soared back into the air, out of reach.

"It'll take the Air Force to bring him down," Tye said. "And then . . . the secret will be out. Despite everything we did . . . this is it."

She looked up at the dragon. "But we have our own air force."

Tye frowned at her.

Jumping to her feet, Lily grinned. She felt magic vibrating inside her. Her bones sang with it. "Come on—ride a dragon with me?"

Quickly, Lily and Tye crossed to the magic world.

The tiger man was in the yard, coordinating the aftermath of the battle. He listened to Tye's explanation and then ushered them to the concrete stadium across campus.

A few minutes later, Lily was ready. She was strapped to a ruby red dragon's back with leather belts, and she held reins in her hands. On the back of a second dragon, Tye signaled that he was ready too.

Tye's father yelled to them, "Keep them over campus! We

have to limit exposure!" He slapped Tye's dragon on the leg. "Now, fly!"

The two dragons flapped their enormous wings and then leaped into the night air. Pumping, they shot upward. Lily felt the wind hit her face, and the trees' song fell away. Flanked by griffins, the dragons flew toward the gate. At Nassau Hall, the griffins peeled away, leaving the two dragons with their riders alone for the final approach.

Tye's dragon flattened his wings, extended his neck, and tucked up his talons. He shot down toward the gate. Lily's dragon dove after him.

Seconds ahead of her, Tye's dragon bashed through the iron decoration, sending the Princeton seal spinning through the air.

Lily's dragon flew right behind him. She felt the impact as the dragon's flanks scraped against the stone pillars. The pillars cracked. White light flashed. And then they were through.

On the other side, the dragons veered up over Nassau Street, silhouetted against the backdrop of the starry sky. Lily spotted the Chained Dragon instantly. He was weaving between the chapel spires, a gray shadow against the dark blue sky. "There!" Lily shouted, but the dragons had already seen their kin.

Talons extended, the Chained Dragon dove toward the plaza. Lily screamed. Her dragon echoed her scream with a trumpeting roar. Below, she saw figures: Grandpa, Jake, other

Old Boys. All of them were looking up at the three dragons.

The Chained Dragon broke his dive. Rearing back, he rose in the air in front of one of the chapel's stained-glass windows.

Lily's dragon took the lead. Blasting flame from his jaws, he seared the air in front of the Chained Dragon. Lily felt hot wind on her cheeks. Dodging, the Chained Dragon fired back a burst of orange red flame.

Shooting fire back and forth, the three dragons spun in a spiral higher and higher over the chapel. Lily saw stars spin above her, streaking into circles of light. Suddenly, the Chained Dragon broke out of the spiral and shot away from the cathedral plaza. Lily's and Tye's dragons chased him.

They flew over the classrooms, the gardens, and the dorms. Ahead, beyond several fields, Lily saw a string of car headlights on Route 1, the highway that marked the border of campus. She thought of the tiger man's warning. They couldn't let the dragon leave campus.

Red sparkles burst over a soccer field. A stream of silver white chased them. *Fireworks!* She heard a band playing John Philip Sousa below them.

As they flew over the field, the sky lit with umbrellas of silvery sparkles. Fireworks whistled and screamed. All three dragons veered away.

Lily yanked on her dragon's reins. "Listen for the whistle, and watch for the streaks!" she shouted to her dragon. She pointed toward a thin strip of sparks that then exploded into a white burst of light. "Drive him toward those!"

Tye followed. Together, they chased the Chained Dragon over the soccer field. Using the reins, Lily guided her dragon around the about-to-explode fireworks. With no one to help him watch for the telltale streaks, the Chained Dragon spun erratically through the air, twisting and turning to avoid both the two dragons and the umbrellas of embers and hot ash.

As the Chained Dragon flailed in the air, Tye and Lily circled around him and began to drive him back toward the chapel. A crinkling sparkle of white yellow light singed one of the Chained Dragon's wings. He screamed and dipped, and the two dragons closed in.

Talons extended, the two dragons flew above the Chained Dragon's back. They forced him into a descent. He twisted and spat flame at Lily. Lily's dragon veered away, skimming the tops of the trees. Song from the trees burst into Lily's head.

She had an idea.

"Drive him toward the gardens!" she shouted to Tye. Snapping the reins, she urged her own dragon faster. They overshot the Chained Dragon and beelined for Prospect Gardens.

As they flew, Lily unhooked the harness belts from around her waist and wrapped them around her arms. Taking a deep breath, she leaned over the side of the dragon's neck. She reached out one hand and touched the treetops.

Leaves brushed her palm, and she felt song crash through

her so loud and strong that it felt as if the notes were ramming themselves directly into her veins. She put a picture in her mind of the Chained Dragon and of the trees reaching up to him. "Grab him!" she ordered the trees. "Bring him down!"

Approaching rapidly, Tye's dragon rode above the Chained Dragon, driving him lower and lower. Circling the gardens, Lily slapped at treetops, repeating her command until every tree she touched now strained toward the stars, branches reaching.

Just before the gardens, Tye's dragon slammed down hard on the Chained Dragon's back. The Chained Dragon jolted lower. As he hit the top branches of the evergreens, the trees snapped together. They knocked into his wings, they battered his stomach, and they caught his legs.

The Chained Dragon tumbled out of the night sky.

"Land!" Lily cried to her own dragon.

Her dragon abruptly dove. He skidded to a landing on the walkway outside the gardens. Lily was tossed forward into his neck. Tears sprang into her eyes as her chin smashed into a scale. She didn't let it slow her, though. She flung herself off the dragon and ran into the gardens.

Above, in the treetops, the Chained Dragon thrashed. Lily heard the trees scream.

Dropping to her knees at the base of the trees, she plunged her hands into the ivy that wove between the evergreens. She pictured what she wanted: vines growing and wrapping themselves around the beast's legs. "Grow to him," she ordered the vines. "Tangle him."

Obediently, the vines stretched and wound their way up the trees toward the suspended dragon. The ivy snaked around the dragon's body as he opened his jaws and spurted fire. The nearest trees burst into flame.

Lily grabbed more vines. "Smother the flames," she commanded. Again, she formed the clearest picture she could in her mind: the vines weaving into a mat and blanketing the fire. She didn't wait to see if they succeeded. Jumping to her feet, she ran to the trunks of the trees that held the dragon. She threw her arms around the closest tree. "Pull him down!" She repeated her order with all the nearby trees. "Capture him!"

Mimicking the image she had sent them, the trees began to enclose the dragon's legs in bark. As the bark thickened, vines crept around his torso. The tree trunks creaked as the dragon fought.

Lily ran to the flower beds. Bending down, she touched the tulip petals with her palms as she ran through. "Block his eyes!" she said. "Fill his mouth. Blind him. Gag him."

Pulled by the branches and the vines, the dragon tumbled to the ground. He crashed into the fountain in the center of the gardens. The tulips shot toward him. Brilliant yellow and red petals filled his eyes and mouth. Above, Tye's dragon hovered, silhouetted by the moon, blocking the Chained Dragon's escape.

The dragon thrashed, and the force of his flailing snapped trees and crushed flowers. Lily saw the vines strain. She needed more!

Lily sprinted up the hill to the rosebushes. She thrust her hands into the leaves. Thorns scraped her palms, but she ignored them. "Pierce him," she ordered. She felt her muscles shake as the magic flooded out of her and into the roses.

The rosebushes spread down the slope toward the heart of the gardens. They wove themselves around the fallen dragon. He fought them off, breaking the branches. Lily concentrated, picturing the magic pouring out of her and into the rosebushes. "More!" she cried.

Filled with her magic, the roses multiplied as they flowed down the hill, over the gardens, and to the dragon. Blossoms burst into red and white bloom as they snaked around the beast.

"Thorns, grow," she commanded. She imagined the thorns thickening and stretching until each was a living sword.

The thorn swords stabbed the dragon.

She heard the dragon scream, and for an instant, she faltered. The roses felt her hesitation and withdrew.

"Don't stop!" Tye shouted down at her. "He killed your father! He killed my mother! You have to end this now!"

Closing her eyes, she sent more thorns into the dragon.

Rose thorns pierced the dragon's heart.

In the distance, dimly, she heard men and women shouting. The dragon screamed as the Princeton knights burst into the gardens. Releasing the roses, Lily sagged to the ground.

The rosebushes retreated up the hill. The tulips fell out of the dragon's mouth and slipped from his eyes. The vines shrank and slithered back to their trees, and the trees themselves rose to stand tall around the gardens like silent, broken sentinels.

Swords raised, the knights, led by Jake, raced toward the downed dragon.

In the center of the gardens, covered in petals and blood, the dragon lay still.

CHAPTER Eighteen

Six months later

ℒily straightened her sword arm. "Is this right?"

On the benches behind Vineyard Club, Tye lounged as he bit into a cheesesteak. "Sure," he said around the oozing ketchup, "if you want to topple over."

She glared at him. "Very funny," she said. She pushed her hair out of her eyes. She'd been sweating so much that it had started to frizz. She wished she'd worn short sleeves, but she hadn't expected to sweat so much in December. It was all Jake's fault, of course. He thought she needed extra practice.

"Jake, wanna show her?"

Flashing her a smile, Jake rammed his shoulder into hers. Naturally, she flew sideways. She landed on the frozen grass with a thud. "Ow," she said. "Totally proves nothing. He could topple an elephant."

Always the gentleman, Jake held out his hand to help her back onto her feet. "You are nothing like an elephant," he said gravely.

As compliments went, it wasn't impressive, but she'd accept it. She dusted flecks of dirt off her shirt and jeans as she smiled at him. "Thanks, Jake."

Tye scowled. "You're flirting with my girlfriend again," he complained.

Jake's ears turned pink as he blushed. "I'll, um, get the practice swords."

Putting down his cheesesteak, Tye jumped off the bench and crossed to Lily as Jake went inside the club. He wrapped his arms around her waist. "Just so you know," he said, "I am planning on sweeping you away tonight, feeding you ice cream, and then taking you to watch a phoenix rise."

Lily grinned and wrapped her arms around his neck. "Not the traditional dinner and a movie?"

"No dinner. Just an ice-cream cone," he said. "Your grandfather thinks I'm a bad influence. I have to maintain my reputation."

"He said that?" She'd have to talk with him. Again.

"Not in so many words." Tye wound his fingers through Lily's hair and then cupped her cheek in his hand. She felt the familiar tingle as their magic fizzed over her skin. He drew her closer and kissed her. His lips were soft and gentle and wonderful.

A familiar voice interrupted them. "I do think you're a bad influence. Please refrain from slobbering over my granddaughter in public." Tye and Lily jumped apart as Grandpa strode out of Vineyard Club. "Jake said I'd find you back here."

"Thanks, brother o' mine," Tye muttered.

"Grandpa . . . ," Lily began.

He held up a hand. "You have a letter," he said.

Lily felt her heart hammer faster. "Oh?"

"You're delivering—," Tye started. "Ooh. Right. *The* letter."

Lily wiped her sweaty hands on her jeans and told herself to quit being nervous. The Old Boys had promised, and her application had been solid. She'd transferred to Princeton High School for senior year in order to be closer to Mom, but she'd kept up her grades and even taken on an extra AP class. "Big envelope or small?" she asked.

Grandpa's face was blank as he handed her a business-size envelope. She held it to her chest for a moment, trying to force her heart to calm down. It couldn't be a rejection, could it?

"Seriously? You're nervous?" Tye asked.

It was such a small envelope!

"Lily, you're amazing," Tye said. "Any school would say yes."

She studied the seal on the return address, and then she

flipped the envelope over and ran her fingers over the back. *Just open it,* she told herself. *Quit it with the melodrama. It has to be a yes.* Unless the Old Boys didn't have the pull they thought they had . . . Unless that "unprepared" in gym class hurt her GPA too much . . .

Tye rolled his eyes at her. "Bet you submitted other college applications, too," he said. "Just in case."

She blushed.

"Lily!"

"Only Harvard," she said.

Grandpa frowned. "Why?"

"Well . . . everyone needs a safety school."

Grandpa guffawed, slapping his thigh.

Tye plucked the envelope out of Lily's hands, ripped it open, and handed the letter to her unread. Taking a deep breath, she read the first sentence, and then she punched her fist with the letter into the air. "Yes!" she yelled.

"Congratulations, Princeton girl," Tye said. He grabbed her and kissed her forehead.

Brushing Tye aside, Grandpa scooped Lily up and swung her in a circle exactly as he had when she was a little girl. "I am so proud of you, my tigerlily."

She beamed at him.

"Never mind the ice-cream cone," Tye said. "I'm buying you a banana split."

Over Grandpa's shoulder, she said, "You're on."

Lily read through the entire letter to make sure the first

sentence hadn't lied. She couldn't stop smiling. Everything inside her was singing, not just the trees.

It was finally really, truly, irrevocably real.

"I need to tell Mom. Want to come?" she asked Grandpa.

He hesitated. "Love to, but I can't. We had another emergency—some alum has sold his photos to an obscure tabloid. We're maneuvering to buy the tabloid." Since June, the Old Boys had had their hands full pulling strings, leaning on the media, and planting information to try to bury the truth of what had happened. "Sometimes I wish I'd never left the flower shop," Grandpa said, making a face. Lily knew he didn't mean it. He was the new leader of the knights, and Lily had never seen him so happy. He whistled all the time, often starting at six a.m., which was less than charming, especially since her new bedroom was next to his. "Tell your mother that I'll come on Sunday."

"Will do," she said. She hugged him.

He frowned at her. "Put on your coat. Your mother would never forgive me if I let you freeze."

Obediently, Lily fetched her coat. She kissed his cheek, and then she grabbed Tye's hand and headed across campus. He laughed as she dragged him faster down the sidewalk and through the 1879 Hall arch.

Both of them waved up at the monkey gargoyles, and the monkeys waved back. One of them skittered down the brick. Tye paused to scratch him under the chin, which made a sound like scraping stone. Lily waited for him impatiently.

They crossed the rest of campus in less than three minutes.

Together, they plunged through the gate. Tye waved up at the gold eagles. "Hey, guys. Guess what?" He pointed to Lily's letter. She grinned as the eagles screeched approval. "You go ahead," Tye said. "You should tell your mom the news without interlopers."

"You're not an interloper," Lily said. "She likes you."

"I'll report to the council," he said.

"Thanks," she said. This time, she pulled him closer and kissed him. Above, the gold eagles whistled. Both Lily and Tye laughed as they moved apart.

She headed into the forest. Touching the bark of an evergreen, she felt its song whisper through her. The ferns and underbrush spread away to create a path for her. Lily broke into a jog and then a run as the path opened before her, leading to Mom's grove.

Mom was waiting for her. She looked as beautiful as a green goddess. Her pale green hair wreathed her head like a crown, and flowers clung to her skin and her dress. Ivy vines were twisted around her arms and calves, and tiny rosebuds filled her pockets. "Lily, is anything wrong? The trees told me—"

Lily barreled into her and hugged her. "It's real! I'm in! Look!" She waved the acceptance letter in front of her.

Mom laughed.

Without knowing exactly why, Lily began to cry. She hugged her mother, and her mother hugged her back and laughed and cried, too.

"Your father would be so proud of you," Mom said.

Lily wiped her eyes. "You remembered more?"

Mom's smile lit the grove like a mini sun. All around, leaves burst out of the trees in defiance of winter. "Oh, yes," Mom said. "I remember him perfectly."

"Tell me everything," Lily said.

Tapping the ground with her foot, Mom caused a tree root to buckle up through the earth. She sat down on it and patted the spot next to her. Lily sat. "Your father was a wonderful man," Mom said, "for a human."

"Mom!"

Her mother laughed. "He had your eyes and your laugh, and he loved you so much. One time, when you were just a baby . . ." Around them, the forest fell silent, as every tree listened with Lily.